ILLICIT SENSES

ILLICIT MINDS #1

REBECCA ROYCE

Illicit Senses (Illicit Minds #1)

Copyright @ 2019 by Rebecca Royce

Original Publication 2016 called "Eye Contact" by Rebecca Royce

Ebook ISBN: 978-1-951349-10-3

Print ISBN: 978-1-951349-11-0

Cover art by Glowing Moon Designs

Content Editing: Heather Long

Copy/Proof Editing: Jennifer Jones

Final Proof Editing: Meghan Leigh Daigle

Formatting: Ripley Proserpina

Published by Rebecca Royce

www.rebeccaroyce.com

❁ Created with Vellum

A DECISION

Every major news network carried the story. As the President of the free world, he had no choice but to address the issue. He stood in front of his podium, the symbol of freedom positioned behind him in the form of a red, white, and blue flag, and told the world they'd run out of options.

Too many new cases of the Condition had emerged. It was past time to act. Before that day and his announcement, no one had ever used that particular word to describe it. The bizarre manifestations had appeared in small numbers, but at a rate that had garnered the interest of public health officials everywhere.

The media was responsible for much of the attention. First, the incident with the Collins boy in Manhattan, one year earlier. The blond-haired, four-year-old cherub with cheeks still chubby in the way that was only cute on toddlers, had arrived at the police station with his mother.

"Murder," she'd whispered to the clerk behind the desk. If there had been any doubt of her terror, the way she held her son's hand in a death grip would have given her away. The little guy had witnessed a murder in *his mind*. She'd assumed it to be only a nightmare brought on by exposure to the media, until she'd seen the incident on the news exactly as he'd described it.

For months following her report, the child had been referred to as "the psychic cherub" and worshiped as if he were the second coming. The documented case of true second sight had seemed miraculous at first. If all the children thereafter had helped law enforcement, that would have been one thing, but several had seen visions of state secrets and made the mistake of speaking about them publicly.

It wasn't okay to be openly ridiculed at a negotiation for oil rights, because a ten-year-old boy couldn't keep his mouth shut on matters that were none of his business.

Even so, they might have been able to contain the occurrences less dramatically, until the violence began. In Denver, a five-year-old girl blew up her father's car with her mind; in Dallas, a two-year-old boy killed a would-be intruder in his parent's house; and in San Francisco, eight-year-old twins stopped their grandmother's pacemaker and watched in horror as she died.

Every day, more and more documented cases appeared on the President's desk. It was no longer a containable *Condition*. So, he stood at his podium and spoke with his countrified manners and his folksy ways about the need to "help" the children, to keep them and everyone else safe, to assure everyone they could be brought back to God and the American way.

The next day, the notices went out. They arrived in mailboxes around the country. If anyone missed them, they were posted for everyone to see in newspapers, magazines, and on signs at the post office. In case anyone should doubt their origin, they were written on an official letterhead with the insignia of the Commander in Chief affixed to the top.

To whom it may concern,

All children who show any of the list of symptoms below are to be brought to one of six safe houses to be observed, protected, and trained to behave in humane, normal, and productive ways.

Some of the symptoms of this illness are, but not limited to:

Psychic visions—including any and all predictions of the future

Mind control

Telekinesis

Pyrokinesis

Telepathy

If your child has these, or any other symptoms of abilities not considered normal, please bring them to one of the addresses listed below.

Be warned: Any parent, guardian, or relative who fails to bring an infected child for examination will be arrested, their wages will be seized, and they and their family will be considered hostile persons with terrorist intentions against the United States.

The notice went on to list the six locations designated as safe houses. People began to line up. Soon, they needed a lot more houses, and the safe houses became camps.

Where America led, the world followed.

ONE

Addison Wade couldn't keep her legs from shaking. Her movement started as a tap, tap, tap of her left foot on the ceramic tiled floor, and progressed until both legs trembled together. She sat in an uncomfortable straight-backed chair, and tried to concentrate on anything other than the noise her feet were making as they hit the floor beneath her. She glanced at the clock on the wall. It ticked; she could listen to that. One minute had passed since the last time she'd looked. *Ridiculous.*

For twenty-six years, she'd been trained to take over the Wade Corporation upon her grandfather's retirement. All that education wouldn't do her any good in this situation, or in any other future crisis, if she couldn't get control of herself.

She shifted and tried not to sigh. She was a Wade, and Wades didn't show that they were uncomfortable, not in public—not even in private if they could help it. Even the sound of her Aunt Morgan's whispers on her cell phone wasn't enough to distract Addison from the sense of doom.

It had filled her thoughts since she'd awoken and grown worse as the day passed.

Addison hadn't been this terrified since she was a child.

She'd actually had to resort to her old methods to help her cope—the silent chanting—to get out of bed. Maybe the problem was that she'd hardly slept. How could she? Jeremy was out there, and he needed to be found. Only four years old, he didn't deserve what had happened to him. She'd promised herself she'd take care of her nephew as though he were her own after her sister's tragic death.

So, she'd started the chant again. Over and over, until she'd managed to calm her mind and find her famous steadiness.

A, my name is Addison, my mother's name is April, we come from Albany, and we eat apples.

B, my name is Brenda, my mother's name is Britta, we come from Boston, and we eat bananas.

C, my name is Caroline, my mother's name is Christa, we come from Concord, and we eat chocolate.

She hated having to do it, but it was beyond her control. Her father would have been glad, if he were alive, to see that it still helped her rein herself in. In the month since Jeremy had disappeared, it had become increasingly clear she wasn't going to get through this with her mind and secrets intact.

Hence the desperate decision to reach out to *these* people for help. No other reason in the world could have motivated her to walk through the institution's doors and wait in the outdated, uncomfortable room to be seen by the director of Safe Dawn. She'd rather have spent hours in a dentist's chair than the ten minutes she'd sat in the stiff, leather monstrosity. She already knew no one in this place would want to assist her in any way.

Addison rubbed her head as she looked around the room. It looked like whoever had decorated it had chosen the seventies as their central motif. The seat cushions were pleather, and pictures of men and women wearing bell-bottoms decorated the walls. The clock on the wall, its endless ticking about to give her a migraine, was the brightest neon pink she'd ever seen. Not to mention, there was a distinctly musky smell that made her think a leak had, at some point, created mold. Someone needed to turn on a dehumidifier.

Or maybe she scented the hate toward her entire family that radiated from every inch of the building. It was no secret that everyone there held Wade Corporation in the lowest regard, owing to her grandfather's involvement in the testing that had taken place thirty years prior. Of course, once he discovered that she'd gone to them against his wishes, he'd blow a gasket and she'd spend years working to make up for it. She took another deep breath and exhaled loudly. At least she could always say she'd tried. Whatever happened, she had to keep her promise to Jeanne.

Jeremy came first.

"Why yes, but you know how my nervous condition affects me." Her aunt's whispers into the phone were so loud she might as well have given up the pretext of quiet. "This whole thing. The poor boy. You can imagine how desperate we are to even consider this. Addison says it's our very last hope, and you know she's not one for over-expressing things."

Addison rolled her eyes as she gave her aunt a disgusted look, which Aunt Morgan either didn't see or ignored completely.

"Aunt Morgan, it's time to get off the phone."

All she needed was for the woman to spill all their business to the wrong set of ears, and the media would have a field day. She could almost see the headlines now. It would be displayed as another "Wade mystery," and the conspiracy theorists would arrive in droves on their doorstep. It would be a nightmare.

"Yes, okay, Addison would like me to get off the phone and stop ignoring her."

Addison bit her lip to keep back a grimace even as she sobbed on the inside. Her dear aunt couldn't have been more wrong. As much as she loved Aunt Morgan, the woman was all heart and very little common sense, and she could try Addison's nerves on a good day.

This didn't qualify as anywhere near a good day.

The phone snapped as her aunt set it down. The woman couldn't handle a smart phone. The flip phones were all she could manage. No texting either and for that, Addison was grateful. The woman would text all day and night if she could work it out. Addison cleared her throat. "Who was that?"

"Beatrice Haifa."

Addison nodded. She'd known the woman for most of her life. Morgan and Beatrice had grown up together, and, at the very least, Beatrice could be counted on to use discretion with whomever she chose to share their troubles. It was really just a matter of time until everyone knew anyway. Even close friends liked to gossip about the Wades.

"Now, my dear, I'm so glad you took my advice and brought me with you."

She patted her aunt's leg. "I'm glad I brought you, too." And she was. This ordeal would have been so much worse if she'd had to make the drive by herself. Too much time alone with her own thoughts gave her migraines.

"I know you're capable of handling this on your own.

Lord knows, you've been doing just that for weeks now. But they built these places before you were even born, and you've never had to deal with the odd ones. They're going to try to take advantage of you." She lowered her voice until she was doing that loud whisper thing again. "They might even try to steal your thoughts."

"The odd ones" was the politically correct term for the residents of the institution. Other less charitable phrases included freaks, demons, and Satan's helpers.

Those phrases irked Addison terribly, and they were relatively kind compared to the way people in more religious parts of the country discussed them. She'd heard the last phrase, Satan's helper, from her third cousin in San Francisco. Even in New York City, where Addison lived, most people would prefer to be pelted with eggs than labeled as Conditioned. Addison swallowed. If not for her father's decision to hide her strangeness, she herself would have been raised in this place, and forced to live in the shadows or face the scorn of the world.

But her Aunt Morgan didn't know that, and with any luck, she would continue to live in ignorance of Addison's true nature. Unless the rumors were true, and even setting foot in this place would expose her for what she was.

She blinked as she realized her aunt was still expecting an answer. "I'm sure they can't steal the thoughts from your mind."

"Did you read the report that Kristof printed out for you?"

She had. When she hadn't been able to sleep the night before, she'd read through the report so thoroughly she had all but committed it to memory. They had come to the institution known as Safe Dawn to beg the help of William Rhodes. Nearly eighty years old, if Kristof's report was to be believed, Rhodes had run Safe Dawn since its creation roughly thirty years earlier.

Rumored to be just as strange as the children in his care, Rhodes had turned a jail for unusual children into a community that thrived and worked—when necessary and only with Rhodes' say-so—with the outside world. It was said that the odd ones held the deepest loyalty to Rhodes, and would follow him into the pits of Hell if he asked them to.

If needs be, Addison would beg the man to ask one of his people to travel there with her. Hell would be nothing compared to what they would face.

Kristof hadn't been able to find out exactly how many people lived in Safe Dawn. For obvious reasons, Rhodes had gone out of his way to hide the number of odd ones from public knowledge. As diplomatic as the man had been over the years, he was fiercely protective of the lives that seemed to—literally—be in his keeping.

Rumor was that Rhodes eliminated the ones who wouldn't cooperate. But all that speculation remained merely rumor, since Kristof's research had, for the first time ever, turned up almost no new information.

"Ladies, Mr. Rhodes will see you now."

The first thing Addison noticed about the man who stepped through the door was his shortness. It had been a long time since she'd seen such a tiny person who wasn't female. She rose and walked in front of Morgan through the door he held open. As she walked by, he arched an eyebrow. Oh God, had he heard her thoughts?

She was so flustered she nearly lost her footing. Morgan reached out and grabbed her arm to steady her.

Muttering her thanks, Addison forced herself to stare forward at the hallway that stretched out in front of her. It had to have been her imagination. There was no way the man who'd ushered them inside could have known what she'd *thought*. Not really.

That was the stuff of myths. Sure, it was possible that people had extrasensory abilities. She knew that better than anyone. But to actually read someone's mind? Not likely. Maybe he knew her mind because everyone noticed how petite he stood. What was he? Five feet or slightly under?

The tiny person scooted in front of her and opened the door to let them in. As he touched her arm, he smiled. She had to look down to make eye contact with him.

"Relax." His voice was gruff. "This is a safe place."

Anxiety had formed a lump in her throat, and she had to clench her hands at her sides to stop them from shaking. She was Addison Wade, and there was no way in hell any of these people would learn her secret. She was in control, and if Jeremy needed them, then she could make this work.

Morgan's stammering brought her attention back to the present. William Rhodes was leaning up against his desk. He still had a thick head of silver-gray hair that fell to the middle of his back—a look she was more used to seeing on younger people. As she watched, he pulled it back and affixed a ponytail holder to it. His cheekbones were high and pronounced, giving her the impression that he had a Native American background.

Unlike his assistant, Rhodes stood well over six feet tall, and all of him was hard muscle. Whatever it was he'd been doing to stay in shape, Addison wished he'd give her the instructions so she could look that good when she was his age.

Behind her, Morgan was actually twittering. In her whole life, Addison had never seen her aunt react that way to anyone, male or female. Morgan had always seemed completely unaware of anyone sexually. Evidently, it had taken someone like William Rhodes to get a reaction from her.

"Ladies." Rhodes extended his hand and indicated toward the two chairs in front of him, as he walked behind his giant oak desk.

Sparing her aunt a warning glance that she hoped told the older woman this really wasn't the time to lose their cool, she sat in the chair to the left.

"Thank you for seeing us, Mr. Rhodes." Addison schooled her features into an agreeable mien, the one she usually reserved for boardrooms and charity events. Jeanne used to call it her "professional Addison" look. The expression promised the world they wanted to do whatever it was she asked of them.

"It's not every day that Wade Corporation requests a visit with us. I have to admit I was intrigued. What can I do for you?" He glanced briefly at her aunt. Addison was impressed by how quickly Rhodes assessed the situation and turned his attention to her. Most people took a little longer to realize the pecking order, which was mostly because Morgan had forty years on her niece.

"We're not here today on behalf of Wade Corporation, but for the Wade family itself." Addison crossed her legs and hoped her strange new habit of foot tapping wouldn't plague her.

"You have my attention."

"I'll cut right to the point." There was no conceivable reason to make small talk with the man or deal in double-speak. After the incident in the hall, Addison was becoming more and more convinced her aunt hadn't been wrong when she'd suggested the Conditioned could take the thoughts right out of her head. That meant she would say exactly what she wanted them to know and not think of her strangeness at all, lest the thought be ripped from her mind. Except, of course, she'd just done it again. Damn it.

"Please do." His voice was like velvet. How many people had underestimated him because of it?

"Almost a month ago, my nephew, Jeremy Wade, was kidnapped from his bedroom sometime between one and six in the morning. We can't be more specific than that because we simply don't know."

"I assume you've contacted the authorities."

Addison nodded. "Yes. The police are trying to handle this quietly, but it's not going well. They haven't been able to find a single piece of evidence. Not a fiber they can run in their labs, no sign of forced entry, nothing. It was as if one second Jeremy was in his bedroom and then—poof—he was gone."

The sound of tapping on the floor made Addison realize she'd started again. She sighed as she pushed down on her knee, hoping she could keep her foot steady with some pressure on the top of her leg.

"So, you've come to us." It wasn't a question. "How old is Jeremy?"

"Four. He's the only child of my older sister, Jeanne, who died during a ski vacation three years ago." The word didn't begin to describe what had happened.

Silence. Then the sounds of sirens traveling up the mountain. Addison bit the inside of her cheek to force the memories away. This was neither the time nor the place to revisit them.

"And the boy's father?"

"We have no idea who his father is. Jeanne always refused to name him. We're the only family Jeremy knows."

"And it's taken you a month to come to us?" Was that anger flaring in his eyes before it quickly vanished?

Her aunt harrumphed. "It's just not the way things are done." Addison wished her aunt had stayed quiet. She needed to do damage control.

"What my aunt means, Mr. Rhodes, is that the Wade family has certain obligations to our shareholders. Those duties, if you will, require us as a family to behave in a certain way. Not to make problems that might affect the company's stock value. There have been a series of unfortunate accidents over the last few years. My grandfather discussed the situation with the Chief of Police, and decided it should be handled quietly." Despite her screaming and yelling at her grandfather about it.

Every expert on child abduction stated clearly that children whose faces were plastered all over television and the internet were found more quickly, and more often, than children for whom that didn't happen. Addison had spent hours researching the subject. Everything her grandfather had done from the beginning had been inherently wrong, and after weeks of trying it his way, she'd finally had enough. Hence her trip to Safe Dawn.

"I see." Rhodes stood so abruptly that his chair flew backward. Morgan gasped, but Addison only allowed herself the briefest of glances at the now-broken chair, before regarding the man again. She was quite used to displays of temper. They didn't impress her, not in the least. Men who screamed weren't the problem; it was the quiet ones you had to worry about.

"I'm going to be honest with you, Ms. Wade. The last thing in the world I want to ask any of my people to do is help Wade Corporation or your grandfather. As far as I'm concerned, he is personally responsible for every bad thing that has ever happened to a Conditioned person."

"I'm aware of that—"

He interrupted. "However, if you'd allow me to continue, I was going to say that there is a child involved here. An innocent child who hasn't had the chance to be responsible for any of the wrongs in the world." His icy glare told her she'd had plenty of time for the same responsibility to fall on her shoulders.

She returned his glare. There was nothing to hide—not on her part, anyway. Any decisions she'd made, she was comfortable with.

"So you'll help us? You'll send Spencer Lewis?" Excitement and something akin to relief surged through her veins. She could barely keep her composure. "Wade Corporation will, of course, make a large donation to any of the charitable organizations that help your people with their special needs."

"So you read the news reports on Spencer." He kept talking, which meant he hadn't actually meant that as a question. "We will help you, but it's not going to be Spencer Lewis. I'm sorry. After what happened last time, he's earned a vacation. And there were some complications."

"His partner. Yes, I remember." She gasped and covered her mouth. Had she just admitted to Rhodes they'd had a private report commissioned on them? Why couldn't she maintain her professional mask with this man?

Taking a deep breath, she continued. "It has to be Spencer Lewis."

"It can't be. It's complicated. With our people, it's so much more than just a partnership. It's much more... intimate, in a way I simply can't describe. I'm not sure Spence can do what you want him to do anymore. We have other highly qualified people."

Anger surged in her veins, and she fought for control. Highly intense emotions were likely to bring out her strangeness, and this was the last place on Earth where that could happen. Rhodes would likely haul her back into their facility, and have her entire family locked up while they investigated whether or not they'd known about her Condition. No, she needed to get control of herself right now.

A, my name is Addison, my mother's name is April, we come from Albany, and we eat apples.

B, my name is Brenda, my mother's name is Britta, we come from Boston, and we eat bananas.

C, my name is Caroline, my mother's name is Christa, we come from Concord, and we eat chocolate.

Rhodes narrowed his eyes. Just then, the door slammed open.

A man strode in. Instantly, Addison knew she was in the presence of the most intense and possibly dangerous man she'd ever been around. Close to six feet five inches tall, he had a football player's build. Broad-shouldered, he looked like he could be trampled by a herd of elephants and still get back up again without trouble. Power poured from his core, and Addison revised her opinion from football player to outlaw. In times past, he would have led a posse of thieves on horseback. The very sight of him would have had people giving over their prized possessions.

Blond hair covered his head and, even though it was cut short, displaced pieces of it hit the tops of his eyes. Addison imagined he would have to literally shave his head to keep it out of his eyes. On other men, the effect might have softened them. It only made him seem more provocative, like he didn't even take the time to brush his hair. He didn't pretend to be civilized. Just being in the room with him made her survival instincts scream *danger*. Gripping the sides of her chair, she willed herself not to be afraid. Immediately, she failed.

He turned his head to stare at her. His eyes were a dark shade of blue, almost green in the office lighting. Silver circles floated in the centers, creating a hypnotic effect. Addison wondered if his odd powers included the ability to put someone in a trancelike state by just looking at them. She'd heard that some of these people had physical manifestations of their abilities, but she had never seen any before.

Shooting his attention back to Rhodes, he strode to the desk and slammed his hand down on it. "Who the hell is doing that? Did you bring an untrained juvenile here and let them loose on my senses just to make me crazy?"

Rhodes shook his head. "I have no idea what you're talking about. I suppose it's possible one of the new ones is letting off some unknown signals, but I'm not feeling anything. Of course, I'm not as sensitive as you." He motioned to Addison and her aunt. "I was just informing Addison and Morgan *Wade* here that you're unavailable to search for their missing nephew. He's four years old, and he's vanished. Ladies." Rhodes stood up. "This is Spencer Lewis."

Addison gaped. Rhodes was right. They would need someone else. He was far too volatile for her senses, and she'd never be able to maintain her composure.

Someone else would have to find Jeremy.

TWO

Spencer had nearly swallowed his tongue when he'd stormed into the room. He'd been in one of his too-common rages, when he'd stumbled on the blonde with the cold blue eyes sitting in the chair to the left. Stunning didn't begin to describe her. She had made the world stop for a moment.

That she was a Wade didn't surprise him, not in the least.

Despite the heat of attraction, he could almost feel a chill. Then again, the whole family was said to have ice instead of blood running through their veins. Addison Wade sat frigidly in her chair, her expression haughty and removed, as if she was more concerned with not wrinkling her skirt than noticing he was in the room. They'd come asking for help to find a missing boy? She looked like she was making a quick stop before some trendy lunch date.

Spencer had some experience with finding missing children. He was used to the families falling apart, not sitting calmly, looking like they'd just come from a day at a hair salon.

At least they had come.

Surprising as that was. Until then, Spencer would have sworn the Wade family would rather swallow their tongues, than come near one of the institutions. The whole thing was ironic, considering he was in the presence of two of the individuals responsible for the misery that plagued so many of his people and necessitated the continuing use of these places.

He should tell the Wades to go screw themselves. Why was it his problem that they couldn't keep track of their own child?

Even as the thought crossed his mind, he dismissed it. In his life, he'd always helped a child if he could. In this case, the *could* would be the ultimate question. Spencer had no idea whether he was even capable of performing the functions they would need to locate their nephew.

Knowing that every eye in the room was focused on him, including Will's, he turned around to regard the women who sat behind him. Leaning on the desk, he gave Addison a good long stare. If she already thought he was a savage, why not live up to the role? There would be hell to pay from Will later, but just watching her try not to squirm while she maintained her detached expression would be worth it.

"Your nephew has gone missing." He made his statement sound like a question. He knew the kid was gone—Will had just said he was, and Will was, as far as Spencer could tell, never wrong.

"Yes, he disappeared from his bedroom a month ago."

"Spencer, I told them you aren't available for the assignment. I'm going to pull in someone else." Will's dark tones clearly expressed what he thought of Spencer's presence in the room at that moment. "Your other issue, the one that had you storming in here like a lunatic, I'll look into the matter later."

Ignoring Will, Spencer continued his long stare at Princess Addison. "And it took you a whole month to come here? What were you doing?"

"Why, we were too busy to come here, naturally. I had a ski vacation in Aspen, and my aunt needed to get her nails done every day." Addison's sarcasm spat from her mouth and Spencer nearly laughed out loud. So, the cat had claws. What was wrong with him that he liked it so much?

"Temper, temper, Ms. Wade." Spencer ignored the tug in his groin that said he was more than just a little aware of how attractive she was.

"I don't like your implication, Mr. Lewis. For your information, we have been working with the authorities and trying to handle this nightmare ourselves." She looked down, and for a moment Spencer could have sworn she was biting the inside of her cheek. Her foot still tapped on the floor. When she looked up, her gaze was not on him, but on Will behind him. Spencer narrowed his eyes. He didn't like that one bit.

"I realize this is the perfect opportunity to attack and humiliate us. We're sitting here in your office, easy targets. But we've come here in good faith, to ask you for help in our most desperate situation. Can you help us, or should we leave?"

"We can help you. I'll assign you someone." Will walked around the desk to stand next to Spencer, placing a hand on his arm.

Spencer started. When was the last time the other man had touched him? A jolt of psychic awareness filled the room, although he was sure the two non-sensitives wouldn't feel it. Why was Will pushing on his senses so hard?

"But it won't be Spencer here helping you. As I said, he's not capable of doing what you need him to do right now."

Addison's eyes showed relief. "That's fine. We'll be most grateful."

Oh, hell no. "I can do it."

"What?" Will and Addison spoke at the same time.

Spencer crossed his arms over his chest. "I said, I could do it. I'll find the missing Wade child, your nephew."

"No." Addison stood up.

Looking left and right between Addison and Spencer, the older woman Will had called Morgan rose as well, a pained expression on her features showing her worry.

"No?"

"Mr. Rhodes says you're not capable of doing the job. Therefore, we need someone else."

"I said I would do it, and I'm the best there is. No one else can find your nephew as quickly as I can. You do care about that, don't you, Ms. Wade? Or do people in your position, who wait a month to get the services of freaks like us, not care about things like the mental health of the missing child?"

Addison's mouth gaped open, and he had the momentary pleasure of watching her do her best imitation of the number zero. Satisfaction crept up his spine. Let the spawn of all things evil feel lower than low for a while. Nothing he'd ever said had felt better.

Until he saw her hand shaking.

She quickly stuck the less-than-composed portion of her body into the pocket of her neat gray suit jacket.

He narrowed his eyes as he took a better look at the younger Wade woman. She was perfectly put together, and he'd fallen into a trap he wouldn't have believed he still could. He knew better than anyone how deceiving appearances actually were.

Dark smudges hidden by makeup marred the skin under her eyes. Most people wouldn't notice that. He should have recognized it immediately. Psychic ability alone hadn't gotten him the reputation he had. He'd had to learn to be shrewd, cunning, and observant. When he'd heard the name Wade, it had made him momentarily careless. When he coupled that carelessness with the unfortunate sexual pull Addison caused on his nerves, he had gone completely off the deep end.

There was no excuse. He was going to have to do a better job of handling Addison Wade if he was going to find her nephew.

She'd composed herself, and this time Spencer noted how much energy it seemed to have cost her. Addison's eyes shot daggers of hate. His heartbeat picked up; he was more than a little turned on. The whole thing was strange. He liked nice women, and so far, Addison was not coming across as anything close to *nice*. He smirked. It probably didn't help that he'd goaded her.

"I love my nephew." Her voice broke, and he felt a pang of regret. "He's all I have left of my sister." She swallowed, and he opened his mouth to answer, only to have her raise her hand to stop him. Clearly, she was fighting tears. "If you really are the best, and you think you can do it, then I will take any insults you want to dish out without complaint. You can batter at me, and call me names. I don't care. Can you really help us, Mr. Lewis?"

For the first time in more years than he cared to remember, he felt ashamed of himself. Not that he would tell her that. "I can try, Ms. Wade. There are never any guarantees."

Rhodes interrupted. "I'm afraid this is more complicated than that. As much as I would love to send Spencer to you, I'm going to have to put a stop to this. Without his anchor"—at the mention of Priscilla, Spencer's insides went cold—"Spencer can't do more than a peripheral reading for you."

Addison shook her head. "I'm afraid I don't know what that means."

"A surface reading from me is better than a deep one from anyone else."

"You've never been short of ego." Will's voice was harsh.

"Am I wrong?"

"No." Rhodes looked back at Addison. "Despite what movies and tabloids tell you, none of our psychics—not the ones who can do what Spencer does—can work alone. It's too dangerous for them. They can get lost in the vision, in the otherness of it. I can't explain it to you because I don't understand it myself. I don't have that talent. But it takes two people, who have complementary abilities, to navigate the experience. If Spencer were to let himself go too deep into the vision, he would lose himself. His body would be here, but his mind would never return."

Rhodes' incredibly inaccurate description of exactly what happened to a person with his so-called talents when they got lost in the "other place" made Spencer want to roll his eyes.

He'd had only a touch of the experience when Priscilla had died. She'd always been remarkably strong, and somehow with her last breaths, had managed to pull him out. For the rest of his life, he would always be grateful.

And guilt-ridden.

Could she have saved herself if she hadn't been preoccupied with bringing him back?

There was no point in dwelling on it, since there would never be anything he could do about it. People like him had no rights under the law, and even if he'd been able to convince a member of law enforcement to look into the matter, it wasn't considered a crime to kill one of their kind if they were in some way threatening the person who killed them.

You didn't have to prove you'd been threatened. How could you, when the freaks could do things you simply couldn't? That automatically made them threatening, at least under the law. Spencer sighed.

"Regardless, if I do a surface reading, I can go deeper than anyone else."

Addison's aunt finally spoke. "Then we want you."

For a second, it looked like Addison was going to argue, but she seemed to think better of it and stopped. "And your fee is?" She had the good sense to address that question to Will. Spencer had no idea what his fee was. He never saw any of the money.

"Non-negotiable." Will was always clear on that point. "Your check is made out to our facility and not to Spencer. As you know, since your family was pivotal in the writing of the law, he is not allowed to have money or own property."

He continued. "Also, as no one from Safe Dawn can be outside these walls unsupervised, for the duration of the process, Spencer will be living with you and you will be responsible for his welfare."

Addison made no remark to refuse Will's condition, and Spencer was relieved to see she had known that. It was degrading to have to essentially be treated like her child during the time they were together. But those were the rules, and as Will liked to point out to them, until they could be changed, it was better to find ways around them than to beat your head against the wall.

"When will Mr. Lewis be arriving?"

"Later today—much later."

Since her impassioned speech, the rumored-to-be successor to her grandfather as the CEO of Wade Corporation had gone out of her way not to look at Spencer. He was going to have to do something about that. He shouldn't have felt this way, but he missed the way her ice-blue eyes told him he was less than nothing to her until he made her mad.

"I'll send a car around dinner time, seven o'clock?"

Will nodded. I think we'll have concluded our preliminaries by then."

"Then we'll take our leave." Addison turned to the door.

"Thank you for your time."

The two women walked almost soundlessly to the exit. After watching them cross the threshold into the hall, Spencer waited until the door closed tightly behind them, before turning toward Will.

"Why would you assume I can't do my damn job?"

Will pounded his fist into the desk. "Why would you take unnecessary risks?"

"I don't see how it's a risk. The kid's been gone a month. We both know I'm going to be leading them to find his dead body, rather than running into some kind of trap."

"It's not your physical well-being I'm concerned about, and you know it. You can handle yourself better than anyone in that kind of confrontation. You've never done a reading without Priscilla. Since you haven't been able to successfully match up with anyone else since she died, you're going into this one solo."

"Are you insinuating that I can't do it by myself? We both know I can."

"I'm not saying anything of the kind." Will took a deep breath. "I think you need to give yourself a little more time."

"I didn't die. Sooner or later everyone is going to have to stop treating me like I did." He'd finally said the words that had been itching to explode from his body since the moment he'd returned from the hospital. Apparently, they'd all been worried he might decide to follow Priscilla to the grave.

"If everyone is treating you that way, it's only because they care."

"I know that." Which was why he hadn't said anything earlier.

"Fine." Rhodes pointed a finger at him. "But if you can't handle this, I expect you to say so and let someone else do it. Despite what you think, I know you didn't die, but I refuse to bury you this year, too."

Will had practically raised both Priscilla and him. No one could have done better under the circumstances. The last thing he wanted was to make the old man worry about his welfare.

Spencer needed to complete this job. It served the Wades right, after all they'd done to make his people miserable, that they'd had to turn to the "freaks" for help in finding their missing family member. Spencer loved irony, and the way it suddenly cropped up as if the universe were making a giant joke of everyone.

Plus, he couldn't deny that Addison Wade called to him sexually, and he didn't normally find snobby girls attractive. She had gotten beneath his skin. She was clearly a woman with hidden depths. Her hand shaking had only been the beginning of his interest in what she was hiding. Her constant downward glances and the tapping of her foot were all physical manifestations of a mental war he wanted to be a part of. He would enjoy exposing her secrets until her soul was stripped bare in front of him.

Then he might satisfy them both sexually for a few moments before he sent her back to her life. He was sure that entailed a lot of time figuring out how to destroy the existence of people less fortunate than she was.

"Why did you push Addison Wade so hard?"

Spencer shrugged. "She bothered me."

"Obviously. She *bothered* me, too." Will crossed behind his desk and pulled out a bottle of Jack Daniels. He put two shot glasses down in front of them and poured them each a portion. He handed one to Spencer as he raised his own. "To Priscilla."

Spencer waited for the sadness that always hit him when discussing Priscilla, but felt only the slightest tug on his heart. He'd loved the woman... like a sister. Sure, there had been a time, when they'd been only slightly older than teenagers, where they'd gotten naked. It had been years since they'd done that. Even though right before her death she'd made overtures to try again, he could say without much hesitation that neither of them had been particularly satisfied with the other in the sack.

Priscilla wanted romance from her lovers. She liked kind words and heartfelt sentiment. Spencer didn't have those kinds of emotions. Not when it came to his bedmates. All in all, he preferred a really intense couple of hours rolling around in the sheets—the wilder the better—followed by an evening spent away from the person he'd rolled around with.

Both of them had preferred being friends. She had been his partner, his guide, and his most trusted ally. He would always miss the intimacy of her mind touching his, as she kept him from staying in the dark places only she could share with him.

"To Priscilla. Why are we drinking in the middle of the day?"

Rhodes smiled. "There was another reason I thought it might be better for someone else to handle this."

"You didn't answer my question."

"Patience." Will's eyes gleamed, and Spencer groaned. His mentor had formulated a plan. For thirty years he'd watched the man work, and he knew there would be no putting him off of his track now. No matter what happened.

"This, my friend, is an opportunity."

"To find the child?"

"Yes, of course."

"Of course."

Will rubbed his hands together. "But also, to earn the everlasting gratitude of the Wades, and to show them that we can be trusted. Maybe then, they will support the legislation going in front of the board later this month."

"I don't think my turning up the remains of their dead nephew is going to earn any kind of thanks." Priscilla's death had proved how dangerous it could be to tell people what they didn't want to hear, truth notwithstanding.

"But you can show them how human you are, how you deserve to be treated with respect." Will narrowed his gaze, and Spencer felt twelve years old again.

"You can do that, can't you, Spence?" His tone spoke of skepticism and doubt.

"I can try." He could. He hoped.

"Good. Then go and get ready. And try not to antagonize Addison Wade too much. Keep your head down, get the job done, make yourself approachable and not at all scary, and then you can come home and regale us all with stories of just how awful Addison is to be around."

Spencer shrugged. "Maybe she's not that awful."

"Don't be fooled. I've dealt with the Wades my entire career. They're as awful as you think, and then some."

"Now you sound like a Wade."

"Out."

Spencer smiled as he headed toward the door, his mind already turning to packing.

He stopped in his tracks. "But seriously, Will, look into that juvenile who's projecting like that. It's awful and dangerous. It would just take one bad mind to push through those shields, and then you've got a brain-dead psychic on your hands."

"What were you hearing?"

"One of those obnoxious children's rhymes."

"Which one?"

"One of those where you fill in the letters."

"I don't know it."

"It's like, S, my name is Spencer, my brother's name is Shawn, we come from Sarasota, and we eat sundaes. T, my name is Trevor, my brother's name is Travis, we come from Trenton, and we eat turnips."

"Over and over again?"

"Yes."

"We'll look into that. Too much time spent with that as a shield would make a person crazy."

THREE

Oliver turned off the power on his cell phone so he wouldn't be disturbed. His granddaughter, Addison, hadn't answered when he'd called. It was unusual, but not enough to get worked up over. After all, in this modern day and age, women had the same rights as men—and that included the right to disappear if they wanted to. Besides, he had a council meeting to get through. All his attention needed to be focused on that task, and not on why his granddaughter had temporarily disappeared.

At least he hoped it was temporary. His family had an unusual habit of going missing and winding up dead.

He stared out the noise-blocking windows that lined the outside of the room.

Wade Corporation held the patent on the design, and they worked like a charm. Inside the room you couldn't hear a thing that went on outside. They could have been anywhere in the world, for all you could tell from inside. But they weren't; they were in his favorite place on Earth, two blocks north of the Natural History Museum in New York City, on Central Park West.

It had always seemed the perfect place from which to run the world—a merging of the historical with the modern —and so beautiful, no one noticed anything amiss as the scenery overwhelmed them.

The committee had met in the same room for thirty-four years. Every time Oliver entered its familiar surroundings, he mused remotely over how odd it was that life-changing decisions could be made in such humble surroundings. Plain black conference table, hard-backed red chairs, a screen on the wall to allow for the rare videoconferences. He supposed it could have been a board meeting anywhere.

It wasn't the space that made the place one of a kind; the people who arrived in New York City once every three months to conduct their meetings created the uniqueness of this environment.

He shifted in his leather chair and looked out the window. The meteorologists called for rain, but it looked bright and cheery over Central Park. Someone coughed, and he turned his chair to regard the room again.

Oliver Wade knew more private details about the lives of the other six members of the council than they could possibly imagine. He'd made it his business to know. None of his colleagues—if you could call them that—could legitimately make that claim about him. For eighty years, he'd kept his own counsel and played his cards close to his chest. He'd grown up the son of a coal miner, with a mother who'd been drunk more often than not. Those days had taught him that the only reliable person in the world was himself.

That wasn't to say he didn't consider himself a family man. He'd built his empire for his family. He just needed to keep them all alive long enough to let one of them inherit.

That had, over the years, proved to be more difficult than he could ever have imagined.

As the last member of their group arrived with muttered apologies, it occurred to him that none of the attendees had any idea that his great-grandson was missing. He would commit murder to keep anyone from knowing. Weakness in the family structure affected stock prices.

He looked around the room and smiled as he considered them carefully. He knew, because he always knew these things—that was why he was Oliver Wade—that one of the people in his presence was responsible for Jeremy's disappearance. *Which one?*

That question plagued him.

To his left, staring at her laptop as she always did, sat Grace Ann Charters. Forty years old, the mother of six children and heiress to a liquor dynasty started by her great-great-great-grandfather, she'd also inherited her father's place on the Committee for the Protection of Free Society. She was five feet five inches tall, and her hair fell straight, dyed black, and looked as though it had been plastered to her scalp with hairspray. Her eyes matched her hair in color. A slew of freckles covered her face and she did nothing to hide them, as so many women did.

For fifteen years, she had been married to her second husband, Paul, and they had three children together. Her first marriage, which no one discussed, had lasted two years. For the most part, it was like it hadn't happened. Except that Oliver knew about it, like he knew about the small incident in college involving a hit-and-run and three ounces of cocaine.

Was she the one who'd arranged for Jeremy's kidnapping?

Her views on the council were remarkably consistent

with what her father's had been. As far as the woman was concerned, they shouldn't have locked up the people who showed symptoms of the Condition—they should have killed them. Oliver had personally talked her father out of a plan that would have included the torching down of buildings, and possibly the implementation of killing squads.

Was she out for revenge because he'd halted her family's plans?

Evidently, neither the man nor his daughter was a follower of history. They didn't know how that plan would have eventually blown up in their faces. No, Oliver had known the only way to keep people safe was to put the Conditioned safely away, where they couldn't harm the general population. It was better that Ma and Pa Everyman had no idea how close the bogeyman of their nightmares lived to their colonial farmhouse.

It was better that only Oliver and the other council members ever knew just how dangerous things truly were. It was better that he alone knew how close they had all come to destruction. As long as he lived, he would keep the world secure.

As if feeling his gaze, Grace Ann shut the computer with a click and looked around the room. She held the role of group moderator. They rotated the position, the idea being that none of them would ever become more powerful than the rest. That was, of course, bullshit. He'd been in charge since day one, and everyone knew it.

"Now that we're all here"—Grace Ann eyed the latecomer, George Rainier, with a brutal glance to match her tone—"we can begin. I think our first order of business should be to figure out what we're going to do about this ridiculous request sent over by William Rhodes, the director of Safe Dawn."

"Why is it ridiculous?" George took a drag on his hand rolled cigarette. His fingers were always dyed slightly orange from the tobacco he regularly handled. George had been the first person Oliver had considered as a potential suspect in Jeremy's kidnapping. His ruthlessness almost matched Oliver's, and that made him a serious threat.

The completely bald, sixty-five-year-old man had been raised in South Carolina and, other than to attend these meetings in New York City, Oliver didn't think the short, stout force of nature left the Palmetto State.

It was unusual that George had been so late to the meeting, and Oliver made a mental note to find out what he'd been doing. If something important had made the other man late, Oliver would know what it was by the end of the day.

Grace Ann sneered. "Because there is no way we can start arbitrarily handing out travel passes to people who, for good reason, have been sent to live away from society."

Oliver cleared his throat. "I don't think he's asking for that." Whether they liked it or not, he would achieve his agenda by the end of this meeting. The trick would be convincing the six others in the room that he didn't *have* an agenda.

The woman Oliver considered least likely to have taken Jeremy finally spoke.

"We locked them away for a reason. I have no interest in letting them out and about unsupervised." Karen Monroe, daughter of the late Turner Monroe—the well-known industrialist who'd been responsible, before his passing, for one of the most notorious sex scandals of his generation—slammed her fist on the table to add emphasis to what she'd said.

He often speculated whether she ever wondered how

her father had been caught that day in the orgy that would destroy his reputation. Oliver could have told her; after all, he'd been the one to send the photographers to capture the scene.

George interrupted. "It's not *all* of them, and it's not a total lack of supervision. They wouldn't just be wandering around. But a few of them—those who are deemed worthy because of their helpful behavior and abilities—should be given passes out into the public. It will silence the critics who say we've locked them up, kept them prisoner, and abused them."

Oliver rose from his chair. He walked to the back window and looked down at the street as if contemplating something. His early days building sets at the back of the 9th Street Theater in Manhattan had taught him a thing or two about showmanship. Just to drive home his point, he placed both hands on the windowsill as if he needed support. Let them think he was weakening; it would draw them out sooner.

"There was a reason we talked the President into creating the facilities thirty-four years ago. Four of you were with me when we made that decision. The other three... well, you've heard the stories."

Mumbles of agreement met his statement. "But we're not monsters. We didn't put them in ghettos; we didn't starve them to death, or force them to work as slaves." Some of the people in the room had wanted that, and he hoped his subtle reminder would bring up whatever small amount of shame the Council still had left. "We tried to fix them. Wade Corporation is still trying to find a way to ease the burdens of their ungodly behavior."

Grace Ann nodded. "How is that going? Any progress?"

"As always, the progress in helping the damned is a

slow-moving vehicle. It is out of my hands. I am merely a vessel for God's work." No one could talk the language these people wanted to hear better than he could. "We placed the right people in charge. Rhodes, Drummond, Cooper, Starlight. All people with minor manifestations they had under control. But they're all getting older now. As am I. And, like me, they are looking to find new leadership to take over when the inevitable happens and they are—hopefully, despite their sins—allowed to enter God's kingdom. To adequately assume this role, they need to know the ones they've placed in charge can balance the needs of the outside world with the requirements of the unfortunate who live within the facilities." Oliver threw his hands in the air. "I'm afraid I can see no other option than to give a chosen few travel privileges."

He would handpick those few, and they would work for *his* agenda and on *his* terms. *Unlike Rhodes.* He would have killed Rhodes years before—the one true failure of his career—if doing so wouldn't have created a cascade of problems.

Susan Brilener, one of the quietest members of the Council, who for all her bluster was as pious as she claimed to be, stood, her white hair falling past her waist. Oliver was almost one hundred percent sure she hadn't taken Jeremy. "I agree with Wade. We can't continue to keep people safe from these spawn of Satan if we don't do something to insure the future now." She walked to the window to stand next to Oliver. The woman forever smelled like cinnamon. He wondered if she bathed in it.

"After all, people are already going to them for help, signing them out if you will, for their own needs. They've been most helpful with some law enforcement difficulties, and some of them have cleared up issues pertaining to questions in wills by communicating with the dead."

Oliver could have snorted if he hadn't been so adept at keeping his cool. *That's right. They all call those abilities godless, until they need them for their own personal use.*

"Even Oliver's own family has gone to them."

He shook his head. "To what are you referring, Susan?" Oliver's heart rate increased just a touch. For the first time in more years than he cared to remember, he had a feeling he was about to be surprised with some bad news. The shock of it was that it was coming from Susan. What was her game? His certainty in her innocence regarding Jeremy took a plunge. She was officially back on his list.

"Why Addison, of course. I understand she had some private business at Safe Dawn today."

Oliver crossed to his chair, keeping his expression neutral. The girl had defied him. He had specifically given Addison instructions not to go there to ask for help, and apparently, she had disregarded him entirely. If he hadn't been so furious, he would have admitted it was a sign that she was finally acting like a Wade.

"Oh, Addison has been trying to set up Wade Corporation in some charity work that would help to let the inhabitants of Safe Dawn receive online master's degrees in the subjects of their choice. You know how my granddaughter is. Hell, what twenty-six-year-old isn't a bleeding heart?"

That statement earned him the laughs he wanted and took the pressure off him for a moment. Deliberately, he avoided looking at Susan. Even the slightest eye contact would give the woman power over him she didn't deserve. Just because she'd entered the realm of subterfuge, didn't mean she got to play at his advanced level.

It was time to call for a vote while he still had everyone's attention. Then he would have Addison hauled into his office for a much-needed explanation, followed by a thorough investigation of Susan Brilener, including unearthing the name of her spy at Safe Dawn.

"I think it's time for a vote. Don't you agree, Grace Ann?" He smiled at her and resisted calling her Gracie. Evidently, it was what she liked to be called in bed. Smiling to himself, he remembered that power was in the details, and he was the one with all of those. Susan Brilener would be nothing but a small blip on the Wade Corporation radar by tomorrow morning. By next week, she'd be off the Council, and if she was responsible for Jeremy's kidnapping, she'd be dead.

Grace Ann stood and asked the members to vote yes or no to granting Rhodes the power to bring to them several candidates for the so-called travel privileges. The yeses voted first and, as Oliver had expected, won the day by one vote. Grace Ann, Karen, and George joined him in granting Rhodes the power he'd requested. Oliver jotted their names down on a piece of paper before folding it and sticking it in his pocket. Susan, even after the speech that had alerted him to her hidden agenda, had stayed on the no side of the fence.

He could eliminate the nos. Someone who'd voted yes had kidnapped his great-grandson. A power shift had just begun in the council, and it hadn't been started by anyone who'd voted against him. As with all the best schemes, one of his so-called allies had betrayed him in the deepest possible way. He knew these things, not in the way the *aberrant* knew them, but just enough to have become hugely successful.

He accepted Grace Ann's suggestion that they all go to

lunch at the newest high-priced gourmet eatery that had opened down the block.

ADDISON WALKED STRAIGHT-BACKED into his office an hour after he returned from his overpriced, tasteless meal. Her eyes were distant, her demeanor set as though she had nothing in the world to fear or worry about. If he hadn't been so angry, he'd have been proud. No one outside their small family circle had any idea Jeremy was missing.

"Come in, Grandchild, and close the door behind you."

She did as he asked before crossing to the leather chair she always sat in when called into his office. Addison was nothing if not predictable and organized—up until she'd visited Safe Dawn despite his orders not to. Now, he had to wonder what else his darling granddaughter was hiding.

"I got your message and came as quickly as I could manage. I was across town at a meeting with the garment suppliers. I think this entire venture is going to be a huge success. A thinner bulletproof vest. It was a brilliant idea, Grandfather."

It had been, but he hadn't called her here to discuss that. He cleared his throat and leveled a look at her that had made grown men whimper. She didn't even lower her gaze.

"Do you want to explain to me what you were thinking?"

"I'd be happy to, if I knew to what you referred."

Insolence. Addison knew exactly what he wanted, and still she was going to make him say it out loud.

"I want to know *what* you were *thinking* going to Safe Dawn this morning."

Now she shifted in her seat. Maybe he'd been wrong; maybe she hadn't known what he wanted, or she'd been hoping it was something else.

"I was thinking that I want my nephew found."

"And the insinuation there would be that I *don't* want that."

"I'm just not clear why you aren't doing more to locate him."

"My methods and my decisions are none of your concern."

She crossed her legs. "Except, of course, they are."

He gripped the edge of his desk. Usually Addison backed down immediately. He had clearly not prepared enough for this meeting. "Since when are the decisions I make for this family your concern?"

"As I'm a member of this family—one fourth of it—I would say that your decisions are very much my concern. But even more than that—and here is where it's going to get really tricky—Jeremy is almost entirely my concern, as he was entrusted to me specifically."

Oliver wanted to explode. If Addison continued down this path, it was going to take her into shark-infested waters. He raised an eyebrow. Maybe he'd been wrong. Maybe her foray into deception meant she could handle this.

The question was whether he was willing to let her make the attempt.

"You do understand that when you deal with these people—maybe it's not fair to even call them that—there is always a hidden agenda. You think you're hiring them for their abilities, and you end up owing them something. You end up caught up in the web of destruction that caused us to lock them up to begin with."

She paused before speaking. "I did get the impression

that William Rhodes is playing many cards at the same time, and certainly Spencer Lewis is a handful, but they are both well within my ability to deal with." She sat forward in her seat. "I can handle them. This won't be a problem for the Wades. The only thing Safe Dawn, William Rhodes, or Spencer Lewis will be getting from us is money for their services. We will find Jeremy."

She looked down at her hands, and for the first time Oliver wondered how much of Addison's affectations had been learned from him. Was she playing him with her apparent insecurity?

"Don't punish Jeremy because I went against your orders. If you don't think I can handle it, take it over, but let them find Jeremy for us."

He stood and walked around his desk until he towered over her. It was keenly important that Addison understand the severity of this situation. For a moment, as he gazed at her, he was struck by how much she looked like his late wife. Nothing like her own parents, who had been dark-haired, Addison had Sharon's blonde hair and blue eyes.

Blinking, he let the memory fade away. This was no time to pick up sentimentality.

"I don't know who took Jeremy, but I'm working on it. Unlike the authorities, I believe if Jeremy were dead, we would have found a body by now. Someone *has* him. The question is *why*." He studied her clasped hands. Standing this close to her, he could practically feel the tension radiating from her body. "If you must hire Safe Dawn, then hire them. But I need you to remember something. I sit on the council. If something goes awry with them, I, unlike the average citizen, will have no choice but to bring in the Fury to handle it."

Addison gasped. *A-ha.* He had shocked her. "I thought the Fury was a myth."

He shook his head. "Not a myth. Keep that in mind when you deal with Lewis or whomever Rhodes sends you. Ask yourself if you want death and mayhem on your hands."

FOUR

An hour later, Addison sat in the back of the town car, staring out the window as the landscape changed from urban Manhattan to rural New Jersey. It always amazed her how fast everything altered outside New York City. In under an hour, she'd gone from cityscape to farmland. She wished more of her life could be that way, as if she could just make a small adjustment and switch the landscape of her own existence.

Her mind whirled.

The Fury was *real* and her *grandfather* was so powerful that he controlled them. How was it possible that she'd never known any of this? She'd known he sat on the Council, and understood that he was one of the richest men in the country, but she hadn't realized just how involved in things he actually was. No wonder Rhodes had been so interested in what she'd wanted from them.

She ran her hands through her hair to flatten it as she tapped her foot on the floor of the car. "Gregory, when we get there—when you get to Safe Dawn—could you please pull up front and park so I can run inside and retrieve Mr. Lewis?"

Why on Earth had she thought it was a good idea to go pick up Spencer Lewis? One misstep on his part and her grandfather would call in the Fury, and then he'd be dead. She'd be lucky not to follow him to that end. Maybe she wouldn't die; maybe she'd simply wish she had.

"No, ma'am, I'm not letting you inside that place without me. No way, no how."

Addison smiled. Greg had been with her family so long, she wasn't even sure the exact year he'd started working for them.

Even her grandfather couldn't bully him. He always said what he thought, at least to her. He liked to remind her he'd driven her mother to the hospital when she'd been in labor with Addison. That had given him some rights.

Who was Addison to argue with logic like that?

Greg was approaching sixty—the same age her father would have been if he'd lived—completely gray, with a belly that was getting bigger every year.

"It's okay, Greg. Aunt Morgan and I drove down there this morning. It's perfectly safe."

"Well, you didn't have me with you this morning, Addison, and if you had, I wouldn't have let you and Ms. Wade in there without me. Which, I might point out, is precisely why you drove yourself."

He was right; it was why she'd done it.

"So, then, I suppose you'll be coming with me?"

"Damn right I will. Your grandfather is crazy letting you come here without a man to protect you."

Addison rolled her eyes. She'd long ago stopped arguing with Greg about how capable she was. Besides, it was nice to have someone left in the world who cared what happened to her. Her grandfather barely thought of her at all, and her Aunt Morgan only concerned herself with her when she needed something. Her sister had understood the character of the people in their family perfectly, which was why she'd entrusted Jeremy to Addison.

For a month, she'd done things the way others wanted her to do them. Now she would trust her own instincts. The Fury be damned.

Even thinking of that organization caused shivers to cross her body. The rumor—which had proved, incredibly, to be true—was almost too much to believe. Thirty-four years earlier, when the President had decided that people with the Condition were too dangerous to be left out in society, he'd opened six institutions to relocate the dangerous *creatures*. In his private memoirs, he would later say the Conditioned had to have been spawned by Satan and couldn't be left amongst the good, decent Americans just trying to live a simple life. Even the ACLU couldn't help. People had rights only if they were actually considered to be *people*, and not dangerous manifestations of evil.

But it hadn't proven so easy to institutionalize them. Hell, some of the children who'd shown the strange, dangerous abilities could blow up a person's brain with just a thought. So how had they managed it? The public line had been that eventually, through negotiation, the parents of these children had seen the benefits of placing their offspring in the care of people who could handle them better. Professionals who could keep them safe, keep them from hurting innocents. That had never made sense to her. For most parents, it would take a little more than persuasion to give away their children.

Addison shuddered now that she knew how the children had been taken away. Quietly, the rumors had persisted. The whole thing had happened eight years before Addison had been born, but she still heard them discussed in private where public ears couldn't listen. The council, some said, had taken it upon themselves to find a way to police the Conditioned from within the community itself.

The Fury had been born. Chosen for their special abilities to control those like themselves, they'd trained to work for the council and been given the freedom to live in secret outside the institutions because they tracked down and identified—hunted, really—people like them.

Try to hide your child? The Fury would find you.

Try to escape your institution? The Fury would take you back... or kill you.

Even non-Conditioned children were terrified of the Fury. It was every little boy and girl's fear that they might be falsely identified by the Fury and taken away from their families. Now, it looked like the Fury would be monitoring Addison during her time with Spencer Lewis.

Bad news, considering she'd already had to take out her childhood rhymes to keep her mind from doing funny things. If she wasn't completely careful, Spencer could be killed and she would be exposed. The possibility made her stomach turn.

The Fury is real.

"We're here, Addison."

Jolted back to reality, she looked up as they pulled into Safe Dawn. If possible, the facility seemed even more imposing to her than it had earlier. Everything about it seemed to scream, "stay away." The building was large, but not huge. Behind the facade, surrounded by walls and guard towers that made it all but invisible to public view, was a small village of houses and apartments serving as homes to the Conditioned. The gray-and-beige-bricked building with the black roof was only the public part. It was off-putting. The big problem was that having come this far, Addison couldn't obey its unspoken commandment.

After she and Greg showed their identification cards, they were waved through. It took about two minutes for the car to reach the main building. Addison expected Gregory to have to look for a parking space until she saw Spencer standing outside.

He leaned a shoulder against the guard post in a lazy pose. Addison narrowed her eyes, wondering if she could be reading the situation wrong. It looked to her like Spencer was actually joking with the guards who surrounded him. He said something, and the one holding the machine gun cracked up and slapped him on the back.

Well, it appeared that the guards weren't afraid of him, so maybe she didn't need to be either. Of course, it could just be that they were holding guns and could blow off his head.

"Pull up right there, Greg. Mr. Lewis is already outside." Did her voice sound as stiff to Greg as it did to her own ears?

As the car slowed down and finally stopped, Addison unbuckled her seatbelt and opened the door. She smoothed down her gray skirt before she stepped out of the car. She tried her best to smile as she met Spencer's sharp gaze. Her head felt fuzzy and unclear.

"Hello, Mr. Lewis. I'm sorry if we kept you waiting."

He shook his head. "You didn't." He motioned to the guard standing to his right, and she followed the direction with her gaze.

The other man was holding out a clipboard. After a moment, he snorted. "You need to sign him out."

"Sign him out?" She was having a hard time following

what was going on. She felt confused, and she could only blame Spencer Lewis' presence for it. The man was dangerous to her nerves.

"Yes, like a Jet Ski from a resort in the Caribbean." The fat guard snorted, and Addison bit her tongue. She should tell the man that at the type of resorts she stayed at you didn't sign out a Jet Ski. Someone ran and got you one or bought another one if they were out. But he wasn't worth the effort, and he wouldn't think any better of her for the jibe. In fact, he would probably think she was a stuck-up bitch.

"You're responsible for my welfare and those I'm around while I'm not here." Spencer's voice was like the warm apple cider that she loved in the fall. "Will explained this to you when you were here earlier."

He paused and ran his hands through his hair. She watched, transfixed, as his golden locks seemed to move in slow motion through his fingers and back down onto the top of his head.

"Are you okay?" Spencer's voice sounded far away.

"Huh?"

Whirling around, he stared at the gray fortress behind them.

"Ben, cut it out."

Blinking, Addison felt her thoughts speed up, and for a moment, she was dizzy. She shook her head, her mind finally not feeling sluggish or confused. "What's going on?"

"Ben is fucking around with your mind a little bit. Go on, sign me out so we can get this over with."

"What do you mean he was fucking with my mind?" Addison signed the paper that gave her responsibility for Spencer, a daunting thought at the very least. Her hand shook, and she hoped no one noticed.

"He's a teenager and should know better. But he's completely harmless—he's not capable of doing any damage, just sort of confusing you. He thinks he's amusing, like somehow it's funny that you can't follow conversations. Another minute and he would have exhausted himself."

Addison felt rage pulse through her bloodstream. "That's an invasion of my privacy. It's illegal for him to do that to me." She was shouting, and she didn't care. Not only had this *Ben* violated the sanctity of her mind, but he could have affected her coping mechanism and then she might have exposed herself as being afflicted, as being Conditioned.

Spencer pointed to the exit of the complex. "Right through those gates, it's illegal. Where you're standing right now, it's annoying." Gripping her arm, he ushered her back to her car door and pushed her gently inside. "Just another reason to get you out of here. Later, when you return me, you can lodge a complaint with Will. I'll witness it. Ben will end up doing kitchen cleanup for a week. Unless, of course, you have more important things to think about than getting a fifteen-year-old you will never see again punished for a harmless mind trick. Like finding your missing nephew."

Addison felt a moment of shame and immediately resented Spencer for bringing it on. How dare he lecture her on what she should or should not be offended by? She opened her mouth to tell him so and closed it. This was not going well.

Sliding in closer to her, he shut the door and looked around the inside of the car.

Nodding toward Greg, he grinned. "Who is he?"

"This is Gregory Bradley. He's worked for my family for a long time. He's our driver."

"Hi, Gregory, I'm Spencer Lewis."

Addison could see the driver's face in the rearview mirror as he nodded his hello.

"Greg, would you mind closing the divider? I need to speak to Spencer for a moment. It concerns company business." Gregory nodded and raised a window between them.

Spencer motioned to the divider. "Do most town cars have that feature?"

"No. Grandfather had it custom-made. He doesn't like driving around in a limo, but he wanted the privacy that a limo allows for business transactions, so he made his town car limoesque."

"If I could drive, I would never let anyone chauffeur me around."

"You can't drive?"

Half of his mouth raised in a smile. His eyes glowed with an emotion Addison couldn't identify. "Ms. Wade, you just had to sign me out. Do you think they let me operate a motor vehicle?"

Addison's cheeks warmed in embarrassment. It had been an honest mistake, but a silly one. Damn it. In less than two minutes, he'd made her feel foolish twice.

She would try again. "Then I guess this must be nice for you, to get out of Safe Dawn and see the world outside those walls."

"Why would you say that?"

He shifted in his seat, and she admired the strong lines of his profile. Spencer seemed to radiate heat, more so than most men she knew—more alive, somehow more vibrant.

"It must get trying, always being stuck in the same place."

"Actually, I prefer it. Very few things tempt me away. Missing children happen to be one of them."

"How can you prefer it?" The idea of being stuck

behind the walls of that place and never allowed to leave made her shudder.

"Would you want to be somewhere where everyone around you treated you with suspicion and disdain? Even if you were doing them a favor? And that's all I do—favors—considering that I can't get paid, not directly."

And strike three. She'd officially stuck her foot in her mouth in all three attempts to speak to him. "I can see how that would be... difficult." She took a deep breath. Everything with Spencer was proving to be complicated. She couldn't seem to say anything at all without it being the absolute wrong thing. "But surely there must be something you'd like to one day see outside Safe Dawn?"

He nodded and turned his head to look away from her to stare at the scenery. Evidently, his brief nod was the only response he intended to give her. Well, two could play at that game, and why did she care what he wished he could see? He was a means to an end to find her nephew, and a potentially dangerous one at that.

"Why don't you tell me about your nephew? Finding him will be in the small details."

"I thought you'd just go into his room, do a reading or whatever it is you do, and then you'd be able to tell us where he went or who took him."

"That *would* be efficient, wouldn't it?" He turned his attention back to her, his blue eyes claiming all her attention. Was it her imagination, or did the temperature in the car rise several degrees? In another few seconds, she was going to start sweating.

She cleared her throat and took off the gray jacket that matched her skirt. Underneath it, she had put on a simple white blouse that she wished was short sleeved.

Spencer's eyes followed her every movement. She

wondered what he was thinking about. Whatever it was, she imagined it was intense, because his eyes seemed to glow with some unknown thought.

Nearly shaking now with nerves, Addison knew she was about two minutes away from having to resort to her rhyming. Once she started doing that, she would barely be able to speak at all. That meant she needed to answer all his questions before it was too late, and he became suspicious or somehow the Fury caught on. Addison had no idea how it worked. Could they be monitoring her in the car?

Spencer reached out and grabbed her shaking hand. She jerked but didn't pull her hand away.

"I'm having a terrible time figuring you out, Ms. Wade."

Her tongue felt dry in her mouth but she was glad to find it still worked. "I don't know why you think you need to figure me out; you're working for me, nothing more."

Even as she said the words, her brain could only think one thing: liar. Spencer was proving to be much more than an employee; if anything, he was going to be a hazard to her health. But she'd be damned if she'd let him know that.

He smiled, but there was no joy in his eyes. "To answer your earlier question, if Priscilla, my anchor, was still with us, then I could easily go into the boy's room, do a deep reading, and with a ninety-percent certainty come out with at least a sense of where he is. Even if he were dead that would still be true. Now that I have to keep the reading shallow, it may take more than one shot at it to find him."

"Jeremy."

"What?"

Addison huffed out her frustration. "My nephew's name is Jeremy. I would prefer that you didn't call him 'the boy.'" She didn't know why it mattered so much to her, but it did.

"Okay. Jeremy." Was that admiration in his eyes? "I might be able to locate him in the first attempt just by going to the room where he was taken, and then we'll be done. But I might need more than that. We might have to go to his school, to the park where he plays. I might have to handle his favorite toys. I don't know. So, I'll need you to keep thinking of things that are inherently 'Jeremy' and keep throwing them at me until we come up with something that works." He took a deep breath. "I'm sorry it's not going to be an exact science."

"We'll do whatever we have to do. I'm not losing Jeremy."

Spencer shifted in his seat so she could see him even more clearly. His eyes were bottomless pits of blue, like the color of the sky on a perfectly clear day when she managed to be far away from the city. There was something else, too. The very center of his eyes... they seemed to swirl with color. Not just blue, but gray and green. How was that possible?

"What if you've already lost him? Are you prepared to deal with that?"

Letting go of his hand, Addison sat back in her seat and crossed her arms. She put on her best-practiced haughty expression and shot daggers at him. Forget looking at his amazing eyes. What did they matter when they belonged to a man with no feelings at all?

"It's not possible."

"Addison..."

"I said it's not possible." And that was all she was going to say on the subject. She knew what her expression said, since she used it often enough in business. It dared him to contradict her if he was brave enough. Actually, she kind of hoped that he would. It might be cathartic to really let loose her temper and damn the consequences. Bring on the Fury.

Forcing herself to swallow her anger, she tried desperately to get her thoughts back on track and off her distaste for Spencer Lewis. Jeremy was what mattered. She needed to stay focused on that.

"All right."

She shook her head. "What?"

"All right, he's not dead. If ever there was someone who could keep a missing child alive through sheer force of will alone, it would be you, I suspect. So, for right now, I'll acquiesce and say that he's alive."

Nodding, she bit down on her lip. Little did he know he had just described her grandfather, not her, to a T. Most of the time, Addison was missing the Wade gene that let her control the world with just a thought.

"Thank you."

"You're welcome." He moved closer to her, and she abruptly pressed up against the wall of the car to try to put some space between them. Spencer countered this by pressing even more tightly against her. She gulped.

"Someday I would like to see the ocean."

Addison's eyes filled with tears and she blinked them away. He'd never seen the ocean, and she took it for granted that she got to see it all the time. "Which one?"

"Doesn't matter. The open sea. That's really all I wanted in the world."

"Past tense? Wanted?"

He raised an eyebrow. "Let's just say that now there's something else I want even more."

He was so close she could smell the ivory scent of his soap. Using every bit of willpower she possessed, she stopped herself from taking a deep breath to bring his scent even further into her mind. He would know immediately what she had done, and she refused to give him that kind of power.

He moved back in his seat, giving her space again. As she tried to regain her breath, she couldn't help but feel that she'd just been warned. He wanted her. That much was clear.

His face had turned back into the mask she couldn't read, and she felt momentary disappointment because, despite her best intentions, he made her heart flutter. And she wanted him.

FIVE

All Rhodes had asked of him was to behave around the Wades, to make a good impression, and yet Spencer couldn't seem to help acting like a brute in front of Addison Wade. Two more minutes in the car, smelling the sweet vanilla wafting from her hair or the natural, clean scent of her soap, and he would bang her over the head and drag her off to some cave where he could ravish her. Hell, maybe he could just bang her in the car.

He was usually better at controlling his baser instincts. What the hell was wrong with him? He didn't harbor sexual fantasies about skinny blonde cheerleader types with pissed-off attitudes. He liked his women curvaceous, with black gypsy eyes and long, glorious dark hair. Women who were confident in their own sexual appeal, who didn't try to hide it, who said what they wanted and did what they desired.

Addison Wade was so bundled up in her plain gray suit, with her ordinary nude pantyhose and sensible black shoes that he wanted to scream. And there was nothing rational about his reaction.

What would it be like to push her down on the seat and screw her until her pouty, strained mouth smiled with sensuous desire? This woman, for some bizarre reason, was causing his senses to go into overdrive. It wasn't acceptable. He needed to get it under control before he embarrassed himself. If there was one thing he could be sure of, it was that Addison Wade, granddaughter of the man who had practically invented torture for the Conditioned, was not going to be spreading her legs for him.

She probably thought he was less than an animal, which was why she stared at him with so much contempt. Hell, the woman could barely stand to be in the car with him. Her hand shook from the strain of being in his presence. He rolled his eyes. So what on Earth had possessed him to tell her he wanted to see the ocean and was desperate to have her?

Maybe he was as deranged as people thought his kind were.

"We're here." Her voice, which was only slightly above husky, broke his internal musings, and he raised his arms to stretch his body. Addison looked down and tapped her foot again. What should have been an annoying habit was, for no discernible reason, adorable when she did it.

"Before we go inside, I have to tell you something."

He rubbed his jaw, surprised by how much stubble he felt there. When was the last time he'd shaved? Lately, he forgot more and more to do that type of thing.

"What's that?"

"My grandfather is furious that I brought you here."

"You did this without telling Oliver Wade?" He didn't know if he should have been impressed or horrified. As a member of the community Wade had devoted his life to trying to destroy, Spencer knew better than anyone just how dangerous he could be.

She nodded. "Jeremy is mine. He was entrusted to me. I'd walk through the gates of Hell for him if I had to."

"Do you love him like he's your son?"

"I do." She nodded. "I really do. He knows I'm not his mother. He's only four, but he remembers Jeanne, and he loves her. But he comes to me for mothering, and I can't imagine I could ever love a child more."

Just when he thought he could categorize Addison Wade as a spoiled, entitled brat, she went and said something like that. "So I should watch out for your dear old granddad, then?"

"He said if you got out of line, he'd call the Fury down on both of us."

Spencer saw terror pour out of Addison's ice-blue eyes. She wasn't even doing anything to disguise it. Before he could stop himself, he reached out to grasp her hand in his and wasn't surprised that it shook. "If that's what is scaring you, don't worry. I always have the Fury watching me when I leave Safe Dawn. They might even monitor me when I'm inside the walls of the institution. I have no idea. If they were going to kill me, they would have done so when they let the police take Priscilla's life."

Her eyes widened even farther and he bit back a curse. He was trying to comfort her, and evidently he'd only added to her fear.

"What happened?"

Nope, he wasn't going there. "It has no bearing here. Priscilla did something stupid."

"So the Fury only went after her because she broke the rules?"

He wouldn't go that far. They were unfair laws, and he

wasn't going to act like they were otherwise. "It's all a lot of bullshit. She didn't do anything a human being shouldn't be allowed to do. But, yes, technically she broke some rules." He needed to get off this topic before the anger made him let loose on the woman in the car. If that happened, he might not be able to help people anymore.

Spencer didn't have much to qualify him for salvation, but when asked to help people with his strange powers, he always did his best. That much he would be able to claim if he was ever in front of the pearly gates.

Of course, if people were to be believed, he was doomed to Hell simply for having been born the way he was. But Rhodes didn't believe that, and Spencer had never known the older man to be wrong about anything.

Gregory, who had not shown himself through the screen since Spencer had first gotten into the car, pulled the vehicle to a stop in front of a large building. Moments later, the door opened from the outside as a doorman made his greetings to Addison. She stepped out onto the street and Spencer followed her.

Leaning back, he tried to see the top of the building the Wades called home. It wasn't the biggest building on the street, but it screamed money and prestige. Looking to his left, he caught sight of a street sign. They were nearly on the corner of Madison Avenue and Seventy-First. Not that he'd be going anywhere without Addison, but he always liked to have a general idea of where he was, in case he needed that information later.

Two seconds standing on the street, and he was thoroughly impressed with the sound proofing in Addison's town car. He'd been to New York City before, and the noise of the place was always what struck him first. There was so much traffic on the streets that the automobiles almost took on a life of their own. Cars honked, people shouted, and hammers and construction drills blasted all around him. It was a huge change from the quiet of Safe Dawn, where there weren't even any neighbors for miles around.

He liked New York. He liked the energy, and the way the city seemed to be just as alive as the people who lived and worked there, as if it had become a living, breathing life form from having sheltered so many souls over the years.

"You okay?" Addison stood in front of the building and stared back at him. Her blonde hair whipped around her in a halo of gold and yellow. For a moment, he wished he could paint so he could capture her at that exact second and look back on its perfection for the rest of his life.

He walked toward her and the doorman rushed ahead of Addison to pull open the entrance to the dark-gray concrete building. The awning they walked under was burgundy, a similar shade to the aging doorman's nose and cheeks. Spencer wondered if he was cold or if he'd spent too many years drinking and now his face was showing the effects. He smiled as Addison introduced him, and nodded. She seemed to know all the people who worked for her on a first-name basis.

Addison called the man Charlie, and Spencer held his breath as he waited for the ice-blonde goddess to inform the other man just who Spencer was. All pretense of politeness would disappear. He waited. Addison moved forward to the elevator without explaining his presence.

Spencer took a deep breath. What the hell? They—meaning the people he was signed out to—always told everyone around them who he was and what his purpose was. Addison hadn't. What was she playing at?

He followed her to the elevator. The doorman, who acted as the first line of defense for security in the building, should know who he was. If Addison belonged to Spencer, he'd be pissed as hell at her for not telling the people who were supposed to protect her that she'd deliberately brought danger into her apartment. Spencer knew that, if he was nothing else, he was dangerous to those around him.

Stepping into the elevator, Spencer waited for the doors to close, sealing them in before turning to her. "Why didn't you tell Charlie who I really am?"

She shrugged. "It's not his business. He's two seconds away from losing his job, considering someone got in and out of this building without his noticing. Turns out he was asleep. There's a rotating group of four personnel who hold that job. It was designed to prevent anyone from getting tired and doing just what he did. Grandfather hasn't fired him yet, but it's coming. He won't want publicity about Jeremy, so he'll find another reason to do it, or he'll have one of the other tenants get the co-op board to do it."

"Or he was drugged."

"We considered that. Grandfather had him tested. He was totally clean. He just fell asleep."

"Oh, your grandfather had him tested." He couldn't help the sneer in his voice.

Addison narrowed her eyes. "Yes, he did. Grandfather wants Jeremy found as much as I do."

Just not enough to come to Safe Dawn himself. Spencer did have some sense of self-preservation, which fortunately let him keep that particular thought to himself. He didn't want to make the woman any more defensive than she already was. Even if Oliver Wade's tests were legitimate, his gut was telling him this was more than just a story of an employee falling asleep at his post.

Maybe the man had been in on the whole thing. Maybe he'd been manipulated psychically to fall asleep. There were any number of possibilities. None of that was his concern. His job was to get a psychic reading, get a sense of who'd taken the kid, figure out, as best he could, where the child was, and get himself back home.

The conspiracies involved could be the Wades' personal problem. They had nothing to do with him, and he needed to stay out of them unless it related to Jeremy.

An image of Addison standing on the street with the wind in her hair appeared before his eyes. Usually, he didn't have visions unless he tried to. Controlling when they happened had been part of his training. This felt different. It was channeled, but not from the dark place; it was more like his mind wanted him to see her like that again.

He couldn't imagine why. He'd taken a pretty good look at her the first time. Her glorious hair floating like that had made him take temporary leave of his senses and think whimsically. There was something else, though; something he could see now that he couldn't earlier. She had looked so... unguarded.

He blinked as he cleared his mind and looked down at Addison as she stood with him. Hands at her sides, back straight, eyes focused directly ahead as if there were something interesting happening at the front of the lonely elevator.

"What floor do you live on?"

"Grandfather, Jeremy, Aunt Morgan, and I reside in the penthouse."

"Must be sort of awkward."

She shook her head. "What?"

"Living with your grandfather and Aunt Morgan. You and Jeremy must get very little alone time."

"Aunt Morgan is around quite a bit, when she isn't

living in the house in Grand Cayman. Grandfather spends most of his time in the office."

The elevator dinged and opened directly into the apartment, which Spencer gathered meant that they literally lived on the whole floor of the penthouse. He'd never been able to accumulate wealth of his own, and he didn't care very much how rich his so-called clients were. For the most part, it was only the exceptionally wealthy who came to Safe Dawn looking for help. Rhodes never told the residents what he charged for their services, but he guessed it was pricey. He'd once asked the old man if he would turn away the poor if they came to him for help. Will had said that of course he wouldn't, but never—not once in the thirty-four years he'd run Safe Dawn—had they been asked by anyone who couldn't pay.

Since they didn't advertise, it might have been fair to say that only people with influence in the upper crust of society knew they were available for help.

The Wade apartment had clearly been designed to impress and possibly to intimidate. He raised an eyebrow as he looked around. The walls were painted a deep gold beneath a silver trim. A crown molding jutted out from the top of the wall directly beneath the ceiling and accentuated the colors. The actual design of the molding looked to be something circa turn of the nineteenth century, and Spencer wondered just how old the building was.

The older the facility, the harder it could be to go into the dark spaces he would need to visit to find Jeremy. In the past, people had been more superstitious and taken steps to ward their homes, even if they hadn't known they were doing it. Lately, since the Condition had started appearing more regularly, people had returned to old-fashioned notions of paranoia. Some of those theories, it turned out, had been completely correct. They built buildings with materials that made shifting into the other level of consciousness more difficult. For most readers, if there was lead-based paint on the walls, it was downright impossible to get into the dark land. Not to mention not healthy for the people who lived there, but that part wasn't his problem.

Of course, he managed it.

Spencer crossed the room to a large window—there were six total in the foyer—and looked down at the street below. "So it's not likely they carried him out of the window. Someone down below would have seen."

"Do you want to see his room now, or can I get you something to eat? Would you like to rest?"

He grinned and turned to look at her. "We can go now. Then maybe you can return me tonight and be done with this."

"You talk about yourself so strangely. 'Return you' and 'sign you out.' You can't possibly think of yourself as property."

"I don't, but you do, so it makes it easier if I speak the language you're comfortable with." He walked toward a large, ornate, black-rimmed staircase that stood at the left side of the room. Now that was impressive; he'd never seen a two-story apartment in Manhattan before. "Jeremy slept upstairs?"

"Don't presume to know how I think, Mr. Lewis."

She'd gotten formal, which must mean that he was in trouble. "My apologies."

"You know, from someone else that might be genuine, but I can't get over the feeling that when you say things like that you're just being condescending and disguising it as manners. I do not accept your apologies, Mr. Lewis, and yes, Jeremy lives upstairs. Follow me."

He walked behind her, pissed off about being called on his bullshit. Nobody ever did that, not even his friends back home or Will. Where had she gotten the courage? Wasn't she afraid he was going to mind-rape her or set the curtains on fire with his outrage? After a moment, his attitude changed considerably as he noticed the sway of her hips and the firm, supple mound of her behind.

Without too much effort, he could reach out and grab her firm rear end and give it a pinch. Her squeal might be worth it... up until the point she called the police on his dumb self. The escapade would be far from worth it. Or maybe not.

He shook his head. What the hell was the matter with him? He hadn't been this desperate for a woman since he'd lost his virginity at sixteen. The longer he stood in the apartment, the more aggravated he became by it. Everything in it was so formal; it looked like it belonged in a museum, just like her gray skirt. Addison had to be less than thirty years old, and yet she seemed to grow more ancient by the minute.

All he could do was hope that he got this job done quickly, before he did something stupid and told Addison Wade that she was too hot to be so cold and too young to be so *gone* already.

She whirled around, her eyes venomous as she pointed her index finger at him. Wow. She was really mad, and it made him even harder. He wished he could find a subtle way to adjust his pants, except he didn't see how that was possible. She hadn't spoken a word yet, but she was like a cyclone, ready to whirl and destroy whatever was in her path... which at that moment happened to be him.

"I do *not* think of you as property. I can't get over that you said that to me. I came looking for help." Her hands swung left and right as if of their own volition, and he realized just how distressed she really was.

"Addison..."

"I have no idea whether you're dangerous, whether you or anyone you live with needs to be locked up. I didn't make the rules. All that happened eight years before I was born. I know Grandfather is terribly involved and that Wade Corp did things, when I was a small child, to make things even worse for you, but I would never"—she poked her finger hard into his chest—"ever, ever think of you or treat you that way."

He grabbed her shoulders and pulled her closer. She gasped and stared up at him with huge blue eyes that looked anything but ice-cold now. They were fuming with anger and heat. "That was very unfair what I said to you. I'm not a nice guy."

"You're *actually* apologizing?" She seemed confused as she chewed on her bottom lip.

"Yes." He let go of her shoulders and brushed her blonde hair off her forehead.

It was softer than he'd expected, like cotton balls. "I was wrong. Let's start again. I'm Spencer Lewis. I can travel to dark places, read energies, and find missing children, but I'm currently without an anchor, so I'm working at half capacity. It's making me edgy, and I'm not a nice guy when I'm in a good mood, so a bad one makes me even worse. And you?"

The smallest smile appeared, and her eyes seemed to glow with mischief. "I'm Addison Wade, spoiled granddaughter of the third wealthiest man in America. I'm desperate to make a name for myself in my family's company. I'm not good with people, and I act haughty when

I'm uncomfortable. I need you to find my nephew. I miss him *desperately*."

Her last word ate at his soul. What must it be like to be missed desperately? To have someone care that much? Anger made his head pound. This child was loved, and someone had dared to remove him from that love. Spencer didn't know love but, if it was possible, he'd find a way to give Jeremy back to Addison,

"Let's go to his room, Addison Wade."

Forcing himself to move, he took a step back. Maybe it would be smart not to touch her again. It had been too perfect, too right, and God knew he was not entitled to those kinds of feelings. At least not in this lifetime.

SIX

Jeremy's room had always been a haven for Addison. At the end of the day, she would find him sitting on the floor playing, his nanny having just gone home. Joining him was like having a chance to enjoy part of the childhood she'd been too terrified to actually have. Now it just felt empty, deserted—the way she imagined Hell would be. Complete and utter loneliness.

She crossed to the bed. Too rattled by her explosion at Spencer, she picked up Jeremy's brown, slightly tattered teddy bear and squeezed it. It was going to lose an eye soon, which meant she'd have to find someone to sew it back on, since she had no idea how to do that herself.

"This is it, then?" Spencer walked around the room. Someone else might have called his gait aimless, but she could see that he was zigzagging purposefully to cover the most space in the least amount of time. A serpentine maneuver, it was an impressive approach.

"This is his room, where he was taken." Saying it hadn't gotten any easier in the month that had followed her first horrifying discovery.

"And it was what time?"

"Sometime between one and six in the morning."

"How do you know he was here at one?"

She sighed. "I checked on him at one."

He stared at her in the way that made her feel like her insides were about to melt. He was doing it again, whatever it was that made his eyes swirl in the strange hypnotic way she had noticed earlier. "Do you do that every night?"

"A lot of parents check on their kids every night."

He shrugged. "I guess. I wouldn't know. I grew up sleeping in a hospital bed in a room I shared with fifteen other boys. No one checked on us till morning."

Her heart broke a little, and she swallowed the lump that formed in her throat. "Oh." There really wasn't anything else to say. He'd been so matter-of-fact in the way he'd said that—it hadn't seemed like he was trying to elicit sympathy.

Experience told her that men in general didn't want to be pitied. As Spencer seemed even more macho than most of the men she knew, she thought it better not to test that theory on him.

"Besides, that wasn't the question I asked you."

"What?"

"I asked if *you* checked on him every night."

He wasn't going to let this go. Even having just met him, she could tell by the hard line on his brow that he was going to be stubborn about this. Maybe she could still get away without him knowing about her issue. She just needed to lie... a little bit.

"I check on him every night before I go to bed. One in the morning is a little bit late for me to look in on him, but I happened to be up getting a drink of water, so I peeked in again."

His eyebrows furrowed, and she wondered if he didn't believe her. Wow, if she couldn't even convince him of that small untruth, she was never going to get through this ordeal without him finding out what she was.

None of that mattered. For Jeremy, she would expose herself, if need be.

"And then at six in the morning, he was just gone."

"That's right."

"Let's see if we can do a reading." He closed his eyes and took a deep breath.

Just at that moment, the door slammed open and Aunt Morgan ran in.

"Addison, dear..." The other woman's face went slack with horror. "Oh, *he's* here." She gripped the doorway like she might fall over.

Spencer's eyes popped open, and Addison gasped and covered her mouth. For a moment, before he blinked, his eyes had been pitch-black. Almost immediately they returned to their natural blue and not even the swirl in the center of them was noticeable.

Addison rushed to her aunt. "It's okay, Aunt Morgan. This is Spencer. You met him earlier today in Mr. Rhodes' office." Her aunt wasn't usually so delicate.

"I just didn't realize what it would do to me to have one of *them* in the house." Her aunt said them like she might say the word plague or cancer. "Oh, I think I might faint."

Holding her aunt's side, Addison looked over to where Spencer stood. If she hadn't known it was impossible, she would have sworn he'd become a statue. His gaze was straight ahead, his expression unreadable. Gone was the passionate, exasperating man who had made her lose her temper earlier, and in his place was someone she didn't recognize, even though he looked exactly the same.

Morgan started to shake in her arms. "I'm sorry, Addison, I'm so sorry, but you have to get it out of Jeremy's room. It's too much; it's just too much."

"You can't be serious. He's here to help us. He's going to find Jeremy for us so we can bring him home." What the hell was going on?

"Addison..." Spencer's voice startled her.

Aunt Morgan turned around, pulling out of Addison's arms, evidently able to stand. "Don't you use her name, you freak of nature. Don't you dare address Addison Wade as if you have the right to use her first name."

"Aunt Morgan," Addison yelled, wishing the other woman would just shut up.

"I apologize that my presence here offends you, ma'am." Spencer's voice was cold. "As you recall, you came this morning to Safe Dawn to seek me out." He turned his attention to Addison, and his tone did not change. "Perhaps, Ms. Wade, you might tell me where I can find the room you want me to stay in, and I'll wait there while you determine whether or not you actually want me to do what you hired me to do."

Addison wished she could close her eyes and disappear. An ache started in her chest. He sounded so removed, like the whole thing didn't matter to him, but she could hear, could feel it. He was hurt. He'd let his guard down with her, something she'd all but forced him to do by reprimanding him in the hall, and Aunt Morgan had just slammed into him like a freight train.

"It's two doors down on the left." He started to the door.

"You can't let it wander around the house by itself, Addison."

She had always loved her aunt. The woman was remote, spacey, and childlike. She had never married, never wanted children, but she'd doted on Addison and adored Addison's parents. Jeremy was like her plaything; she treated him like you might treat a puppy. Right now, Addison wanted nothing more than to hit her in the face.

Clearing her throat, she stared at her aunt as Spencer walked down the hall. "First of all, I think that starting immediately you will cease referring to Mr. Lewis as 'it' and begin calling him 'he,' which he obviously is."

"I can't help it, Addy. He's not human, not really. That's why they're locked away."

Addison wished she could die. If ever there was an answer to the question that plagued her about how her family would treat her if they knew about her own oddities, it was right there. No wonder her father had worked so hard to teach her control.

"He *is* human, and he is here doing us a favor. I insist that you treat him with respect while he's in this house or working for us. If you feel you cannot do that, I will book the plane to take you to Grand Cayman right now."

Her aunt huffed, her cheeks puffing quickly in and out. "Well, I..."

"In fact, I think that's an excellent idea. I'm going to call Kristof right now." Addison walked into the hall and picked up her cell phone. She called her assistant and instructed him to make the arrangements to send Morgan away. Ten minutes later he'd called back to tell her it had been done. Her aunt would return to her island home in the Caribbean and remain there for the foreseeable future. That was exactly what she'd wanted.

She'd never given very much thought to prejudice against the *aberration*; she'd been too busy trying to hide her own oddities. But now, with prejudice facing her in her own home, she was absolutely humiliated. Spencer must think...

Oh, she couldn't bear to think what Spencer must think. She closed her eyes and took a deep steadying breath. Opening them, she turned on her heel and headed down the hall to the guest room. She tapped lightly on the door, which flew open almost immediately. Startled, she jumped back a step.

Spencer raised an eyebrow, his eyes still dead to emotion. He turned around and picked up a pair of sunglasses he'd pulled out of the small bag he'd brought with him. Gregory must have brought it inside. She never thought of small details like that, they were just done for her, and for some reason at that precise moment, it bothered her to think that.

Without comment, he covered his eyes with the dark glasses and stepped out into the hall.

"Would you like me to continue, Ms. Wade?"

He wasn't calling her Addison. The sound of the syllables "Ms. Wade" had never sounded so remote and unfeeling; it made her want to vomit. They'd been at each other's throats the whole car ride home and had only been civil for minutes, but somehow he'd come to mean something to her. This stranger about whom she knew so little had plowed past her defenses. The fact that he'd pulled away so quickly had left a hole that she would have to find a way to fill again.

"Spencer." She just couldn't bring herself to call him Mr. Lewis again. "I'm so sorry about my aunt. She's always been sort of simple, and I'm afraid that the stress of all this, of Jeremy being taken, has pushed her over the proverbial edge of the cliff, as they say."

"Ms. Wade, you certainly don't owe me an explanation. I'm not a citizen; I don't have rights. I'm here to perform a function because my handler, William Rhodes, gave me this job. I will do it, and then you will return me to where I belong."

He moved past her and stopped abruptly. His back stiff, he didn't continue forward. "Do I have your permission to reenter Jeremy's room?"

She nodded before she realized he couldn't see it because his back was turned.

"You can go anywhere in the house you'd like."

"Then I guess I won't have to ask your permission to use the bathroom." On that note, he turned the corner into Jeremy's bedroom.

After taking a moment to try to regain her equilibrium, she followed him in. He still wore the glasses as he stared down at the bed. She felt bereft at not being able to see his eyes.

"Why are you wearing shades?"

"To spare you the unseemly view of my non-human eyes while I go into dark space."

"You've used that phrase before—dark space. So did Rhodes. What does it mean?" Better to ask him that than tell him to take off the glasses so she could gaze into his baby-blues. Or to beg his forgiveness for the behavior of her family. Neither of those options would do her much good. Besides, it wasn't in her nature to ask for forgiveness. She'd removed her aunt from the premises; it would have to be enough.

"Where I go, when I go to the 'other,' the place only I can see that lets me read energies and see things that have happened, isn't a real place. Well, it's real to me. It's like I'm here, but I'm not. I can see this room, I can see you, I can see this bed, but it's permeated by darkness. Dark clouds, dark sounds, crystal stars bouncing off things. None of it is solid. The deeper I go into the darkness, the more accurate my predictions can be. Most people who can do what I do have to keep a little light around them. You can go mad without it. The sensation that you'll never see the light of the sun again hits you very hard and very quickly."

He shrugged. "I have very little fear, and I've always been able to go deeper, push farther than anyone else. Priscilla could go into the same spots as me, but she couldn't see anything. She could feel things, with instincts that told her if something was dangerous. She could also tell if I was going too far and guide me back to here, back to reality."

Addison swallowed. She knew what he meant about feeling that things were dangerous. That was what had made her check on Jeremy at one in the morning. All day she'd just had the feeling that something was wrong, that something was going to happen to the child. Compelled to investigate, she'd gotten up and checked on him every hour from nine o'clock on. After one, she'd convinced herself she was cracking up and had taken a pill to go to sleep. That had been her biggest mistake. If she'd trusted herself... Well, she couldn't go there.

"So you're going to do that now. Go into dark space, but not as deep as you would have gone in if Priscilla were still alive."

Spencer ran a hand over the stubble on his chin. "If you'll be quiet, Ms. Wade, and let me work."

"By all means."

She walked to the window and pretended to look down at the street. The desire to stare at him while he went to that other place threatened to overwhelm her.

The skin on her arms tingled as every hair on her body stood straight up.

"This is Jeremy's room?" Spencer's voice behind her startled her, and she whirled around.

"Yes, I've already told you that."

"Doesn't feel like Jeremy's room. The only energy I see here is yours."

What? "I've been sleeping here since he was taken."

"I can see that. You're all over the bed."

"What do you mean, I'm all over the bed?"

"Your particular energy is all over the bed."

"How can you tell?"

He exhaled. "Look, it's complicated. It's like taste. You can taste a glass of wine and suddenly you can remember where you were the last time you drank it. You might even remember what you ate, where you sat, who you were there with, what the weather was like."

"It's sense memory. I get that. I took acting classes in college." It had been a disaster, but she remembered the concept.

"I know your particular energy. I've spent time with you. My senses have digested the essence that is you, and I can see you on the bed." He turned and faced the left side of the room. He pointed at the door that joined her room and Jeremy's. "And through there. Is that your bedroom?"

"That's right."

He nodded. "You permeate through the bottom of the door."

"Is it just that Jeremy has been gone a month, so his essence has vanished from here?"

"No." Spencer shook his head. "I've been places where people have been gone for years and their essence is still there. Damn it. It's like someone has wiped him from the room."

"Psychically wiped his energy? That's possible?"

Spencer swore and ripped his sunglasses off his eyes. As Addison watched, his eyes turned from black to blue in a matter of seconds. This time she didn't gasp but was transfixed by it. "I've never seen it before, and I've seen just about everything. Someone would have to have that particular talent—or sin, as your aunt would put it."

"Let's stay focused." Addison didn't need any reminders of the damage Morgan had done earlier. "Someone with the talent to psychically remove Jeremy's energy from the room kidnapped him."

"At least to the point where I can't see him in such a shallow read." He swore again.

"If you could go deeper, could you tell?"

"I have no way of knowing. I pushed a little farther than I should have just to see if it was there. It would take a real deep read to know for sure, and I can't do that. That far in without an anchor, and I wouldn't come back. I wouldn't be able to communicate with you about what I found anyway."

"And without Jeremy's essence, you can't go any further."

He smiled and the hairs on the back of her neck stood up. "You catch on quickly, Ms. Wade. Most people aren't at all interested in the logistics of what I do."

"What do we do now?" Her heart pounded hard. She placed her hand on her chest, hoping that she could will it to slow down. Truthfully, she'd counted on Spencer being able to help them. She'd risked everything on the idea that he could.

Spencer took a step toward her and stopped. "There are two things we can do. The first I'll do." He shook his head. "With your permission, of course, I'll call Rhodes and see if he's ever heard of an aberrant with the power to erase people on the psychic plane."

Addison felt some of the tension in her shoulders leave. There was still a chance this might work. "Oh. Okay.

Rhodes must have a database, right? Or the council does? Of all the various powers people have and how they manifest themselves."

"No, he's always refused to complete a database. It's one of the few things he's denied the council over the years. It would give them too much information about us. He tries, when he can, to protect us. However, if there's anyone who would know, it's him. Then you're going to take me to Jeremy's school, the playground, wherever he goes, and I'll see if I can find him there."

She looked at the clock. "It's too late tonight to go to his school."

Spencer ran a hand through his blond hair and blew out a breath. "You're right. I get a little carried away when I'm on a chase. Okay, tomorrow morning, first thing. I'll call Rhodes now then go to bed." He started to move in the direction of the door and stopped. "If I have your permission."

Narrowing her eyes, she felt her blood start to boil. "Stop doing that. Of course, you can use the phone. You don't have to ask. Cut the crap with the permission bullshit. You're not really asking. You're just trying to piss me off by reminding me that you have to, as if I personally imposed these rules on you. Reminder, Spencer, I wasn't born when these laws were enacted. I didn't create these problems."

"You're not afraid I'll make hundreds of dollars' worth of long-distance phone calls on your dime?"

That was *so* not the reaction she'd expected from him. His face was passive, no expression readable, not even a twinkle in his eye so she could see whether he was kidding.

"I think we can afford it."

"Most likely."

"Spencer, wait."

Halting, he turned, his expression smoldering. Addison forgot to breathe. She had no idea why she'd stopped him. It had just felt like she couldn't let him leave just yet.

"What is it, Ms. Wade?"

"Aren't you hungry? We could have dinner."

He raised an eyebrow. "You cook? Or you have someone here to do that for you?"

"Neither, actually. Jeremy's nanny cooks for him. Grandfather and I usually eat at our desks at the office. Um, we could go out."

Spencer stalked forward. "Nanny?"

"Loretta Farris. She's been so distraught since Jeremy went missing that she's holed up in her house. She won't see anyone."

"Take me there right now."

There went dinner. "Why do you want to see Loretta? She wasn't here when he was taken. She only works days."

"Because I can't find her energy in here either. Someone erased her as well. That means she's either in big trouble, or she's someone Jeremy's kidnapper doesn't want us to find."

SEVEN

Spencer had never been to Brooklyn before. He looked out of the window of the Wade town car and watched the buildings, mostly smaller than their counterparts in Manhattan, pass by. They crossed over the Williamsburg Bridge into the new borough, and Spencer closed the window to keep the rain that had just started from getting into the car. As Addison explained about the gentrification of Williamsburg, Spencer tried to make sense of all the things that had happened in the previous twenty-four hours.

Well, *almost* all the things that had happened. If he stewed over the events in Jeremy's bedroom with Addison's Aunt Morgan, he'd get pissed off again. Really, what the hell had he expected? That Addison would jump to his defense and tell the woman to go where the sun didn't shine?

In all honesty, that had been what he'd wanted. As a rule, he didn't get involved with women outside the institutions. A certain kind of woman liked to have sex with men she considered "bad" or "naughty." Men with the Condition automatically fell into those categories. Spencer had never found that particular type of woman attractive, and preferred to interact with women who didn't see him as some sort of life experience they could later tell their friends about over drinks.

Or write about on internet chat boards.

For a moment, with Addison in the hallway, he'd decided to throw away that rule. Why not see if it was possible to meet a high-quality person outside the walls of Safe Dawn or one of the other institutions? There were always stories of such relationships working. Cinderella tales in which a Conditioned person met someone from the outside and ran away to happily ever after. Spencer had never bought that. The Fury would never let anyone have that fairytale ending. Not a freak from Satan, anyway.

He grinned despite his bad mood. In that story, he would be the Cinderella character. Spencer found that vaguely amusing.

"What are you thinking? It must be more pleasant than what I'm dwelling on." Addison's slightly husky voice caught his attention, and his mirth faded. There was no way in hell he was telling her.

Although he'd just closed it earlier, he lowered it again to get a little fresh air, he hoped she'd let him change the subject as easily as she let him mess with the opening and closing of the car window. "What are you *dwelling* on?"

"Jeremy, Loretta, that someone can wipe people's energies from the psychic plane, and the fact that someone anticipated that I'd bring you in on this and went to the trouble of doing that to begin with."

"Loretta may be sitting in her living room calling in job prospects on the off-chance that she no longer has one."

Her eyes flared with anger. He liked her that way, angry

and full of spirit. Not beaten down and nearly defeated. Maybe that was why he kept baiting her.

Maybe.

Or maybe he was just a sick son of a bitch.

"She doesn't need another job; she will go back to taking care of Jeremy in no time. We have, of course, continued to pay her."

"Because if you stopped doing that, she might tell someone, and you'd have to address what happened to Jeremy. That would be bad for stock prices."

She looked away but recaptured his gaze seconds later. "The second you tell me you can't find him, Spencer, I'm going to the press."

He liked hearing that. She'd defied her grandfather to bring him in, and she was willing to go even further. "Aren't you worried about the devaluation of the company?"

"I suppose I should be." She rubbed the back of her neck like it ached, and he resisted the urge to give her an impromptu massage. "I worry about the people who work for us, about them losing their jobs if Wade went under. However, I find the possibility of that occurrence based on a scandal about the Wade family very remote. Worst-case scenario, my grandfather is removed as CEO and Chairman of the Board. I lose my job. We're still obscenely wealthy. Jeremy comes home. It's a positive outcome. Best option, we get media attention, Jeremy is found, there's a blip in stock prices, which recover quickly, and we all continue forward."

Spencer doubted any of it would be that simple. Whoever had orchestrated this whole thing had at his or her disposal the ability to remove someone's existence from the psychic plane. He hated to agree with Oliver Wade, but going to the media might just infuriate them more. Not that he was going to tell Addison Wade what she should do. It wasn't his place to comment on the decisions she made about Jeremy.

Part of him—the part that was most likely deranged—wished it *were* his business to care about the choices Addison made, or to know and love Jeremy. The thought disturbed him, and he decided instead, to take in the scenery around him. Anything not to go down the impossible path his mind wanted to travel, where there was nothing but a world of hurt waiting for him.

"How far are we?" He crooked his neck, hoping to work out the knot he couldn't seem to get rid of.

"About eight blocks."

"Can we walk?"

"In the rain?" She gave him a look that said he was nuts. "Why do you want to walk?"

"I don't want to pull up in a car that screams Wade, in case anyone is waiting for us. Do you melt in the rain?"

Addison laughed, a long, hard sound, and he grinned in response. He hadn't expected her to be amused. "Gregory, stop the car here, we're going to walk."

"Ah, I don't know, Addison."

Spencer leaned forward and patted him on the back of the shoulder. To his credit, Gregory didn't flinch at being touched by someone with the Condition. "I won't let anything happen to her. She's less likely to be attacked if they don't know we're coming."

He hoped he was right, but he meant what he'd promised. Nothing would happen to Addison while she was with him. He hadn't protected Priscilla—hadn't known he'd needed to until it was too late. He wouldn't make the same mistake again.

The thought stopped him short. Priscilla had been his friend, his partner, even his lover at one point in time. When had Addison begun to exist in the same league?

He pointed to a spot up ahead next to a Mexican restaurant and asked Gregory to stop the car again. This time the older man obeyed, and Spencer followed Addison out of the car onto the street. Looking up, he noted that the street sign said Grand Avenue.

He looked around to take in his surroundings. A taxicab behind them honked at Gregory to move the car out of the way. It was only then that Spencer noticed the "No Parking, Standing, or Stopping" sign in front of them. Smiling, he realized Gregory had risked the wrath of New York taxi drivers by letting them off at a taxi stand and getting in the way of the taxis and their fares.

"Do taxis run in all the boroughs?"

"They do. But you usually have to bribe them to come out here. They don't like leaving Manhattan. Sometimes it's easier to get a ride share, but my grandfather doesn't like to use those or to have us use them. Too many people could see us that way." Addison shrugged and tugged her black pea coat tighter around her body. "But I suppose it doesn't really matter. A lot of what once was is changing. Brooklyn has become pretty trendy. They have to bring more and more people out here."

He gripped her small, dainty hand in his and crossed the street. He liked the feel of it.

"Worried I'm going to run away?" She looked down at their joined hands.

"No, I just want to be able to pull you with me without saying anything if I get a sense that we need to run."

It was true. He wasn't going to sugarcoat it for her. He'd never been able to predict the future. In some ways, that particular ability would have been easier than the ones he had.

The rain was cold on his face, but he didn't give in to the urge to put his head down and look at the ground as he walked. There was no way he wasn't going to watch where he stepped. Addison stayed silent, which he appreciated. A lot of chitchat would have put him more on edge than he already was.

After stopping at two lights, and being obligated to move out of the way of a box truck backing into traffic, they finally arrived at a large brick building. Immediately, it struck him as unusual. Surrounded on all sides, and even across the street, by small, four-story buildings, the building where Jeremy's nanny lived was a skyscraper by comparison. It had to have been more than twenty floors high.

"Kind of unusual for the neighborhood, isn't it?" Spencer had to shout to be heard over the wind, which had decided to pick up speed and strength.

"It is. I've only been here three times. Once to drop Jeremy off to play with Loretta's nephew, and the other two times to bring her a paycheck. She's more like a member of the family than an employee, and I had to make sure she didn't need anything because she was sick. I never thought about it, but you're totally right." She shrugged. "I wonder who thought it was a good idea to put this here."

He walked toward the door and pulled it open so Addison could walk through ahead of him. "Do you know much about architecture?"

"Not at all." She cleared her throat. Her eyes were bright and her cheeks red from the cold. Wet blonde hair that looked silver from the rain fell everywhere, having been blown out of its neat bun sometime during their eight-block trek. "Do you?"

"A little bit." He motioned to the guard, who had been staring at them since they entered the building. "Do we need to sign in with him or anything?"

"He'll let us up."

"After he calls Loretta?" Spencer was still hoping for an element of surprise, although that was becoming less and less likely, as the building was more secure than he'd anticipated. Then again, Jeremy had been taken from a building with security the equivalent of that in a bank vault while his aunt slept in the other room.

"No." She grinned. "Wade owns this particular building." His look must have told her that he wished she had told him that when he'd asked about the building earlier. "You asked me if I knew about architecture or if I thought the building was unusual here. I don't know about architecture, and I didn't build it, so I'd never thought about its oddity."

He was going to have to remember that Addison was capable of leaving out very important pieces of information to suit her needs.

He grabbed her arm and stopped her as she moved forward. "Is that usual? Do you guys house most of your employees? The ones that work for the family, I mean." There was no way they could house the entire population that worked for Wade Corporation as a whole.

His mind moved at a thousand miles a minute. Everything was so intricate, so put-together. It felt like if he could just see all the pieces of this puzzle, he could get a better sense of it. So far everything led back in one direction: Oliver Wade.

"Grandfather thinks it's a good idea to keep the people who work for us happy. He pays them well and makes sure their needs are met. That way, they're less likely to steal."

"And less likely to leave."

"How do you figure?" Her gaze bored into his. She squinted, seeming to concentrate hard on looking at his face. The intensity in her baby-blues made his groin harden.

"If they're totally indebted to you, not only by where they work but where they live, they may feel trapped, as if not working for you would be next to impossible. It's similar with the institutions. Sometimes, people want to know why we don't stage a coup or an uprising, but where would we go? None of us have any skills or abilities that would make it easy for us to survive. The only thing I can do is follow energies. I'd give myself away pretty quickly or starve to death."

"Well, they'd take one look at the swirling thing your eyes do and they'd know right away anyway."

"What swirling thing?"

"In the center of your eyes, when you're using your ability, a thousand different shades of blue, gray, and green move around your pupils."

No one had ever said that to him before. "Really? I've never heard that. Are you sure you're not just imagining it?"

"I'm positive." She laughed. "It's not like you can see your own eyes."

"That's true, but you would think someone would have told me."

"Maybe they're just not as observant as I am. Anyone could see the blackness that comes when you reach dark space, but it's the light colors that swirl around in there when you're sensing something that's really captivating."

Addison moved forward and out of his grip as she approached the guard. Did she have any idea what she'd just said? She'd just called his eyes captivating. Part of him wanted to strut like a rooster. The other part was horrified. Addison Wade was becoming a tax on his well-being.

Maybe in another lifetime they could have been just a man and a woman getting to know each other...

Focus, he commanded himself. He was in a tall building in Brooklyn. A building that just so happened to be owned by Oliver Wade. Jeremy was missing.

Addison was hot. He wished he could bang his head against something. Even when he tried to be stone cold in his thinking, she snuck into his head like a bad cold he couldn't get rid of.

She walked back, smiling. "We can go up."

Silently, he followed her to the elevator and waited for it to arrive. She smelled good, too, something like vanilla, as she had earlier, and now also coffee beans. Damn, the situation wasn't getting any better for him. He needed the day to end. It was funny how some days flew by, but this one, in particular the time he spent with her, seemed to move slowly, as if every second counted.

The elevator dinged and they entered. It was noticeably colder inside, by at least a few degrees. "They need to turn down the air conditioning in here. It's winter."

Addison laughed, and he was delighted by having made her do that again. "So, you were saying you know about architecture."

"I know about it in the ways it relates to me." Spencer made note that she pushed the top floor button. Interesting. So not only was Loretta an employee of the Wade family, but she warranted the penthouse? "Does your family do construction?" That would be new information on the Wades.

"No, but there's a division of Wade that invests in real estate. Or at least there used to be. I think we just sold off that division. Grandfather said we owned enough for a good long while. We kept the property we owned. The rent is good income for the company, but we got rid of the division that did the purchasing."

"You say that like you're very aware of how it went down."

"One of the other people from the council bought it. Grace Ann Charters. I guess they're trying to branch out from liquor."

The name made his skin crawl. Five years earlier, that woman had rewritten the rules of conduct for people with the Condition. One of them had been that no one from an institution could act at all violently outside the institution walls. That had meant that when Priscilla had pushed the man trying to kill Spencer, she had deserved the bullet that had been put in her brain moments later.

Priscilla should have let him—Spencer—die. He shivered at the memory. It had been the gunshot that had brought him back to his senses. The gunshot and the bridge Priscilla had kept open for him in her mind while she died.

Not wanting to give Addison a chance to notice his distress, he opted to keep talking about the building. It gave him something else to think about as well. "Certain kinds of architecture affect certain kinds of conditions differently. Most of the 'freaks' that can control the weather have to be standing on solid ground to do it. A lot of people with my abilities can't trance properly in buildings made of lead or steel."

"But you can?"

He nodded. "Easily. I'm that powerful." It wasn't bragging. He just wanted her to know so she understood the kind of technique it took to do what he was about to do. "Your home, and this one, are all built with those same substances."

"Is that standard?" Her face took on the strained, panicked look again.

"For old buildings, yes. For this more modern one, no."

"Because of the lead."

"Yeah. The health problems associated with lead paint made people stop using it in their building materials."

The elevator doors opened and they stepped out onto the floor. While she walked briskly to the door on the left with the number 2 on it and knocked, Spencer made note that there were only two apartments on the floor. He stepped out of the elevator and followed her slowly as he glanced at the other door. The fluorescent light that lit the hallway was out over the doorway marked 1.

"She's not answering. Do we wait?"

He shook his head. "Not if we want to make sure she's not dead."

"I could try calling her." She'd suggested that before they left her apartment, and he'd told her not to. If she wasn't dead, he didn't want her to know they were looking for her.

"Nope." He took a deep breath. "I'm going to break the law now. If they catch me doing this, they'll put me to death."

"All punishable offenses are death offenses."

She'd quoted the Conditioned law, and he had to admit he was impressed. Well, maybe he needn't be—she was going to inherit her grandfather's place on the council when he retired or died. She could probably recite all the different ways to torture them in her sleep.

"It's the most awful law." She visibly swallowed, and he forgot his internal rant about her future council seat. Maybe it would be a good thing when she took over. Maybe they'd become more humane. He would look forward to that day. "Would it be the Fury that killed you?"

"Maybe. It might also be the police." The police had killed Priscilla.

Her eyes got huge. "They'd just shoot you? No questions asked?"

"Like they'd put down a dog." He kicked hard at the door. It vibrated but didn't open. Addison's gasp made him smile. "I'm not really kicking down the door. That was just for effect."

She groaned. "Not funny."

"I wish I was action-movie strong. I'm afraid I'm more nefarious than that." He bent down to look at the lock. "Give me one of your hairpins." Her messed-up hairstyle was going to prove useful for more than just tempting his senses and making him think about sex.

"You're going to pick that lock with a hairpin?"

"Unless you have a better idea."

"I could try to talk the guard into giving us the spare key."

"Somehow you're not getting the idea of stealth here."

She put her hands on her hips. "I guess I'm not that good at subterfuge... and you kicked the damn door. Not exactly quiet."

She had him there. He let his gaze roam her body for a moment. "You're obviously not good at spy tactics, but you are good at secrets. I just haven't been able to figure out which ones you're keeping yet or why." He pointed to the hairpin. "Give that to me."

She handed it to him, and he didn't miss that she didn't contradict him. Better to say nothing, he supposed.

Straightening the pin, he pushed its ridged side into the keyhole. A few good strokes and it opened for him.

"How did you learn to do that?" Addison whispered.

"Why are you whispering? If she's in there and she hasn't opened the door by now, she's dead or in a coma."

"You didn't answer my question."

"Funny how that works. I guess we're both good at keeping things to ourselves." He motioned to the open door. "Shall we?"

EIGHT

Addison didn't know what she was more nervous about: breaking and entering Loretta's apartment or Spencer's announcement that he knew she had a secret. Couple that with her attraction to him, which she couldn't seem to get under control, and she was one giant mess.

Loretta's apartment was frighteningly quiet. Dark shadows danced across the white walls and the sound of a ticking clock was the only noise. She wasn't sure why it was bugging her so much. Places were always silent when no one was in them, but something about the space struck her as ultra-hushed. Maybe she just watched too many movies. Spencer wasn't acting at all concerned.

He walked quickly from the entranceway toward a door on the left and disappeared from her view. She almost called him back before she decided that would be incredibly cowardly of her. She really didn't want to come across as terrified, even if she was.

She took a deep breath as she looked around. The apartment was small, but it had a beautiful view of the Williamsburg Bridge and Manhattan behind it. One bedroom stood to her left, where Spencer had disappeared, and where she assumed there was a bathroom. The kitchen was to the right, visible above a wall that reached only halfway to the ceiling.

She walked toward the eating area of the kitchen and scooted around the wall to open the small refrigerator. It was stocked with all the essentials—milk, butter, eggs and orange juice, as well as fruits and vegetables. Not things you would buy if you knew you were going out of town. That meant either Loretta was simply out of the apartment, or she'd been taken.

"Doing a little detective work?"

She jumped. "I was just trying to see if there was anything missing."

Spencer raised an eyebrow. "Is there?"

"Truthfully, I have no idea. The fridge is pretty stocked."

He moved next to her, and she felt strangely comforted by his warmth against her body. "So now you're wondering if she's coming back and if we're about to get caught."

"Is mind-reading one of your strange abilities?" He'd been frighteningly close, except for missing the wild sexual fantasies she had in addition to her terror. She was sick in the head, which was the only explanation for the inappropriate feelings she couldn't get under control.

"No, just following the logic." Spencer touched the coffee pot that stood on the counter next to a small, silver toaster oven. "It's still warm."

That must have some significance she wasn't following. "So?"

"Do you go out of the house and leave your coffee pot on? At the institute we're all very careful not to leave electrical equipment on if we're not present."

"I don't know if we leave it on or not. It's always on when I get up in the morning and off when I come home at night." She raised her hand to stop what she assumed he was going to say. "I know. I'm spoiled. You don't have to tell me."

"I wasn't going to say that." His eyes flared with an unreadable emotion and she was reminded of what a mystery he was to her.

"Oh." Why had she gotten so defensive without cause? The last time she'd cared what people thought about how she lived, she'd been a teenager.

"We have to turn off our electrical equipment because there are lots of juveniles running around the institutions with their powers not under control. One of them could accidentally blow up an active coffee maker and then we have a fire on our hands. I don't know how people behave out here. So I'm asking you—should she have turned it off?"

"I really have no idea. I think most people try to turn things off, unplug them. It saves money on the electric bill and saves energy, which is good for the environment."

"All right." He nodded. "So Loretta is Jeremy's nanny. She lives in a building owned by your grandfather. She's on leave, waiting for Jeremy to be returned home and has told no one what has happened, or else by now it would have leaked to the media. Her bed is unmade—I just checked— the fridge is stocked, and the coffee maker is on."

Addison's heart pounded hard. "You think she ran out of here fast."

"I do. I think when we go back downstairs, we're going to discover from the guard that she ran out of here a few moments before we arrived."

"How could she know we were coming? We parked eight blocks away."

"Addison." Whenever he said her name it sounded so much nicer than the way anyone else said it. "I just don't know how insidious this whole conspiracy is. The light is out over the neighbor's doorway next door. Extreme uses of power by Conditioned people or sudden bursts have been known to shatter light bulbs. I need to do a reading in here and see if I can find Loretta, or even Jeremy, since you said at one point he was here."

"Okay." She didn't like this one bit. Loretta had been Jeremy's nanny. She had *trusted* the woman to be with him when she couldn't. They had done extensive background checks. Hell, once a week they had gotten coffee together and talked about reality TV dancing competitions.

"I'm going to be very exposed while I'm in dark space, even though I'm only doing a shallow reading. I won't hear anyone coming or going. If anyone approaches, like say Loretta returning home, shake me very hard or shout. I'm not concerned so much about me, as I am about leaving you unguarded."

"I can take care of myself." Even though the thought that Spencer wanted to protect her made her warm somewhere deep in her soul—somewhere that she'd thought would be cold forever—she didn't want him to think she was incompetent.

"I know you can, but I'm not going to get into the habit of having women injured on my watch."

Priscilla. He was talking about her. The part that had started to warm cooled off again. It wouldn't do for Spencer to be around another woman who got hurt. Why had she thought it had anything to do with her? He didn't care about her or any of this. It was all a job to him. If she was honest, he'd probably been instructed to flirt with her to gain favor with Wade Corporation. It burned her insides to realize she was so easily manipulated.

"What's going on in that head of yours?"

"Nothing. Do your thing. I'll keep watch."

"Addison." The way he said her name made her heart flutter. He stepped forward and grabbed the back of her head in his large hand. With surprising gentleness, he squeezed. "We'll find him."

He thought she was upset because of Jeremy. She closed her eyes in shame. That was what she should have been focused on. Why couldn't she keep her mind on the end game? Forcing her lids open, she stared into his blue, swirling depths.

"There they go again. Your pupils are floating in seas of blue, gray, and green."

"That's impossible. I'm not picking up any psychic senses right now. Are you *sure* you're not just imagining it?"

That was the second time he'd accused her of having an overactive imagination. "Trust me. They swirl."

"I'll have to take your word for it." He took a step backward and closed his eyes. When he opened them again, they were pitch-black.

"If you're so out of it that you won't hear anyone coming, how come you can talk to me?"

"Right now I can. The longer I stay in here, the harder that gets."

If it was anything like dreaming, she could understand that. It was always easier to be woken earlier in the night. "What's it like?"

Spencer moved slowly around the room. His expression blank and removed, his eyes pitch black, he looked like a reflection of himself. The body was there but the soul had gone somewhere else. Addison shivered at the thought.

"It's impossible for me to describe it to you as anything other than dark space. Everything exists here, but life becomes a shadowed version of itself. It is, but it isn't, and I know that doesn't make much sense. The only things that are real are the essences we leave behind. Our permanent signatures." He took a deep breath. "I'm going now. I will be farther inside, and it will be harder for me to speak. No Jeremy yet."

"Spencer." Her voice cracked when she said his name. She hadn't even known she was holding back so much emotion.

"Yes, Addy?"

At the use of her childhood nickname, she nearly stopped breathing. No one had called her that in years, yet the sound of it didn't come off as foreign on his tongue. She shook her head to bring back her attention, as she was rapidly losing time before he wouldn't be able to talk.

"Don't get lost in there. Don't go too deep. Come back."

The blank expression left his mouth and was replaced for the briefest of seconds with a half-smile. "No worries. I'm good at this."

He stood still, seemingly staring out into nothingness. She pushed away her fear as she walked farther into the kitchen and leaned against the bluish-gray countertop. It was pathetic that she felt uncomfortably alone even though Spencer was in the room with her.

There was so much to consider, so many ideas taking shape in her head. First Jeremy had gone missing. Now she knew that he had been erased on the psychic plane that only a few people could see. Her nephew had never shown even the smallest sign of the Condition, as far as she could tell. But then her own weirdness, which she tried so hard to hide, was so unpredictable. It had been four years since she'd had any issue with it, but since Jeremy had gone missing, it had been a problem nearly every day to control it.

She ran her hands through her hair and finally gave in and closed her eyes, momentarily stopping her fight against the migraine that wanted to form in the space between her eyes.

"Not one trace of him, and I went as deep as I could go without a guide back."

Addison reluctantly opened her lids to stare at him. "I'm not surprised. Everything is so odd. First Jeremy, now Loretta."

"I think it's worse than that."

She wasn't sure how much more she could take. "What is?"

"There's no trace of Loretta here either."

"So whoever has them has erased her, too?"

"No." Spencer took a step forward and reached out to grasp her arm. He pulled her forward against his chest. She gasped as she smashed against his hard body. "Relax. You look like you're going to fall over."

Like her skin might absorb sun tan lotion, her pores seemed to be sucking in the maleness that was Spencer. "I'm getting a migraine."

"I hear those are brutal. Let's get you home."

"Tell me what you meant first. Whoever has them didn't erase them?"

"Loretta did the erasing."

She pulled her head back and stared up at his face, straining her neck as she did so. "How could you possibly know that?"

"The psychic plane is buzzing in here, like someone just did some hardcore work on it."

"Someone could have come in here and grabbed her

and done the erasing. It didn't have to be her." No. She couldn't believe it. She wouldn't. There was no way her instincts and the background checks on Loretta could have been so wrong. Damn it, she had chosen her to be Jeremy's caregiver. No one else had had anything to do with that decision; it had been hers alone. That made her solely responsible for this. It wasn't possible.

"If your pulse picks up any more, your head is going to explode from the pressure."

Realizing she was still in his embrace—and why had he done that to begin with? Why had she let him?—she pulled away and started to pace. It was either that or let him see her lose it, which might make her Condition appear, and then she'd be done for. Spencer would probably love hauling her in to an institute. William Rhodes would hold a press conference informing everyone of her years of deception. Her grandfather would disown her.

"Addison, calm down. You're going to pass out. Let me explain."

"Please do. How can you possibly imagine Loretta is behind this?"

"I'm not imagining anything. Look around. You're extremely bright. Do you see any signs of a struggle in here? Anything that would indicate to you that someone was abducted?"

Everything was in order. She sighed. "Let me see if I can follow your train of thought here. Loretta comes to work for us. She isn't who she seems to be. In fact, she wants to kidnap Jeremy."

"Or she works for someone who wants to."

"Okay." She tried to steady herself. Through willpower alone, she managed to stop pacing. "For some unknown reason either Loretta, or someone she works for, wanted to kidnap Jeremy, so she came to work for us. Loretta has this ability to erase herself on the psychic plane. Why not take him right away?"

"I don't know. Maybe she was waiting for official orders to do so. Maybe they were waiting to see if they needed to. Despite my feeble attempt at this, I'm really not a detective. I'm Conditioned, remember?"

"How could I forget with you constantly reminding me?" She didn't care if she sounded snippy. The fact that Spencer's eyes showed amusement instead of anger did nothing to cool the inferno raging inside her. Her head pounded, she was starving from having eaten no dinner, she'd just been given a blow to the heart because it looked like Loretta had betrayed them, and he wanted to play the Conditioned card again?

"Why take Jeremy? Why not go after Grandfather or me? They haven't even asked us for any money."

"Then it's not money they want."

"What could they possibly want from Jeremy?" She heard herself shout after she'd already done it. She wasn't a child. Why was she losing it?

"Why don't you tell me?"

She stomped forward and pushed against his chest with both hands. It didn't budge him. "What the hell is that supposed to mean?"

"I'm not an idiot, Addison. Whatever you're hiding is completely related to this. That's why you look like you want to die whenever I bring it up."

"No." She hated even to admit she was hiding anything at all, but denial was getting pointless. "It's my secret, and it has nothing to do with Jeremy at all."

He exhaled like he was searching for patience, and she wasn't sure if she wanted to deck him or kiss him. Wow, he was making her crazy.

"If you say so."

Deck him. That was the decision. Only she'd never hit anyone in her life and Spencer Lewis would probably not be a good start.

"Here's what I think happened." As he spoke, he moved to the center of the living room. "Loretta takes Jeremy. She's then tipped off that we're on our way over here. She cleans the room, using so much energy she blows out the light across the hall when she's on her way out, and rushes downstairs, getting away before we can get to her."

It felt right. Even though everything she thought she knew about Loretta protested it, in her gut, it felt correct. Damn. "I should have just asked the guard if she'd left before we came upstairs."

Spencer shook his head. "I would have wanted to come up anyway and look around." He paused. "You like her." He didn't phrase that as a question, and she appreciated that. "You trusted her, and this is hard for you."

"*Liked*. If she did this, we will put that word in the past tense. If she did this, I want her dead."

The depth of her feelings on the subject didn't surprise her, but saying them out loud for the first time felt strange: freeing, but odd nonetheless.

"You just sounded like your grandfather."

"Have you spent a lot of time with him to know what he sounds like?"

She needed to get out of this apartment. Out of the space where the woman who had most likely betrayed them had lived on the Wade's dime. Storming toward the door, she didn't spare a backward glance for Spencer.

Her anger fueled her forward. Spencer could keep up or not—at that moment she really didn't care. She pressed the elevator button as she heard him shut Loretta's apartment door behind him. She felt the need to move more than ever before in her life, and she rocked back and forth from her heels to her toes while she waited for the elevator to travel to the top floor.

"Someone tipped her off that we were coming." The man had no sense of when he should just not speak.

"Wait."

"What?"

"Don't say another word about it until we get downstairs and I can confirm this with the guard."

"How will you kill her? Will you do it yourself or pay someone else to do it?"

She whirled around and shoved him with all her strength. He grabbed her arms and pushed her up against the hallway wall.

Breathing heavily, he looked down at her. "Shove me again, and next time I'll kiss you for it."

Her traitorous body came alive at the thought. Wetness pooled in her core.

"Why, Spencer, do you like it that way? Hard and abusive?"

"Trust me, Addison, with that look in your eye, I can tell you wouldn't complain about anything we did together."

Damn him for knowing that.

"Let go." Even as she said it, she wasn't sure she meant it.

"Or what? You'll get your grandfather to call the Fury?"

"I still need you to find Jeremy. You let go or I'll knee you in the groin." Just to demonstrate how serious she was, she adjusted her leg just a smidgen closer to his private parts.

Raising a blond eyebrow, he seemed to get the message, and he released her arms. "You fight dirty."

"I'm a Wade. You can make it sound like a bad word if you want to. It doesn't change the fact that I was born to head one of the largest companies in the world. I've trained for it, planned for it, and dreamed of it for years. Now someone has come along and taken the one person on this planet who means more to me than all that time and training. If I want to indulge in a little death-wishing, that's my business, and you don't get to judge me for it." Her chest heaved as she tried to catch her breath.

The elevator opened, and she stormed in. She jabbed the button for the lobby as Spencer stepped in beside her.

"You're getting into the habit of assuming that I'm judging you or thinking ill of you in some way. First the whole bit about the coffee pot and now the death threat. What makes you think I don't want her dead? She took your nephew. He's a child. The same age I was when I tried to run for my life to escape the Fury and failed. Your nephew has to be out-of-his mind afraid. Maybe it makes me a bad person—I'm already doomed for Hell—but I was more concerned with the method, not the motive."

In a million years, she wouldn't have expected him to say that. Turning to stare at the hard lines of his profile, she smiled. "I wouldn't have kneed you in the groin."

"Yes, you would have, and I have to say, I kind of like that about you."

NINE

Spencer leaned against a pillar in the lobby and watched Addison's face as she got the news he'd known she would. In this case, he was conflicted over how he felt about being right. On one hand, knowing now that Loretta was, at the very least, involved in Jeremy's disappearance would be helpful. He hoped she hadn't had time to hide her energy everywhere she went, so if they could find it somewhere, they could trace her instead of Jeremy, and perhaps be led to the boy.

However, it pained him more than he cared to admit to watch Addison suffer a betrayal. Who did she have in her life that she could count on? The question made him sad, and he looked down at the floor so as not to give away his mood. Even he, who spent a great deal of time unable to travel freely, had friends who amounted to family. Who did Addison Wade have to call in the middle of the night when life was too much to handle? Her grandfather? Where was the son of a bitch? He should have been helping her with this, not staying at the office to work late.

Or maybe nine o' clock wasn't late for him. Maybe she never saw him at all.

That was even more depressing.

As she walked toward him, her spine stiff, her eyes hidden away in the mask she wore, he realized he wasn't done hurting her yet. His insides went cold at the thought.

He took her hand. She gave him a questioning look he couldn't answer, because normally he wasn't really a touchy-feely kind of guy. But he wanted to hold it, so he did. He did what he wanted, when he wanted, within the constraints of the system that had kept him jailed for the majority of his life.

They walked out into the dark night, and she shivered from the onslaught of rain and cold air.

"Here." Pulling off his coat, he wrapped it around her.

"No. You'll be cold."

"I don't really mind. I like the feel of it. Somehow, the sensation reminds me I'm alive." He smiled at the skeptical look in her eyes. "Besides, I'll have eternity in Hell to feel the heat."

"You say that like you're joking, but I'm starting to suspect you believe it a little bit."

"Don't you?" He was baiting her, and he knew it, but he wanted to hear her response.

She rolled her eyes. "I'm not a religious scholar. I have no idea who's going to Heaven or Hell, but I can't believe that someone who spends all his time helping other people is going to burn in Hell."

He'd never heard a non-Conditioned person speak like that before. They either avoided the subject or condemned him to Hell. Maybe there was hope for the universe if someone as well-known as Addison Wade thought he had a chance for salvation.

"Before you say anything else, I know what the next thing I have to acknowledge is."

He was confused and shook his head. "What?"

"Gregory."

He stopped walking and turned to face her on the cold, dark street. A distance away a lamp flickered, and he realized it was strangely quiet for a busy avenue. Shrugging, he reminded himself he'd never been to Brooklyn before. It was certainly quieter than Manhattan. Maybe it was just the rain keeping people indoors.

"Someone had to have tipped her off that we were on our way over here. Unless we're being followed." He gave a cursory glance around the street.

"Then Greg tipped them off." She looked at the ground, and he hoped she wasn't about to cry. Addison had been so brave this entire time. If she lost it now, he wasn't sure what he would do. "He's been with my family for longer than I have. He drove my parents to the hospital to have me. He carried Jeremy in his arms when we buried my sister. He takes him back and forth to school every day. How can he have involved himself in this?"

He could only imagine how her world had to be tilting on its axis right now.

"You're being betrayed over and over by people in your inner circle. Tell me about your family. What happened to them?"

"Tell me about yours."

"What?" No one caught him more off guard than she did.

"You tell me your secrets and I'll tell you mine. I can't keep trusting you with all this and know nothing about you. I feel too exposed."

She felt exposed? "I'm trying to help you."

"I know that, but I can't keep sharing all this stuff with you. I'm sorry, but one way or another you're a temporary fixture in my life. People who were supposed to be permanent are betraying me left and right. I think the best thing I can do is stop giving anyone any chance to destroy us."

"You think I have some sort of agenda here? Something other than doing what you asked me to do, finding Jeremy?"

He wanted to punch something. He didn't know why her response bothered him so deeply. She was right. The people she had allowed into her inner sanctum had been responsible for taking Jeremy. The smart thing to do was to close down shop and stop giving anyone the chance to keep doing it. But she'd told him she didn't think he was Hell-bound. That meant something. He should admit it, at least to himself; he wanted her to trust him.

"I think you have a secret agenda."

"Really?" He heard the cold tone in his voice.

At home, people who knew him would have backed off. Addison seemed to have no sense of self-preservation. She pulled her hand from his and placed both fists on her hips. Despite her fuming, he found her sexy as hell. There was nothing in the world he wanted more than to pull her into a doorway and fuck her until they were both panting with pleasure. Instead, he tilted his head to the side to give her an accusing look.

"Everywhere I look I see conspiracy now. Two people I trusted, maybe more, have taken my nephew. They're missing on the psychic plane. I just happen to go and get the one guy who can see that. Hell, even the building I live in is now suspect based on the materials used to construct it."

"The building's construction happened long before either of us was born."

"Are you trying to piss me off? Okay, then the reasons for living in it."

"Yes, I'm trying to piss you off, because you made me incredibly mad. I had two agendas in coming here. One, to find your nephew, and two, Rhodes asked me *not* to piss you off because maybe it would garner some good will with the council. I have failed miserably with the second one."

Addison groaned, and he noticed how soaking wet she was. He hadn't even focused on how much harder the rain was getting.

"How could helping me do that?"

"Don't be an imbecile. Someday you'll hold your grand-father's position on the council."

"No way in hell am I ever taking that job, so you can tell Rhodes he's stuck wooing my grandfather. The Wades will let that spot go to someone else when he dies."

Unable to stand it anymore, he pulled her into his arms. "Whatever conspiracy is going on here, I am not a part of it. Do you understand that? Tell me you at least believe that much."

The tears he'd worried about earlier flooded from her eyes like a dam losing its battle with an onslaught of white water rapids. "I do. I believe you." Her words were muffled and slurred, like it was taking too much energy for her to cry and speak at the same time. As he looked around, he saw a slight overhang that would give them a little protection from the rain.

Keeping her tucked against him, he moved them beneath it.

"I'm sorry, I never cry."

He believed her. Addison Wade was not a woman who got hysterical easily. She was as tough as nails, and he wondered what this display of pain would cost her when she thought about it later. He hoped she wouldn't berate herself for it.

"God, no."

"What?" He looked down, trying to see what Addison meant, but nothing was visible. She strained her eyes closed and tried to pull from his arms. "What's going on?"

"Let me go, Spence." She'd used the name Rhodes called him, and he didn't think she even knew it.

"No. Tell me what's going on."

"I'm going to lose it. It's too much emotion. I can't control it."

"Can't control what?" His heart pounded, and his pulse rang in his ears. In his life, he couldn't remember being this terrified of something he didn't understand. "Explain to me what's happening here."

A surge of energy the likes of which he'd never felt before shuddered from Addison. Behind him, the store window they stood in front of exploded. The sound was deafening. Throwing her to the ground, he had a moment to shield her from the shards of glass that flew everywhere. The woman in his arms shook and sobbed.

She was shouting. "I've got to do the rhyme or it won't stop! I've got to make it stop!" Desperation filled the air from the agony in her voice.

"Calm down." His ears rang, and he had to admit his breath felt shallow. He was frightened of what had just happened. He wasn't sure whether the glass shards had cut him, and he wasn't ready to move yet to find out. If he'd been hurt and he didn't feel it, that wouldn't be a good sign in terms of how injured he was. Clearly, Addison was more than she appeared to be. He could be pissed about it later. For now, he had to get this situation under control, and fast.

"What rhyme?"

"It's something I say to make it stop."

The rhyme. Damn, now he remembered the children's rhyme he'd heard that had driven him into Rhodes' office back at Safe Dawn. He'd heard a singsong nursery rhyme in his head and assumed it was one of the juveniles, but no, it had been *her*. She used it as her shield? The girl had enough power to shatter a window and she used nothing more than a rhyme to stop her power flux? She was lucky she wasn't dead. Hell, the whole city was lucky they weren't dead.

"Okay, let's do it together. I'll help you." And then he'd figure out whether he was bleeding to death.

"I can't even think. I can't seem to say it. What's happening to me?"

"Addison, listen to me." He put his mouth close to her ear and tried to speak softly, hoping that she would pick up his tone and relax a little bit. "You can't say the rhyme because you use it as a shield, and right now you're too upset to properly put your shields in place. So the first thing you need to do is calm down before you break any more windows." *Please don't let her break any more windows.*

"I think I can help with that, Spencer."

His head shot up at the sound of a voice he'd hoped never to hear again in this lifetime: Roman. How had he snuck up on him? Well, he supposed, that was obvious. He was lying on the ground with shards of glass in his back, trying to stop Addison from destroying them.

To be found by the Fury in these circumstances made the agony of the whole thing even worse. What was he going to tell them about Addison? He couldn't allow them to take her. That much he was clear about. He'd find a way to save her from this.

"I'm feeling calmer." Addison's voice shook a little bit less, which was a relief.

"That's because Roman is tempering your power. It's what he does. He's like Rhodes; he can dampen the Condition. But unlike Will, he can also do other things. Terrible things. So we're going to stand up slowly and not make any sudden moves."

Roman laughed. "Despite what you think of me, Spence, I'm not going to shoot the girl in the head as we stand here on the street."

"I take it you two know each other." Addison's voice sounded shaky but steadier than a few moments before.

Spencer had to give Roman credit. His brief seconds with them had done far more to calm Addison down than he ever could have.

Running his hands through her hair, he reassured himself that she was alive, well, and not about to die from a power surge she couldn't possibly control without instruction.

"Careful how you move; you've got pieces of glass all over your back. I can't tell in the darkness if any of them have pierced your sweater." Roman paused. "Why the hell aren't you wearing a coat?"

"Because I gave it to the girl. It's called chivalry." He hoped his tone implied how annoyed he really was by the question. Who the hell was Roman to ask him anything?

"No one has told me how you two know each other yet." He had to give Addison credit; she was determined.

Spencer pulled himself slowly off Addison's back. Begrudgingly, he admitted to himself that Roman was right. He might not have been seriously hurt, but he did have glass on him, and it stung.

"You know the Fury that you were so worried about? Meet one of its primary members."

Addison pushed herself into a sitting position that

vaguely resembled a small ball. Spencer resisted the urge to pick her up like a baby and carry her back to the car.

"So I guess I'm pretty screwed, right?"

Roman placed his hands in his black coat pockets. "You have the Condition, and you've been hiding it your entire life."

Spencer noted that Roman didn't phrase that as a question. Clearly, it would have been stupid at this point to assume anything else. Except that he wasn't letting Roman take Addison. Those who entered the institutions as adults did not do well under their treatments. One out of three died. He didn't like those odds for Addison. Not one bit.

He cleared his throat. "*I* blew up the window."

Roman raised an eyebrow. "You're going to claim you did this?"

Addison looked back and forth between them. She narrowed her eyes, and he knew what she saw. "There's something kind of similar about you two." She stood.

Spencer ignored her remark. "I did. I blew up the window."

"Then why did I feel the power coming from her?"

"It's a new development in my Condition. I can force power on other people. I just can't control it yet."

"And you expect me to believe that Rhodes would let you out of Safe Dawn if that were true?"

"Yep."

"Hold it." Addison's voice held the authority of being listened to and revered for her entire life. He decided it must be a Wade thing. "This is more than just a Fury thing. You two actually know each other."

Spencer shook his head. "It's a Fury thing."

"He's my younger brother by eleven months."

Addison gasped. Spencer could guess what she saw

when she looked at the two of them. Roughly the same height, he was maybe one inch taller than Roman. They were both blond, but where his hair curled at the ends and was forever in his eyes, Roman kept his head nearly shaved to the scalp. If he'd let it grow, Spencer knew his brother would have the same curl problem.

Spencer was built like a linebacker and Roman was even broader. Their eyes were shaped the same way, thin and elf-like, but Roman's color tended toward gray-blue instead of pure blue. He'd gotten that from their mother, and Spencer had always silently resented him for that, among other things, since she was the only parent he remembered. Their noses were the same, but where his face could be considered long, Roman's was rounder, giving him a more approachable look.

Of the two of them, Spencer had been the only one with a visible sign of his powers. His eyes turning black in the dark place had made him obviously Conditioned, whereas Roman had been able to hide his abilities. That was until Spencer had gotten them both caught. Internally, he shrugged. Just something else he could add to his list of things to feel guilty about.

If he really dwelled on everything that had gone wrong in life, everything he was personally responsible for, he'd never get through the day.

Addison whirled on him. "Your brother is a member of the Fury and you didn't think to mention that?"

Lowering his voice, he leaned over to whisper in her ear. "As I stand here risking death to take responsibility for your stunning little display, I would remind you that people in glass houses shouldn't throw stones."

Illuminated by the nearby streetlight, he could see her cheeks heat with embarrassment.

"I did it. I broke the glass. Take me in." Spencer turned back to look at Roman and held out his wrists like he wanted to be handcuffed.

"Liar. You never could pull off even the slightest fib, so knock it off."

"Take me in." Why couldn't his brother just do what he wanted for once in his life?

Roman walked over to Addison and extended his hand. She took it. Never before had Spencer wanted to punch out his brother for nothing more than touching a woman. This time he was damn close to actually following through on his desire to pound Roman.

"I have a bit of a problem here, Ms. Wade. Your grandfather put me on to watch Spencer here. I'm not sure what he'll do if I take you in instead."

"If my grandfather finds out I'm Conditioned, he'll be the first person to turn me in."

"You can't take her, Roman. You know what will happen to her in there at her age."

Addison's cheeks lost their red glow, and she went deathly pale. "What will happen to me?"

"I'm in a difficult position here, Spencer."

Spencer stalked forward and poked him in the chest. "Bullshit. There's right and wrong. This would be wrong, and you know it."

Sneering, Roman rolled his eyes. "The woman just broke a storefront window. We have moments before the police will arrive. How do you suggest we explain it?"

"You tell them I did it. Problem solved."

"Despite what you think, little brother, I don't have a desire to turn you back over for rehabilitation. I don't want to see that happen to you either."

"I survived them once."

"You were a child then. There's no saying you could survive them now."

If his heart beat any faster, it might explode. "Do you worry this much about every poor soul you drag back to captivity?" Spencer spared a glance for Addison, who had crossed her arms over her chest. Clearly, she was terrified. Good, she should be. It was important that she understand the severity of this.

"No. I don't."

Spencer hadn't expected that answer, and he wasn't sure what to say.

Addison moved forward and grasped his arm. Her body heat felt good against him. His back had started to ache and her vanilla scent was like a balm for his bleeding soul. Every time Roman showed up, it played havoc with his sanity.

"Spence, maybe he can help us."

"He can't."

She sighed. "Let's ask him."

"The worst thing we could do is involve the Fury in this."

"Help you with what?" Was it his imagination, or did Roman seem genuinely interested?

"My nephew is missing. Spencer is trying to help us find him."

Roman's silence disturbed him. If he wasn't talking, he was thinking, and that was never a good thing.

"Your grandfather said nothing about that."

She shook her head, and he felt her body shudder. Addison was freezing. They needed to move off of the street sooner rather than later. He opened his mouth, but she grabbed his arm tighter to make him stop.

"I'm not surprised. Anyway, Spence can't find him because someone is erasing people from the psychic plane."

Roman shook his head. "But that's impossible."

Spencer sighed. "Only it isn't. So take me in and not Addison. There are much more important things going on here than Addison Wade and her uncontrolled power."

Roman looked at him. "What does Rhodes say?"

"I haven't told him yet."

"Then before we do anything else, we're going to do that."

Spencer laughed. "Now you're giving orders?"

"Enough," Addison yelled, and she shook hard in his arms. He pulled her tighter against him. "I need to find Jeremy. Let's find him. Then you'll take me in, because despite Mr. Heroic over here, it was obviously me, and I'm clearly a danger to everyone. But first we find Jeremy. Can you help us?"

If Roman said no, Spencer would kill him where he stood.

"I'll see what I can turn up. Talk to Rhodes. I'll find a way to be in touch in three days if I've heard anything."

Like the ghost he'd always been, Roman turned and disappeared into the shadows. Spencer wondered if they'd just opened Pandora's box. Roman Lewis was not to be used lightly. He knew that better than anyone.

Hearing the sirens in the background, Spencer pulled Addison along with him. "Come on, we need to get out of here."

TEN

Addison sat quietly in the car, not daring to utter a word in front of Greg for fear of where his loyalties lay. Part of her wished she could just ask Spencer to beat him up, or that she was some sort of superwoman who could do it herself. The shards of glass still attached to the back of his sweater reminded her that he was probably not up to full speed at the moment.

He might also tell her to go to hell instead of helping her, and she really wouldn't blame him if he did.

As they pulled up to the building, he leaned over to growl in her ear. "Don't go to bed. I need to speak to you."

She waited for the doorman to open the car door and stepped out onto the street. "Thank you, Greg." It wouldn't do any good to tip her hand or alert Greg that she knew he was most likely involved in the conspiracy.

"Goodnight, Addison."

In the future—if she wasn't locked up in an institution or, if Spence and Roman were to be believed, dead—she wouldn't get so close to people who worked for her. She'd pretended they were family, and not spent enough time focusing on making herself a life filled with people who wouldn't hurt Jeremy.

Spencer walked close behind her, so near that she could feel his warm breath on the back of her neck. It made her shiver and long for something she knew she couldn't have. Besides, she reminded herself, sex wasn't usually that exciting for her. It was a lot of work up and not much reward—hardly worth the effort. They walked through the lobby, entered the elevator, and waited while the door closed.

Maybe with Spencer it might have been different. Not that there was a chance in hell she would ever find out now. He had hardly looked at her in the car.

"Spence..."

He held up his hand, one finger over his mouth indicating that she should be quiet. Dear God, did he think they were being monitored in the elevator? What about in the apartment?

They walked into her home, and he closed the door behind them. "And here I thought I'd found a non-Conditioned woman who thought we weren't going to Hell. Surprise, surprise, it was actually a Conditioned woman, hiding it, who hopes we're not damned because that would mean she is, too. Or wait, maybe it's only the ones not lucky enough to be hidden by their grandfathers, who spent their lives hurting people just like their granddaughters."

The sad part of it was that, from his perspective, what he said made total sense.

"Are you finished?"

"This is what you do, isn't it? You act all high and mighty when someone dares to call you on being wrong."

"I was asking if you were done with your pretty little

speech because I have some things to say, but I'm not going to start if you're still planning to rant for a while yet."

He looked up at the ceiling like he was looking for divine help. She wondered if he ever got an answer, because she never did. "You can be such a bitch. Why do I even like you?"

Addison paused. "What?"

"I shouldn't be worrying about your feelings or considering how we're going to protect you. I should be running you into the closest testing institute and throwing away the key. People with your talent are the reason we're all locked up to begin with. Hell, woman, you blew up a glass window. You're dangerous."

Addison could see Spencer's pulse pounding in a vein on the side of his head. He was really, really mad.

"You're all locked up because some ten-year-old-boy couldn't keep his mouth shut about oil trade negotiations. That's how you all became national security risks, and if you think it's anything else that did it, you're fooling yourself."

Spencer exhaled and walked to the couch in the living room. Sitting down, he rubbed at his eyes before he started brushing glass off him again. They'd both been doing that on and off since the explosion. "He killed himself."

"What?" She moved toward him until she stood in front of where he sat on the couch.

"The little boy's name was Penn Rowe. He killed himself when he was nineteen. He hanged himself in the bathroom. I knew him, remotely. He was infamous among us."

"Oh. I didn't know that."

"I didn't expect that you would." Spencer pulled off his glass-ridden sweater, leaving only his T-shirt behind. "Does your grandfather know what you can do? Do you guys have to change the windows in here all the time?"

"He has no idea. He'd be the first to turn me in, I assure you."

"How have you managed to hide it? Do you do that stupid rhyme all the time?"

Her whole body ached. "My father taught me to do that after I exposed myself when I was about three. I couldn't even spell yet, but he taught me letters, and he started doing it with me. I don't think my mother ever knew."

"And for what? For twenty-three years you've done this ridiculous rhyme and it's kept you under control, but tonight you were so upset you blew up a window?"

She sat down next to him on the couch, pulling her legs beneath her. "I've had a few mishaps. However, I've never blown anything up until tonight. The last four years have been so good I haven't had to do the rhyme at all. Only when Jeremy went missing did it come back, and so strongly that I've had to say it at least three or four times a day just to function." She cleared her throat. "Somehow you heard me when I was at Safe Dawn."

"I'm still not sure why. I don't usually tune in to other people's thoughts." He started to pace. "So if you don't blow things up, what do you usually do?"

"I can sense things. I have an idea something is about to happen and then it does. I'm not one hundred percent accurate, but I guess it was frightening enough that when I was a child, I would start to get this sense. It's hard to describe what it feels like."

He moved back to her and knelt down. "It feels like terrible, painful goosebumps. Right?"

He ran his hand up her arm, and a totally opposite sort

of excitement formed inside her. Spencer's touch was becoming an aphrodisiac.

"Yes, but worse. I can sense power inside me. Like my internal organs reshape and alter. Then the power surges out of me. In the past, before tonight's explosion, it would zoom out of my body, and then I would know things." She looked down at the floor. "It's why I checked on Jeremy that night. I had a sense something was wrong the whole day. However, I never had an episode, just a feeling. So I dismissed it." Tears welled in her eyes as she admitted to him what she'd never been able to say out loud before. "If I'd trusted myself, he'd still be here. This is my fault."

"Nonsense. You're entirely untrained. I think all human beings get bad feelings. It's an evolutionary tool. If you had a bad feeling and you ran, then you were less likely to get eaten by the scary animal that was readying itself to run out of the cave and eat you."

She laughed. How was that possible? How could she be laughing when she should have been sobbing?

"Did Jeremy ever show any symptoms? He's four, right? Most of us—and I'm including you as part of 'us' now—show symptoms at three or four. I did, and apparently you did."

"Never." No, she would have noticed that.

"Unless he didn't exhibit the signs to you." Spencer stood.

His eyes were far off.

"You mean he had something happen and Loretta saw it."

"The last person on Earth, save your grandfather, whom Jeremy should have been exposed to. Maybe your grandfather would have been better. Then Jeremy would have been sent to an institute, not taken to God knows where. He's a child; he would have survived the testing."

"If he'd never shown himself before, because he was too young, then that would mean Loretta's first objective wasn't to kidnap Jeremy. What was she sent here to do?" Her mind turning, she answered her own question. "To spy on us from inside. Grandfather is well known for how well he takes care of his internal employees. Greg, the maids, the cook and our personal assistants."

"They took Jeremy when they saw what he could do. It was an opportunity."

"No one has asked for any ransom. Nothing has come out to threaten us in any way." God, she wished it had. It would have been so much easier if this were a case of someone wanting hush money.

"Whatever it is that Jeremy can do is more useful to these people than ransom or extortion."

"And if it doesn't work out, they can always expose Jeremy later and still collect."

Addison was glad she was sitting, otherwise her knees might buckle. "Greg, Loretta... do you think everyone who works here is involved?"

"It's possible. It's also highly likely that we're being recorded right now." Then why had he brought her here instead of taking her to the middle of a park or something? He sat down next to her and stroked her hair. "I never thought I'd say this in my entire existence, but I think we need to call your grandfather."

As if on cue, the door opened and Oliver Wade strode in. She wasn't surprised. The man had always had splendid timing and a sense of how things would work out. Raising an eyebrow, she stood. Maybe it was his own version of the Condition. Weren't they finding out more and more that these things ran in families? A thought struck her suddenly. Had her father known how to help her because he'd also been afflicted?

"Grandfather."

Oliver's eyes didn't meet hers as he looked Spencer over. She couldn't stop the grin that crossed her face as Spencer met his gaze straight on without flinching. She had watched grown men shrink under the scrutiny Oliver was laying on Spencer, yet he hardly seemed to notice it at all. Maybe he was used to being stared at.

"I assume this is Spencer Lewis." Oliver moved forward but didn't extend his hand. "I recognize you from the photograph in your file."

"And I recognize you from the news footage we see of you after every council meeting. It's always a joy anticipating what new form of torture you, the Wade Corporation, and the council will create for us."

"The purpose of the council, as you know, Mr. Lewis, is to keep the general public safe from people who are simply too dangerous to have out and about. Wade Corporation is the second largest company in the world, with operations on four continents employing over three thousand people. We have several contracts with the institutes because it is profitable. I don't need to justify the actions of the council or Wade Corporation to you. As for myself, it has always been my goal to leave the world better than I found it."

Spencer opened his mouth to respond, but Addison interrupted him before it got out of hand. "Grandfather, we've discovered some things regarding Jeremy."

Quickly and methodically, as she always kept things when she spoke to her grandfather, she recounted what had happened to them, leaving out the part where she'd destroyed a window and met Roman.

"So you're telling me you've just discovered that my great-grandson is Conditioned and someone has him for some nefarious purpose that may or may not relate to destroying Wade."

She wished he could sound slightly more emotionally invested, but there was nothing inherently wrong with his description of what had happened.

"Have you both eaten dinner?"

Reminded of her hunger, Addison placed a hand on her stomach. She looked at Spencer, whose face told her he would rather roll around in dirt than eat with Oliver. He was just going to have to deal, because she needed to get her grandfather on board with finding Jeremy. If eating with him was the way to do it, then they would. Plus, hadn't Spencer said they needed him?

"Mr. Wade, before we go into the dining room, I'm afraid I have to point out to you the likelihood that most, if not all, of your home is being bugged or recorded."

Oliver moved closer to Spencer. "Mr. Lewis, I don't need you to point anything out to me, ever. I am always prepared for commercial espionage. I employ anti-spy technology in my own office and in my home, made exclusively for Wade Corporation. No one can plant a bug in here, which would be why whoever did this sent their people into our home."

"So then I guess you're not as protected as you thought you were."

"I think food is the way to go." Addison was going to keep this under control one way or another.

"I'm not hungry." Spencer smiled at her, and she was relieved to see that surrounding the swirls in his eyes was warmth and not contempt when he looked at her. He would never have been a very good poker player. He wore his emotions all over his face.

"Are you sure?"

"I'm positive."

Addison watched him disappear down the hall. She turned and followed her grandfather down the corridor to the kitchen. The room had been a haven when her mother had been alive, the apartment always alive with smells and good food to eat. Afterward, it had become as sterile as the rest of the house.

She took a quick look and found some takeout she could reheat.

She leaned against the wall while her grandfather stuck the food in the microwave, fatigue starting to catch up with her.

"Grandfather, was everything with my parents... normal?"

"In what way?" He didn't turn around when she spoke to him.

"Were they like Jeremy?" *Or me,* she silently added.

He swung around. "Are you asking me if my only child and his beloved wife—your parents—were Conditioned?"

"Yes, sir, that is what I am asking you." Although now she wished she hadn't, since he seemed to be taking the question very badly.

"Let me be clear about this, Granddaughter. No one in this family before Jeremy—who I will assume acquired this Condition from the faulty genetics given to him by God knows who his father was—has ever been one of *them.*"

That answered her question. Should she enlighten the man as to just how Conditioned she herself was, or let him know that her father had possessed a strange understanding of how to control her uniqueness? No, she decided right then and there, she would not. Her father had never told her grandfather, and something had kept her quiet all these years.

After a few minutes of utter silence, which wasn't strained, since she was used to behaving that way with the patriarch of the family, he pulled lasagna and green beans out of the microwave. He motioned toward the dining room, and she followed him in and sat down at her traditional place. They ate together maybe once a month, and their roles were clearly defined.

Before he'd taken a bite, her grandfather leveled a no-nonsense look toward her, and she braced herself for a blow. "What concerns me about this, Addison, is how many people have the potential to know our disgrace."

"Our disgrace?"

"Jeremy's Condition." *A-ha*. "We must make every effort to retrieve him quickly. I had been assuming this was a power play by a member of the council. I still think it is. However, there's so much more to risk now. Your instinct to bring Lewis in on this proved to be completely correct. Had you not, we would not know about this psychic plane business and would never have found out about Loretta." He raised his fork and pointed it at her. "We have to contain this. Do whatever you have to do to get him back, and we'll quietly handle things so nothing ever comes out about this."

"What do you mean, handle things?" Addison was afraid she knew exactly what he meant, and she didn't like it one bit.

"Let's just say that no one who knows about this will be left around to tell anyone."

He clearly meant to include Spencer in that group. As a member of the Conditioned, his disappearance wouldn't rock any boats. There was no way in hell she would let that happen.

Silently, she promised herself that she would rescue Jeremy and make sure nothing bad happened to Spencer because of her. In the little time they'd spent together, he had come to *matter*. He listened when she spoke, his eyes swirled when she looked at him, and he seemed to genuinely care about finding Jeremy when no one else did. Aside from being the most handsome man she'd ever seen, she had finally met someone who was worth knowing. She would protect him... one way or another.

After she finished her dinner, she cleared their plates and took them to the sink to wash and stack them. She muttered her goodnights to her grandfather and finished straightening up the kitchen. If the cook was in on this conspiracy, she should have left the kitchen a mess to make the woman suffer.

Quietly, she crawled into her own bed. It had been a month since she'd slept in it, preferring most nights to be close to Jeremy by staying in his room. The poor baby. Her eyes threatened to overflow with tears again. It was always this time of night when she was closest to losing her cool.

She didn't think her strangeness was about to explode again. Maybe her Condition was exhausted from having been unleashed earlier.

The thought made her remember what she had been desperate not to focus on:

Spencer Lewis was two doors down from her.

The thought of him in bed did strange things to her insides. A warmth deep within her core started as she imagined him naked from the waist up, deep in sleep. Maybe he slept naked or fully dressed, but in her fantasy he was topless. Did he snore? She smiled at the thought. If she slept next to him, it would be a constant reminder that he was in the room, that she wasn't alone, that his presence made her safe.

She shook her head as she tried to force herself not to think about him like that. He was certainly not imagining her half naked. She sighed and forced her eyes closed. The sooner morning came, the sooner they could find Jeremy. It was best not to focus on the fact that getting Jeremy back would mean losing Spencer. Yes, best not to think about that at all.

ELEVEN

He rolled over and covered his head with the pillow. It was no use; he was exhausted but he couldn't sleep. Not with Addison Wade and her vanilla-scented hair down the hall. How long had it been since he'd had a woman? Certainly not long enough to warrant this level of desperation. His cock was so hard it hurt to lie on his stomach.

Besides, he had every reason to be pissed with Addison rather than turned on by her. Maybe that was the problem. The woman made his blood boil when he wasn't mad. Anger only seemed to intensify the reaction.

It was too late to call Rhodes. The man was getting older. Nothing less than a dire life-or-death emergency warranted calling him after eleven at night. Given that he'd just heard the clock in the living room chime midnight, he wasn't going to call with his discoveries. Will woke up ridiculously early, so if Spencer couldn't sleep, he'd just call the other man at daybreak.

He stood up and stretched, letting his arms and back work out the kinks they'd been carrying around all day. Jeremy needed him. He'd never met the boy, but like with most of the missing children cases he'd taken on, he had already adopted the child as his own. When he met him, the feeling wouldn't lessen and it would be harder to leave. In another life, maybe he would have been a teacher or a social worker. Or a father. That thought bothered him so much he made himself forget it.

If he'd been at home, he could have gone down to the gym facility and worked out. As he was deemed safe to be out in public some of the time, he had been granted gym privileges, which allowed him to lift weights and run on the treadmill.

The Conditioned who were too scary to walk among society were not permitted to do things like that. The reasoning seemed to be that the sooner they died, the better, and keeping them healthy was only prolonging the problem. Rhodes had been working to try to change that for years. Like with most things, however, it seemed to Spencer that Rhodes was beating his head against a brick wall.

Having met Oliver Wade, he could see why. The smug way the man had informed him that he was determined to make the world better than he'd found it. Spencer wished he could pound on his geriatric face.

Pulling his pajama pants over his currently too-tight boxer shorts, he opened his door and glanced out into the hallway. If he was going to call Rhodes in the morning, it would be best if he had all the information Rhodes would want. He needed to exhaust every possible angle to look for Jeremy's energy signal. Addison would take him to the school in the morning, but he wanted to be able to tell his mentor that he'd gone as far as he could go here in the apartment.

Quietly, he opened Jeremy's door and glanced around the room. Addison had obviously decided to sleep in her own bed. That was good. It meant he wouldn't have to wake her.

Crossing to the bed, he picked up the pillow and gave it one quick sniff, satisfied when he smelled Addison's familiar vanilla scent over the smell of laundry detergent.

Spencer closed his eyes and let himself drift into dark space. It was like breathing the way it felt in a dream, only this wasn't a manifestation of his internal mind. No sound existed in the space except that which he made himself. He'd also never smelled anything. It was like all senses ceased to exist except sight and touch, and even touch would disappear the farther he went in.

As a child, he had often thought he was dreaming when he'd visited this place. It hadn't been until Rhodes had explained to him what was happening that he'd learned to control it.

Truth was, they shouldn't refer to it as "dark space." It made it sound much more mysterious than it actually was. Human beings lived in two different places. The physical plane, where they ate, slept, had sex—all the everyday things. But there was another place where they existed as well. Their thoughts, feelings and emotions were as unique to each person as their fingerprints. Everywhere they passed, lived or visited, they left a mark of themselves, a fragment that someone with his abilities could see.

The deeper he went, the more clearly he could see the people who had resided in the same space. Jeremy's room looked the same there, except it was shadowed. The whole place was bathed in dark lights broken up by the bright energies swirling through the room that represented the people who had visited it.

There was no sign of Jeremy anywhere. The only lights

visible were his own—a swirling blue-and-white cloud that floated wherever he went—and Addison's bright yellow sunshine. Her psychic energy pulsed all over the space. It was impossible to describe how he had immediately known it was her. In the same way he would recognize her scent anywhere he encountered it, he would know her psychic self.

In the corner, where her aunt had stood, were purple and gray, pulsing and fading, pulsing and fading. The woman had been agitated when she'd been in here, and her energy indicated her turmoil. Well, he'd witnessed it himself.

A tremor started in his head. The shadows were calling to him again, beckoning him to go deeper, to look further. He shook his head. This was what he wanted, what he'd promised himself he would check before he called Rhodes in the morning. Earlier in the day, he'd been too aware of Addison in the room, too distracted to do a proper job, but now, when it was quiet, he should be able to push a little farther in and not lose himself.

He hoped.

Forcing his concentration to sharpen, he let his mind wander deeper into the shadows. The solidness of the room drifted away. All he needed to do was find a spark of Jeremy, one fiber of the little boy, and he'd be able to send his energy out into the universe to track him.

"Come on. Come on." He still saw nothing. The bed looked more distant, fuzzier. At this level of dark space, matter started to lose its solidness and he could see the energy generated by inanimate objects. Everything gave off light. The bed was a brushed green; the lamp looked pumpkin orange. Narrowing his eyes, he pushed his vision a little deeper into the shadows, knowing that he was getting into risky territory. But something inside the darkness beck-oned him on.

Was it Jeremy's energy, begging him to find it?

Smiling, Spencer realized he was starting to wax philo-sophical. Realistically, he knew energies didn't actually speak or communicate with him. Even knowing that, when he was this deep inside dark space, his mind tended to drift into metaphysical matters when he needed to focus on the moment.

"Where are you, Jeremy?" Had he spoken out loud or just in his mind, where only he could hear it? It didn't matter; in either case, there was no one around to answer.

Something caught his attention, and he whirled around. Energy he didn't recognize danced in the gloom of the boy's closet. Was it Jeremy's or someone else's random flow from a previous visit? It was risky to go any farther. He'd never been deeper than this without a guide back. Hell, with Priscilla he could have gone ten times deeper and not gotten lost.

He didn't have that luxury now.

He tried to touch the bed beside him. His hand floated through the object as if it were a phantom version of itself. Damn. He'd already left solid space. Dare he risk it?

He pushed out with his senses to gently probe the shadow that contained the strange energy. Like a kitten nervous to be approached, the colors leaped backward deeper into the blackness. Unlike a live cat, he couldn't coax them back out. If he wanted to see it, he was going to have to go in after it.

A vision of a little blond boy with dancing green eyes appeared to him. He'd only seen a picture of Jeremy once, and very quickly. In his work, the subject's appearance on the physical plane was irrelevant, but sometimes when he touched energy, he could get a glimpse of the physical person who'd created the mark in the universe.

Even if he hadn't known the boy was Jeremy, he would have recognized him as a Wade. High cheekbones, a straight nose, and a stubborn cleft in his chin that he shared with his great-grandfather, spoke of his strong familial genetics. The eyes were not the Wade blue, and Spencer wondered if he'd gotten them from his father. It was odd that they knew nothing about who that man had been or still was; bizarre that Oliver Wade had never investigated it.

Laughter filled his mind, the soft dulcet sounds of true innocence. The boy had lost his mother at a young age, but when he had left his trace of himself, he had still been pure and happy. Spencer could practically taste the unique manifestation of youth in his mouth.

He closed his eyes as the murk plucked at him, gently tugging. Damn. He was going in. There was no choice. Maybe he wouldn't come out again, but he had to give it a try. How could he possibly leave a trace of Jeremy out there without catching it? They'd never be able to follow the path if he didn't grasp on to it now, and the thing was so skittish he might never get this chance a second time.

Spencer would simply have to find a way back. He was the strongest tracker on the psychic plane. If anyone could do it, he could.

Rubbing the back of his neck to relieve some pent-up stress, he pushed all his consciousness forward into the shadow that held Jeremy's energy. Without an anchor holding him, he slammed into the darkness with force, and his head spun from the effort. Regaining his equilibrium, he looked left and right to see where he was.

Drifting in front of him was Jeremy's energy signature.

It was white and blue with some random green spots. He moved toward it, and it hovered away, just out of reach.

Placing a hand out in front of him like a lifeline, he took a deep breath. "Okay, there's nothing to be afraid of."

Usually he didn't talk to the energy around him, but Jeremy's seemed to be skittish. Using his voice meant that he could control his own reactions and energy, thereby, he hoped, manipulating Jeremy's into coming to him. Only once before had he ever had to resort to speaking to the psychic energy he encountered. At that time, he'd been searching for a rape victim who had been kidnapped. Her energy had been as damaged as she had been when the police had found her.

Jeremy's energy didn't look damaged, only afraid.

"My name is Spencer. I need to touch you so I can find the real version of you out there in the physical world. That's what I do; I track energy. Your aunt, the beautiful one with the yellow, sunlight signature, found me and brought me here to find you. I know you've been through a lot. Someone came in here and removed you. It's amazing that you're here at all. Can I do that? Can I touch you and you won't move away?"

Spencer stayed very still and silent. Finally, after what felt like forever but might have been only minutes, he reached out his hand and touched the swirling white and blue in front of him. To his delight, Jeremy's energy stayed still and let him feel it.

With his hands acting like conduits, he took Jeremy's energy inside him. Rhodes had once told him that it was like Spencer took in part of the person's soul when he captured his psychic energy. Although he didn't like to think of himself as doing exactly that, he had to admit it was a pretty good description. Wherever he went, he would always carry part of Jeremy with him now.

Pulling back, he swung around to look for the exit from dark space. Nothing but total blackness surrounded him. Spencer sucked in his breath as his palms started to sweat. He'd gone too far.

There was no light anywhere, and in complete darkness he would never be able to find his path back to the physical world. It was like flying an airplane without equipment in a cloudy area. Without the horizon to show you where you were going, there was no way to tell if you were up or down. If he tried to move and it turned out to be the wrong way, he might end up going even farther into the shadows.

This was his personal nightmare.

Spencer closed his eyes and made himself push down his fears. Only once before had this happened, and he hadn't been nearly this deep or this lost. He'd been only five, and it had been his first experimentation without Rhodes monitoring him. Evidently, Will Rhodes had gone crazy on the outside, found Priscilla—who herself had been only six —rushed her to him, and she had pulled him out.

There wouldn't be anyone to do that today. What pissed him off the most was that he wouldn't see Addison again, wouldn't get to touch her, or tell her that he would now be able to find Jeremy. It was strange that out of his entire life's existence, the thing he was the most resentful about missing out on related to a woman he'd known for such a short time.

How would she find Jeremy without him? He hated the feeling of being ineffectual. He lifted his head as he roared like a trapped animal. Would he just stay like this for the next fifty years until he died? Could he starve to death here? If they kept his body alive on the physical plane, would he continue to live in here?

He tried to push down the insanity that threatened to consume him as he looked around again. There had to be a way out. There simply had to be. This wasn't the way it ended, damn it. His hands shook with fury.

Off in the distance, a light met his eyes. Was it real? He moved cautiously toward it. A few steps more and he determined he wasn't crazy; there was a light beckoning him to return to the physical plane.

Home. The word filled his mind. The light wanted him to come back home. He could have laughed at the silliness of the thought; he didn't have a home, not really. He lived in an institution. Still, it felt good to think he did for a moment. He pushed his consciousness forward, drawn to the light, begging for its guidance. It didn't let him down. Rather than disappear, it got stronger as he approached it.

Priscilla had given him a narrow path to follow; he used to call it his faded gray brick road back home. But this illumination was breathtaking—yellow with crisp gold lines and a stream of silver glowing around the edges. It was easy to follow and manipulate. As he followed where it led, things began to come back into focus.

The bed was to his left. He reached out and touched it. Shuddering, he breathed with relief as he discovered it was solid and sturdy beneath his hand. As his eyes readjusted to the room around him, he looked up and his heart stopped beating for a moment.

It was Addison. She was pushing the light to him; the light that had led him back. How was that possible? Her condition had made her break a glass window. That was in no way connected to conduit abilities. He forced his mind to take him to the physical world.

His first solid thought was that he had fallen to his knees. That was unusual. In the past, he had never moved at all during his trips in and out of dark space.

His thoughts felt clogged, like being awakened at night in the middle of a dream.

For the space of a few heartbeats, he didn't know what was going on.

Cool hands touched the sides of his face, and he raised his head to look at their owner. Addison sat in front of him, and Spencer understood for the first time what sailors lost at sea must feel when they see a lighthouse beckoning them in the distance. She was like an angel sent from Heaven to bring him back from the darkness. If he could have mustered the energy to laugh at that thought, he would have. Heaven was not sending him any angels, not if he was already damned.

Nevertheless, he was grateful beyond belief for her and whatever she had done to bring him back.

"How did you do that? How did you create a path?" His voice sounded rough, like sandpaper.

"You were screaming, I heard you."

"Impossible. I'm silent when I'm in dark space."

Addison laughed. "Well, you weren't this time. It was like you were dreaming, but I couldn't wake you up and you kept screaming. I grabbed you..."

"And?" He wanted to hear the whole story.

"I tried to concentrate on sending my energy to you. Instead of it just flowing out of me uncontrolled and destroying something, I was able to direct it into your mind, and then I could see what you saw... or rather what you didn't see. The blackness was extraordinary. You were lost, but I knew the way home."

Home. She'd used that word. It did feel, right at that

moment with her hands touching him, like he'd come home. Shaking his head, he pulled her into his arms. "Thank you for coming to find me, Addison Wade." He closed his eyes and was glad that she didn't say anything. He wasn't sure he could fill the moment with any coherent speech. It was better to be quiet for a while.

Addison adjusted herself so she could wrap him in her arms. His head pressed against her chest, he could hear the slow, steady rhythm of her heartbeat and smell the vanilla scent of her hair.

A few moments later, he lifted his head. "What kind of shampoo do you use?"

"Some stuff from the salon where I get my hair cut. Why?"

"You smell like vanilla."

She laughed, her eyes dancing in the low lighting of the room. "That's not my shampoo. That's this soap product they make in the Caymans where we have another house. You know, where I sent my aunt. I buy it by the gallon because I like it so much."

"It's natural on you, like it's your scent and not manu-factured."

"I'm glad. I love the Caribbean. The smell reminds me of there."

"Addison." He pulled back so he could look at her. "I found him."

"You found Jeremy?" She shuddered in his embrace.

"Well, his energy field. I should be able to track him now. He was in the deepest shadow. Loretta missed a tiny portion of him. There he was, blue and white with small green dots."

"Spence, you went into the shadows after Jeremy. You risked not coming back out in order to save him?"

"He's a little boy and he should come home. At least for a little while, until your grandfather ousts him to Safe Dawn or one of the other institutions." He hated to think of the laughter he'd heard in his head forever snuffed out by the horror of the institutionalization process.

"I'm not going to let him send Jeremy away."

He squeezed her shoulders hard. "Shhh. The Fury hears us everywhere." He stared her hard in the eyes and wished she were a mind reader so he could tell her how much he admired her resolve to keep Jeremy safe. It was the right decision. No one should casually turn over his or her children. Whatever had to be done to try to keep them safe without letting the government take them was the right thing to do. As wonderful as Rhodes was, he hadn't been a parent to them. Spencer's own mother had died because of him and Roman.

A voice he didn't expect to hear called out, "My brother is right. You don't want to advertise that kind of sentiment."

Not sure where he found the energy, Spencer jumped to his feet. Damn it, was there never going to be a time when he could get away from Roman? "Out." Spencer pointed at the doorway.

"I thought you wanted my help with this." Roman shifted his gaze to Addison.

"I found his signature. I don't need you anymore, and I don't like you stalking about and showing up uninvited."

Addison stood up next to him and grabbed Spencer's arm even as she spoke to Roman. "How did you get in here? Did my grandfather let you in?"

Roman laughed, a cold, sputtering sound. "No, Ms. Wade, I am not here in an official capacity. If I were, you'd be hauled in to Safe Dawn for evaluation. I thought the goal here was to find Jeremy. Am I wrong?"

Addison stepped forward, but Spencer grabbed her by her forearm to pull her back. Roman might have been his brother, but he didn't trust him, not at all. "I just told you, I found his signature."

"That's impressive, Brother, but you're still not going to be able to find him."

"And why is that?"

"Because someone on the council has him, and this conspiracy goes so deep, even your skills in the shadows won't shed light on it."

TWELVE

"Well, aren't you just a ray of sunshine." Spencer rolled his eyes and Addison, pulling out of his grasp, finally managed to step forward.

"Tell me what you found, Roman, please."

She was going to do whatever it took to find her nephew, no matter what their sibling issues were. Roman's arrival might actually turn out to be fortuitous. She and Spencer had come dangerously close to having something spark between them. When his head had been pressed to her chest, it had taken all her willpower not to bend down and kiss him.

But she couldn't focus on that, because she had to deal with his startling brother, who kept appearing at the most inconvenient times.

Roman wore a black leather bag slung over his right shoulder. It matched the rest of his outfit, and she realized he was completely decked out in black, like a cat burglar. Had he scaled the building? As she watched, he swung the bag onto the ground and squatted on the floor next to it, opening the carrier.

He pulled out a dark red folder and placed the contents on the floor. Three stacks of white computer paper lay in front of him. Black-and-white photos stared up at her. Two of the people she didn't recognize, but one of them she did: Loretta. Her heart fell a little. Had she really been foolish enough to hope that somehow Loretta wasn't involved? Yep, her torn up soul told her, she certainly had.

Roman stood, then pointed to the one furthest to the left. "Daniel Monroe. Age: thirty years old. Resident of Safe Dawn." Next to her, Spencer stared silently at the papers and shifted his weight from his left foot to his right. "Did you know him? Were you tested together?" Roman looked directly at Spencer.

"He's dead."

Addison waited for Spencer to say more, but he didn't. The proclamation of death, however, at least seemed to imply that Spencer knew who he was.

"No body was buried."

"I watched him die." Spencer lowered his voice, and she shivered at the tone. If she could go her entire life without ever hearing that much animosity directed at her by him, she would be grateful. Even when he'd baited her, he hadn't sounded so full of malice.

"I repeat. No body was buried. Are you sure he was dead?"

"There was blood everywhere."

"But dead?" Roman ran his hand through his blond hair. "What was the method of death? Suicide, right? He shot himself in the head? Could barely recognize his face."

Spencer shook his head. "I don't like what you're saying here. I watched him shoot himself in the head."

"Did you? Or did you watch the illusion of him shooting himself?"

Spencer fell silent.

Addison cleared her throat. She hated to interrupt, but she wasn't following the conversation.

"It's impossible." Spencer pointed to the third photo, one she didn't recognize. "I know *she's* dead."

"Do you? Did you see *her* die? Weren't you in dark space when that happened? What happened to you just now when you came out? Were you in complete control of your mind?"

"No, but I was deep in there without a path back for a few minutes. That would make anyone disoriented."

Roman shrugged. "I'll have to take your word on that. I'm not that powerful."

Enough. Addison shook her head. "What the hell are you getting at? Loretta is the third picture. Tell me what's going on here."

Raising an eyebrow, Roman regarded Spencer. "Do you want to tell her?"

"My brother is suggesting that Daniel, Priscilla and Loretta aren't dead or missing and are, instead, working as part of this conspiracy."

Roman sighed. "There are no bodies. None."

"Did you go to the graveyard? Are you digging up bodies now?" Spencer turned his back on them and stalked to the window. He reminded her of a caged lion she had once seen at the zoo. It had moved back and forth in its enclosure, deceptively calm. She had known without a doubt that the creature was furious just by the look in its eyes. Never before in her life had she been so glad to have walls and a moat between her and another living thing. Spencer gave off the same sensation.

He was dangerous.

"Not personally, no, but Rhodes has been looking into

inconsistencies in things for some time now. I'm involved in it."

"Rhodes is looking into a conspiracy, and instead of telling me about it he went to *you*?" Spencer swung around to look at Roman.

"Because since Priscilla's death—quote, unquote—you've been so reasonable to deal with? So apt to make the right decision on things? I'd bet there's a lot Rhodes doesn't tell you, even if you are his golden boy."

"Okay. Okay." Addison put herself directly between them, as she could feel violence escalating in the room even though no one had made a physical move. "Let me see if I've followed this, shall I? That man, Daniel, Spencer knows him from Safe Dawn. He was an illusionist? I've read about them. They're never allowed out because they can make you see things that aren't real."

"That's right." Spencer nodded and took a step toward her even as his eyes were still on Roman. "Don't be sure about the not-getting-out part. I think you might find, despite members of the Fury's best efforts, that we do lots of things we aren't supposed to." He said *Fury* with so much venom she was surprised Roman didn't shrivel up. By contrast, Roman hardly seemed to notice.

She continued, trying to keep the conversation moving forward. "But he killed himself?"

Spencer nodded. "Yes."

"No," Roman disagreed.

Addison held up her hand. "You." She looked at Roman. "You think that he didn't. Instead, he gave everyone the illusion of his death. His face was so destroyed no one could recognize him. It could have been anyone, and no body was buried." Turning her back to them, she walked to the closet. She needed a little space, some room to breathe, to sort things out in her own mind.

"Your girlfriend is smarter than you are, little brother."

"She's too good to be my girlfriend."

Addison's cheeks heated. She was glad her back was to Spencer and that the room was darkly lit, so maybe Roman wouldn't notice her blush.

"So Loretta pretended to die too, then, to escape the institution? Before she came to work with Jeremy?"

"She would have been the first to fake her death. Rhodes suspected that Daniel and Priscilla's deaths were not as they seemed. He knows nothing about Loretta, because she wasn't one of his residents. Loretta is from Pine Valley, the one in Arizona." Addison was sure he'd added that last bit of information for her benefit, as Spencer would know exactly where Pine Valley was located. "No one knew anything about her. Tory, the head of Loretta's institution, kept her abilities secret. Loretta was practically shut away from sunlight for most of her life."

"She was so good with Jeremy."

"That was her job in Pine Valley; she took care of the children."

Addison took two steps back toward the brothers. "She had impeccable references."

Roman nodded. "Of course she did. That just means someone with power is manipulating this whole thing."

She narrowed her eyes and let her gaze travel from Spencer to Roman.

"Someone with more power than a Wade?"

"Seems that way." Roman zipped up his pack and swung it over his shoulder.

Anger surged through her veins, and she had no outlet

for it. Raising a hand to massage her throbbing forehead, she stared at Spencer. "What? No obnoxious Wade remark?"

The kindness in Spencer's eyes unnerved her, and she turned around so she didn't have to look at him. "Well." She cleared her throat, something that was on its way to becoming a nervous habit. "There goes our theory about Jeremy just accidentally showing his condition in front of Loretta."

Spencer moved behind her and placed his hands on her shoulders. "Not necessarily. Roman said she was good with kids. She might have been sent here just for that reason. When Jeremy accidentally alerted her to what he could do, her other talent became of use, and the plan changed to kidnapping."

His hands felt good on her shoulders and the slight pressure he was using to massage her was even better. She closed her eyes and let herself feel him for a few seconds. Yes, she could do this; she could stay there with Spencer rubbing her shoulders for the rest of her life.

"Not to interrupt the moment you and the girl who's too good for you are sharing, but if we could just focus on the fact that there are three people not dead. Those three people all have the ability to make it impossible for you to get Jeremy back."

Spencer let go, and she immediately felt bereft. "Rhodes put you on it; you handle it." Was that bitterness she detected in his voice?

"Upset that he kept something from you?"

"A little bit, yes."

Roman opened and closed his mouth, evidently unsure what to say in the face of that honesty. Finally, he looked down before speaking again. "Has Will ever mentioned Guy McKidd?"

Spencer sighed. "No, I've never heard that name before. Who is he?"

"It's another thing your mentor should have told you about, should have told all of his charges about, and hasn't. Ms. Wade, if my brother ever comes to his senses and acknowledges what would be obvious to anyone spending two seconds in the same room with you, give him this."

Roman dug in his pocket and pulled out a business card. Spotting a red crayon on Jeremy's desk, he walked over, flipped over the card, and wrote something. His eyes determined, he walked over to her and held out the card. "And just in case he never comes to his senses, you keep it. I think you're resourceful and you'll figure out what it means."

"So I take it you're leaving?" Spencer moved to block Roman's exit from the room.

Addison rolled her eyes. She'd just gotten everything calmed down, and now they were going to get all macho again? She looked down at the paper he'd handed her. Four numbers were written on it: 18, 22, 64, and 50.

"I have no idea what these numbers mean."

Roman moved out of Spencer's way, obviously not taking the bait. "I hear you sent your aunt to the Caribbean, Ms. Wade. It's beautiful down there this time of year."

Addison shook her head. Okay, she had no idea what that meant either, but Roman had gone. Taking a deep breath, she stared at Spencer for a moment. "Your brother is an odd man."

He smiled, and her heart fluttered. "You have no idea. He basically answers to no one. I don't even know who controls the Fury. They must all have someone they report to, right? Maybe it's Roman."

"I thought none of the Fury knew each other so they could never gang up and take everything over."

Spencer grasped a strand of her hair between his thumb and index finger. "That is exactly correct." He moved closer, and she could feel the heat from his body against hers. "About what you said before..."

"What specifically?" She couldn't help the little tremor that shook in her voice.

Spencer was very close, very hot, and very much invading her personal space.

"About my making a rude comment regarding the Wades."

"What about it?"

"I'm done doing that, okay? You don't judge me based on my family, and I won't judge you based on yours."

Addison stared deeply into the swirls of his eyes. How had no one ever told him they did that? Staring into those depths was hypnotic. It was a few moments before she realized she hadn't answered him. Only the sound of his light breathing filled her ears. It was intimate in a way nothing had ever been before.

"I could hardly judge you by your family, Spence. I have no idea what to make of Roman. He handed me this random business card with a set of four numbers and expected me to know what to do with it, you hate him, and he keeps showing up at inopportune moments. He's the definition of an enigma."

"There's not even a year between our ages." Spencer sighed, and the sound moved through her like a wave traveling to the shoreline.

She smiled. "Your poor mother."

"We don't know whether we have the same father. Neither of us can ever remember there being a man around, so whoever he was, or they were, had left the scene before our long-term memories came in. Lewis was her last name.

Elizabeth Lewis. I have a vague memory of people calling her Betty. She was blonde, tall, and chubby."

"Was she a good mother?"

"I don't know. My memories of her are somewhat skewed."

"You talk about her in the past tense."

"That's on purpose. She's dead. Has been for the last twenty-five years."

There was no pain in his voice. She counted backward in her head and realized he would have been five when she died. A long time to live without someone, but Addison knew from personal experience that there were some losses you never got over, no matter how long you tried. Time did not heal all wounds.

"How did she die?"

"I'm not sure of all the details. She'd turned us over the year before to the institutions. It was my fault; I kept exposing my condition in public. My eyes kept turning black."

She reached out and grabbed his arm. "You were a child."

"True, but so was Roman—and truth is he's probably more powerful than I am—and he could hide his oddities."

"Maybe yours were harder to hide."

He shrugged. "Maybe I'm not good at pretend or secrets." He was probably right.

"Anyway, she took us to a local supermarket where they had collection and evaluation facilities."

"I've heard of those places."

"We'd been on the run for over a year, and she must have been exhausted with two little boys. I guess I was a month over four and Roman must have just turned five. Maybe she thought they'd help us or something. We were in

Columbus, Ohio. Roman kept trying to pull out of her grip. He can sense things. It's one of the reasons he's such a good Fury. He can pass someone on the street and know they're Conditioned. It's really weird."

"What you can do is more impressive."

It was at that moment she realized she'd fallen in love with him. She could have laughed out loud. Decisions always came so fast for her. She'd decided to go get Spencer, so she'd gone to Safe Dawn to do it. She'd decided she'd wanted to run her grandfather's company, so she'd trained to do it. Where other people needed time to muse these things out, she never did. Major revelations came to her and she stuck to them, which was how she knew that even though it had been fast, she would love Spencer from that moment forward without a second thought. It was just how she was built, the crux of her internal nature, the one she rarely showed to the world.

She tried to hide her reaction to the thought as she looked down. Her hands started to sweat and her pulse kicked up a notch. It didn't matter, she told herself. There was no time for love, and he couldn't love her back anyway. Even with his proclamation about not caring that she was a Wade, she knew there were too many differences that Spencer wouldn't be able to get over.

"You okay?" He narrowed his gaze as he looked at her.

"I'm fine. Go on." She wanted to hear the rest of his story. Spencer didn't strike her as the type of person to open up very often. If she lost this opportunity, she might never get another one.

"We got to the front of the line. They were taking children and putting them in the back of this big gray van. I guess they'd had more turn out that month than they'd anticipated, because they were really piled in." He shook his head, and Addison realized he was caught up in the memory. "Mom must have gotten scared then. Maybe the exhaustion wore off or she suddenly came to her senses. Who knows? I was four. I can't believe she took us there to begin with, so I can't even begin to fathom her thought processes."

"It must be awful to think about. My dad hid me."

"To give her some credit, she had been trying to do just that for some time, but there were two small children to care for, and I was difficult."

"Someday you're going to have to forgive yourself for being a child in circumstances you couldn't control."

One side of his mouth curved up in a smile. "Maybe. I'm not good at being out of control." He laughed, one hard spurt of sound. "Anyway, she got scared and tried to pull us out of line but the men were there to stop her. Back then it wasn't the Fury; it was members of the National Guard. One of them grabbed her and held her. He was just trying to get her to calm down. Roman took that opportunity to run. He pulled out of Mom's hands, grabbed me, and we managed somehow to get lost in the crowd. She had dry skin; that's my last memory of her. I was holding her hand, and then I wasn't. I was running with Roman."

"Where did you go from there?" He'd been Jeremy's age. No wonder he was so interested in helping children, so invested in it. In fact, he'd nearly lost his life going unguided too far into dark space.

"I can hardly remember. Roman was in charge. He was, after all, five years old." The last bit was said in a voice laced with irony. "I think we spent several nights in an abandoned warehouse. Roman would leave and then he would return with food. I don't know how he got it. A few days later, the guard caught up with us and we were taken to Safe Dawn."

"And your mother?"

"Rhodes told me when I was eighteen that a year later, she'd joined a group of so-called Institutional Freedom Fighters and tried to burn down Safe Dawn to retrieve us. They were caught, of course. It's stupid to try to take down the institutions; they have a permanent staff that can see the future before it happens. She was shot and killed in the process."

"But she did try to save you." That had to count for something, didn't it?

Addison had fallen so fast for Spencer. How was it possible that she already wanted to ease his pain?

"Too little, too late. Four years later, Roman was taken away again to be made a Fury. I have no idea what his life has been like since he left Safe Dawn. He pops in and out periodically, but we don't spend time together. He blames me for us getting caught. I guess I cried a lot in the warehouse, and there was that whole bit about my not being able to hide the freak in me to begin with."

"He keeps trying to help us."

"Which worries me a great deal." He ran a hand through his hair and smiled before he reached out to touch her cheek. "I know one thing. I need to talk to Rhodes. He has some stuff to answer for. Tomorrow, I have to go back to Safe Dawn. I'm going to need you to take me back."

"Will they let you out again?"

"Jeremy hasn't been found yet, so yes. We're going to have to find a way to beat Priscilla. She's about the only person on the planet who could block me now from finding Jeremy's energy path, but she can do it. If she's alive, I'm going to need help I can only get in Safe Dawn."

"I'll go with you."

He shook his head. "No, it's not safe for you there. If anyone there finds out what you can do..."

"You'll keep me safe."

"I just told you about my mother. From day one, I've been letting women down. Why do you think you can count on me?"

"I don't think it, I know it. Like your brother, I sometimes just know things, remember?"

"All right, but you have to promise me something."

Anything. "What?"

"When the time comes, you'll let me protect you from the Fury. You won't let yourself be taken in."

"I won't let you do anything to put yourself in danger, not on my behalf."

"Damn it, Addison." He hit the wall next to them, and the mirror with the crown molding shook.

"But I promise to do my best not to get taken in." It was the best she could do.

It would have to be enough.

THIRTEEN

Spencer gripped the side of the car as Addison zoomed down the highway at top speed in her red two-door sports car—the only color a real sports car should be, she had informed him.

They'd left at dawn to avoid giving explanations to either her grandfather or the staff. It hadn't mattered that it had been so early; after his adventure in dark space, the encounter with Roman, Priscilla's faked death, and Rhodes' dealings with the Fury, Spencer had been too wound up to sleep.

The only thing that could have made him feel better had been sleeping down the hall. She'd been curled up in a ball with her blonde hair falling over her face and covering her pillow. So what that he'd crept down the hall to check on her long after he should have been asleep? He still wasn't going to pursue a sexual relationship with her, no matter how much he wanted to, no matter how much his body begged to be close to her.

She was a complicated woman, they lived in complicated times, and his life was a mess. It was not the time to get involved. If only he could convince himself he wasn't already involved. That was trickier.

"Do you always drive this fast?"

She laughed. "I thought you liked cars."

"I do. I read car magazines all the time. But I have to say, Addison, I never thought I'd be in one with you driving."

Rolling her eyes, she grinned, and his heart lurched. "That's sexist, Spence. I am as capable of handling this car as anyone." Giving him a sideways glance, she slowed down and came to a fast stop at the side of the highway.

"What are you doing?" Had she seen something? Was there something wrong with the car?

"Get out. Trade places with me."

He narrowed his gaze. "What are you playing at here?"

"I'm going to let you drive."

He leaned back in his seat. It wasn't nice to offer somebody something you knew they couldn't have. In fact, it was downright cruel. "You know that's illegal."

She shrugged. "Who has to know?"

"I'm always being monitored."

"By Roman. Do you think Roman is going to pull us over and demand you go back to the institution? Hell, we're going back to the institution right now."

His gut response was to remind her that Priscilla had been killed for breaking a rule, but then he closed his mouth. The woman he'd known—his friend and former lover—*wasn't* dead, she'd faked it. And he was going to wring her neck when he found her.

He pushed open the door and stepped out onto the shoulder of the highway.

Only a few cars traveled past them. He looked up at the horizon as the red glow of the rising sun illuminated the top of their vehicle. Addison stepped out of the car, slamming the door. She'd placed her hair in a braid, and it was the first time he'd ever gotten a good look at her without her blonde locks seeming to take on a life of their own around her face.

With her hair pulled back, her high cheekbones gave the top half of her face angular definition. The women in Hollywood paid thousands of dollars for such reconstruction, but he would bet Addison had never seen the inside of a plastic surgeon's office. Completely makeup free, she looked young and fresh, like the first day of spring. In the sunrise, she was perfection personified.

Before he could think better of them, words poured from his mouth almost of their own accord.

"Addison, I told Roman that you're too good to be my girlfriend."

She nodded, and her eyes flared for a moment. "I know, you said it twice."

"I meant it. I'm a doomed man. If it's not this case, it'll be another one, but sooner or later, I'm dead. I'll be buried in an unmarked grave and forgotten like I never existed, and I'll very likely burn in the pit of Hell forever."

The blonde angel in front of him pounded her fist on top of her incredibly expensive car. He jumped. "What kind of religion did they drill into you guys in the institution?"

"Not much of one at all, just a constant reminder of why we're locked in there to begin with."

Emotion written on her face, Addison placed a hand over her heart. "Am I doomed, then? If I step out into the line of traffic behind me and die thirty seconds from now, am I heading downstairs instead of up?"

"I didn't say that."

"When you first met me, you didn't know I was Conditioned. You didn't like me, but you didn't automatically assume I was Hell-bound. Now you know, is that where I'm going?"

"If it isn't true, then how am I supposed to live with having been basically locked up for the last twenty-six years? That's your entire life." He really needed to shut up. Why was he putting this on her? What had happened in his life was not her fault.

"That was man-made, Spence." She shook her head. "Now get in the car. I'm teaching you to drive."

"I'm not done."

Addison looked up at the sky for a moment before she met his stare again.

"You're not?"

"No." He extended his hand toward her. "You want me to drive this car. It's like a dream come true to me, but that's dangerous. Don't you understand? You're offering me things I can't have. Two seconds later, there are going to be other things I want that I can't have."

Her eyes were huge. "What? What things?"

"Damn it, Addison, how dense are you? I'm talking about you, for God's sake, about wanting *you*."

"You can have me, Spencer. I'm not off limits."

"No." He kicked a tire. "I can't."

"Hey, watch the car."

"You pounded on it."

"It's *my* car."

The haughty expression on her face did strange things to his insides. How was it that he was most turned on by Addison when she was acting like a superior Wade? No, he corrected himself, it was part of the problem. There was never a time when he wasn't sexually attracted to her. That was the issue. If he was still as enamored as a ten-year-old schoolboy when she acted like a bitch, then he was well and truly in over his head with the woman.

"Fine." He wanted to stomp his foot on the ground, but that had never gotten him what he wanted, not even as a child in the institution. "I can't have you, because it could never just be a one-time thing, and that's all I'm good for. Even with Priscilla, who I thought was my best friend, I had to get out of there as fast as I could when it was over. Somehow, with you, it could never be just once between us. *That's* the reason it can't be."

She cocked her head to the side. "You slept with Priscilla?"

That was the part of the conversation she wanted to focus on?

"A long time ago."

"I see."

"Oh no, no." He shook his head and pointed at her. "You can't be mad at me for something I did long before I ever met you, especially because we aren't together, for the reasons I just explained."

"So what you're saying is, that we can't be together because you're afraid you'll want more than just one time with me."

The sounds of traffic increased, and he noticed the sun was fully over the horizon. He shivered and realized that it was cold outside. He was dressed in a jacket, but Addison wore only a long-sleeved shirt. Why could the woman never dress herself properly? He pulled his coat off and handed it to her over the top of the car, gratified when she took it without complaint.

"Who said I was afraid?"

"I think for such a tough man you're afraid of a lot of things."

"Watch it." He didn't like where this conversation was headed. "Don't presume to know me after so little time."

"Oh, I do know you. You're the man who can go fearlessly into dark space, knowing he might never come back, but you won't start a relationship because you might feel too much. You won't drive a car because it will remind you of what you don't have. Well congratulations, bucko, if you never do it, you'll never know what you're missing. Seems pretty ridiculous to me."

Addison had delivered that whole speech to him without once raising her voice. William Rhodes couldn't have dressed him down better. How had he let this woman get under his skin so easily?

"Give me the keys." He held out his hand, and she threw them to him. Her aim wasn't good, and they fell on the ground just to the left of him. He bent over to retrieve them, and as he stood, he got a glimpse of her shapely legs covered with too-thin-for-the-cold-weather gray slacks as she walked by him to the passenger seat.

If he ever got the chance, he would see to it that she stopped wearing such bland colors. They were her camouflage, her hiding place, and whatever she said about his fears, the woman clearly had some of her own. He'd give her credit, however, as she had gone walking into the lion's den by going to Safe Dawn and risking exposure. That took a lot of guts.

He climbed into the car, closing the door with a thud. She stared at him from her side of the car and smiled when he looked into her eyes. His heart thudded loudly in his ears as he turned his attention back to the task at hand. Sticking the key in the ignition, he listened to the extremely well-built piece of Italian machinery purr.

Suddenly he was more than a little anxious. "Maybe

you should teach me to drive in something less expensive. I don't suppose you Wades keep any old dingy pickup trucks in the back of your penthouse apartment?"

"Sorry, can't say that we do." She reached out and grabbed his arm, patting it twice. "Besides, if this is going to be your only chance at driving, you might as well make it exceptional, don't you think?"

He could see her logic. Still, he wasn't sure he wanted to destroy her car.

"Think of it this way." Her voice held the lightness of humor. "It's my grandfather's money you'll be wasting if you screw up."

He laughed out loud, couldn't help himself, and tried to ignore the budding sadness that formed as he realized that as soon as he found Jeremy, they wouldn't be laughing together anymore.

"Now, actually, this is the perfect situation to learn to drive stick-shift, because we're going to be going straight and maintaining a speed. Stopping and going is much more difficult."

He nodded. "Right."

His palms had begun to sweat. If his nervousness destroyed the leather covering on the gearshift, he figured she could afford to replace it. Most likely it was the cheapest thing in the car.

"The clutch pedal is located on the far left, and you're going to use it when shifting from one gear to another."

"Right." He did know the basics of cars, having avidly read car magazines since he was sixteen. It might not make sense—he'd never own a car—but he was male, and sometimes certain things just felt encoded in his DNA. Knowledge about cars seemed to be one of them.

"In this car, neutral isn't a gear. It's technically, if you want to be particular about it, the absence of a gear."

"So nothing would happen if I raced the engine while I was in neutral."

"Rev is the word I think you want to use. If you revved the engine."

He grinned. They hadn't done anything yet but this was actually kind of fun. "I feel a little bit like you're my mom teaching me how to drive."

The look she shot him was not one of amusement. "If this is going to make you think of me as your mom, I'll stop instructing you right now."

"Hell, Addison, when you get that snooty, uppity tone, I just want to push you down on the seat and do you until you can't breathe."

Her blue eyes got huge, and her cheeks turned pink.

"Is that better?"

She pulled her collar away from her neck a little. "Much. But if you want to do that, why can't we...?"

Because it would destroy me, leave me shattered, and I might not be able to recover. I might end up one of those poor souls in the institution who thought it was better to end their own life than live another day inside the walls.

"Because we can't, end of discussion."

It was so damn unfair. He had this gorgeous, talented, sweet woman coming on to him, and he had to say no. Maybe he needed to have one of the doctors at the institution examine his head to make sure it was actually screwed on correctly.

She sighed. "Okay, back to our lesson, then. If we were driving around town, I would want you to keep the car in second gear, but since we're on mostly open highway, you're going to be driving in third, fourth or fifth gear."

The whole thing was starting to feel like a lot of fun. He put his hand on the gearshift and she placed hers over it. "Let me show you."

With her hand over his, she showed him how to shift from one gear to another. He pulled and she guided his movements. He tried to concentrate on what she taught him, which proved to be more challenging than he'd imagined. All he could think about was the other part of his body he wished she had her hand pulling on.

He gulped. "Okay. I think I've got it."

"All right, let's give it a try."

Maybe it was the years of reading about the experience or maybe he was just a natural at it, but it only took him a few minutes to get the hang of manipulating the car. Before he knew it, he was burning rubber on the open highway, shifting gears and picking up speed.

The car glided beneath him, floated on the road, and the louder the roar of the engine, the more thrilled he got. Addison stayed silent, and he wondered if she understood just how pivotal a moment he was having. This had been a lifelong dream, and even though he'd tried to deny himself the experience, she hadn't let him. She'd been right.

Pointing to the left, she indicated the sign that said they were getting to the exit for Safe Dawn. He turned the car onto the exit, and for a moment, he fiddled with the gearshift. The car groaned, and he grimaced at the sound. Out of the corner of his eye, he saw Addison grip the side of the car. Evidently, she hadn't liked that noise either, despite her earlier protests about not caring what happened to the car.

The institution was only five miles off the interstate— the thinking at the time of its conception being that runaways would be easier to spot on the highways than lost in the backwoods. However, the terrain leading up to the building was desolate. With the exception of one lone gas station and a convenience store where he knew the guards bought lottery tickets and cigarettes, there was nothing built around Safe Dawn.

In retrospect, that had probably been a good call. There were people within its walls who could blow things up if left unchecked. Even Spencer knew that was a bad idea, and he was actually locked up with the human explosive devices.

"Turn right."

He shook his head to disagree with her.

"We're not going in the front door?"

Addison chewed on her lower lip, and he wished he could reach out and plant a soft, adoring kiss on it. Instead, he explained what was on his mind.

"I can't take you in the front door. Rhodes would never allow you inside the walls. The best we could hope for would be the front offices where you and I met the first time. I actually need to introduce you to people the outside world doesn't know exist."

"There are people in there that the committee doesn't know exist?"

"I'm sure your grandfather knows about them. I'm talking about the general public. They'll never be allowed out, so unless Rhodes loses control of the place, they'll live and die without anyone outside those walls knowing anything about them."

"That's a depressing thought."

He nodded. "In more ways than you can imagine."

Never having driven a car before, it took him a few turns and a few more grinding gear mistakes to find the shaded bushes where the guards met with the few smugglers and suppliers who sold contraband in the facility. The foreign bankers Rhodes paid to take some of the Safe Dawn money and hide it for unthinkable situations, away from the prying eyes of the Council, didn't come to Safe Dawn. Will met with them elsewhere, and Spencer was one of the few people on Earth who even knew the older man did that at all.

Coming to a halt, he turned the car off and regarded Addison in silence for a moment. She stared ahead of her, and he wondered if she was even aware they'd stopped. In profile, her long eyelashes shielded her blue depths from him, and he couldn't even begin to guess what she was thinking about.

"Nervous?" He was on a fishing expedition. Well, he'd never been fishing, but he assumed that was what it would be like.

"Yes, and worried about Jeremy as well as other things."

He didn't have to guess what the other things were. Why couldn't life be simple?

Turning his attention back to the matter at hand, he pointed in the direction of the building. "About five hundred feet from here is a door hidden behind that black air conditioning unit. Do you see the one I mean?"

"I do."

"Okay. I'm going to go in the front door, sign in and do the whole shebang. Rhodes will probably schedule an appointment to debrief me for later today. I should be at that door to let you in in about ten minutes." He paused as he tried to decide if there was anything else he should tell her. "If it takes me fifteen minutes it doesn't mean there's anything wrong. I just might have gotten delayed somewhere."

"How are you going to explain it to them that I haven't personally brought you back?"

He shrugged. "I'll tell the guards I pissed you off so much you refused to get off the highway and made me walk. You're a Wade; everyone will expect you to behave badly."

"Spencer, won't we need Rhodes' help with this?"

"Normally, but now that I hear he's making deals with Roman and the Fury, I don't know what to expect from him. In any case, we'll already have you inside, so it'll be too late for him to do anything about that. What's that expression? It's easier to ask for forgiveness than permission."

"And if my power flares up inside? I'll be completely exposed."

"It won't."

She pounded her hand on the dashboard. "How can you possibly know that?"

"Because of Rhodes. It's his power."

"No one knows what William Rhodes' powers are, or if he even really has them."

"No one *outside* the institutions know. We know what he does. He's a power dampener; it's how he can keep everyone under control. As long as he's in Safe Dawn, all is well. It's a very rare Condition, but essential for things to work. When he goes away, things get a little haywire."

"He's eighty years old. Someday he won't be there."

Spencer looked down at his hands as her words reminded him of a truth he'd long avoided. "I know."

Maybe it was the momentary sadness or the way the citrus moisturizer smelled on her skin, but he just couldn't resist her any longer. Leaning over, he pulled her up against him over the center of the car and pressed his mouth to hers.

For half a second, she gasped, before her lips softened and a quiet moan escaped. He closed his eyes and concentrated on living only in the moment. In that second, he was kissing Addison. The rest of the world could go to hell.

She tasted of fruit and peppermint. It was an addictive combination, and he pushed his tongue in farther to plunge into the depths of her mouth. His groin immediately hardened, and since it was the only time they'd be doing any kissing, he tried to show her with his mouth what he wanted to do to her with other parts of his anatomy.

Resisting the urge to explore her body, he pulled back. Her eyes bored into his, pleading with him for more, and he wished he could forget all the reasons it couldn't happen.

He cupped her cheeks with his hands and was more than a little pleased to see how flushed they had become in such a short period of time.

"Spencer, maybe we could find Jeremy and the three of us could run away together. Find somewhere where they can't find us and make a life."

He ran his pointer finger down her nose, tracing the long angles of her face.

"They'll always find me. Roman will always be looking. When this is over, you and Jeremy will run away and I will live knowing you are safe and hidden. That can never be true for me. I'm too well known from the newspaper articles. Wherever I went, people would know who I was. You're Addison Wade; you're probably equally noticeable."

Addison slanted her eyebrows, and he saw a determined look cross her face. She refused to give up the idea that they could find a way around this, which both frustrated and delighted him.

Clearing his throat, he made himself open the car door. "Ten minutes. Fifteen minutes at the most. I'll open that door. Be there."

FOURTEEN

Addison approached the building with trepidation. The gray, industrial concrete hid whatever was inside from the outside world in a man-made glamour of respectability. She'd been mind-altered once already by someone Spencer had called a teenager. In no way did she want to begin to imagine what a full-grown adult could do to her. She tried to convince herself that an adult might actually use restraint.

The door flung open, and she smiled. Spencer was on time. Ten minutes, as he'd said. The smile, however, died a quick death on her lips. It wasn't Spencer standing there at all.

"You know, it's a good thing I always come out and do one more look, because one of you girls is always late to the party."

"Pardon?" Addison looked at the woman who stood in front of her. Five feet six inches tall and curved like something out of puberty-ridden little boys' wet dreams, she was simply gorgeous. Dark, almost black hair that fell to her large and well displayed breasts framed the highest cheek-bones Addison had ever seen.

On some women they might have looked like facial implants, but on her they fit her face; they looked natural. Her eyes, almond shaped, were maybe an inch too far apart to be considered fashionable, but Addison thought it made her look exotic coupled with her dark olive complexion. She was probably of Armenian or Turkish ancestry.

As she pushed away her anxiety, Addison realized she'd been doing that for years—sizing people up with a glance. It was something her grandfather could do; it was why he was so good at his job.

"Are you deaf? Hello?" The other woman waved a hand in front of Addison's face. "Are you coming?"

"You were sent to get me?" She wanted to be clear on that before she went anywhere. Spencer hadn't said he'd do that, but maybe the plans had changed once he'd entered Safe Dawn?

"It's my job. Come on."

She followed her motion to step through the door into complete darkness. Only a feeble neon glow from some-where below the radiators gave any light at all.

Trying to keep up with her guide, she attempted conver-sation once more. "I'm Addison."

"I don't care." The brunette's tone didn't allow for any discussion on the subject.

Who was this nasty woman Spencer had sent to collect her? Where was he? What had happened to keep him from getting her himself? She'd opened her mouth to ask that very question—screw the woman's attitude problem—when they came out of the dark hallway and arrived outside.

Addison gasped. She was standing in a courtyard that could have been found on any small, northeastern college campus. Tiny, dormitory-looking buildings of six floors surrounded a green area that would have been perfect for a game of Frisbee golf or sun tanning on a warm day. No one was using the facility except for a small group of men who stood in the corner of the lawn smoking. She didn't have any time to dwell on her surroundings or how well they were hidden from the outside. Spencer still hadn't appeared, and she was feeling increasingly anxious about it.

"Where's Spencer?"

The woman laughed, and it sounded more like a snort. "Oh, you're a Lewis addict, are you? Sorry to disappoint you, but Spencer isn't here right now. He's out helping some rich bitch who came begging for his assistance, and even if he was here, he doesn't participate in our little games. Spencer likes his women to be only one-on-one, which means you're going to be disappointed. But don't worry, there are plenty of hot freaks to do you the right way."

"Wait, what? Hold on." Dear God, this woman, whoever she was, hadn't been sent by Spencer and thought Addison was there to... to... to have sex with Conditioned people?

"Sorry, no can do. The party waits for no one. This way." The brunette pulled Addison forward, and Addison wrenched her arm out of the other woman's hand only to stumble and fall backward onto her behind. Looking up, she nearly gasped as she saw the woman's eyes glow red.

"You really don't want to screw with me. You paid your money, which means you get to come and do the dirty with a Conditioned man. As was explained to you when you signed up, there are no refunds, and once you're inside the walls you have to be escorted to and from the event location by one of us." The woman seemed to be taking deep breaths. "Now, I'm still under control here, but in a few moments I'm actually going to get angry, and then something is going to burn. I'd really rather it not be your body engulfed in flames, if it's all the same to you. I haven't had to bury a body in almost two months, and William Rhodes gets angry when the police come investigating."

Okay, enough was enough. Addison stood up, narrowing her eyes. She dealt with disgruntled employees all the time. This woman was nothing more than a bully, and Addison wasn't afraid. "Look, I don't know who you think you are, but no one talks to me that way, and no one takes me anywhere I don't want to go. This has been a terrible mistake, and it is going to stop right now."

"I see you're going to be difficult about this. What is it with you freaky women? Last week I had to drag a woman kicking and screaming inside, but when she left here, she could barely walk or stop moaning on and on about how great she felt. I swear, this is my last week doing this, my last frickin' week." The woman spun around and called out to the group of men Addison had noticed in the corner. "Holland, come here, please."

Not sure who Holland was and not wanting to find out, Addison moved closer to the stubborn woman. "Look, I need to see Spencer, okay? He can clear this all up."

"Nice try."

The man called Holland crossed the courtyard and stood before her. Six feet six inches tall and all of it hard, toned muscle, he reminded her of the men she saw playing professional football on television. His skin was a golden tan, unmarred except for a large tattoo on each of his cheeks. One was in the shape of a snake, and the other was of symbols she didn't recognize.

Addison wouldn't have wanted to run into him in a dark

alley, and she was even less happy about making his acquaintance behind walls she might not be able to escape.

She placed both hands in front of him in a gesture she hoped was placating and calming. "There's just been a mistake."

"If she goes home unsatisfied, she might tell the authorities." Brunette looked bored.

"I'm here with Spencer."

"She's a Lewis crusher?" Holland finally spoke, and his voice was surprisingly unruffled, almost reassuring and musical in its tone.

Her nameless tormenter who, Addison was sure she would hate for the rest of her life, laughed. "Seems that way."

"No, I'm not." She was more than crushing on Spencer, so she didn't feel like she was lying. "I'm here *with* him."

"Then where is he?" Brunette raised her eyebrow like the whole thing was so beneath her dignity she couldn't believe she was discussing it.

"Want me to knock her out?"

"No, please don't. I came here with Spencer Lewis." Was that her voice sounding so frantic? If it was, then at least it matched the pounding of her heart in its desperation.

"Do it."

Addison blocked her head with her arms, expecting a blow, but nothing happened. Holland stared at her and narrowed his eyes. She had moments to remember she was in Safe Dawn. No one here would have to lay hands on her to cause her pain. Seconds later, her world went black.

ADDISON AWOKE, sat up with a start, and realized she was screaming.

"What did you do to her, man?"

Her vision was skewed. Around her, all she could hear were voices she didn't recognize. Colors danced in front of her eyes; shapes and flashes of light came into her vision and disappeared again. Nothing had substance or seemed real.

"I just knocked her out. It shouldn't be having this effect on her."

That voice she knew: Holland. She shuddered as she remembered the feeling of losing her will to stay awake. *He* had done that to her.

"Why did you knock her out to begin with?"

It was a man's voice asking the questions, but not Spencer. She would have done just about anything to hear him right then. Even if he was yelling at her for coming into the building without him, even that would have been better than being alone and at the mercy of these people.

"Tara said she was Lewis-crazed and that she needed to be brought here to be satisfied or she might tell."

"Hell."

A cool washcloth touched her face, brushing against her eyes, and a calm, feminine voice instructed her to be still. The colors still danced in front of her eyes, and she would have paid any amount to make them stop.

"Listen to me. I'm not who you think I am."

"Who are you?" The male voice. At least it wasn't hostile like the woman she now knew as Tara, whom she would be making it her life mission to destroy if she ever got out of this situation.

"My name is Addison Wade."

A hush fell over the room. She wasn't surprised. Hers was not a name anyone in their position would want to hear.

"Fuck." The male voice that had been speaking to her hissed the curse. "Tara, Holland, you guys knocked out Addison frickin' Wade?"

"I came here with Spencer Lewis. He's helping me find my nephew."

"This is bad in so many ways."

"I didn't know," Tara's voice finally said.

Addison wished she could deck the horrid beast. "I tried to tell you."

"Here, now." The compress that had been on her eyes was removed, and she was relieved to see that things were coming more into focus. She blinked a few times and could see the world around her.

She was in some kind of bedroom. Her assessment of the quad outside looking like a college campus was matched inside the room. It screamed dormitory and was maybe twelve by nineteen feet. If the size said college, the furniture was all institution.

The bed she lay on was white, with an itchy black blanket and one pillow. The bed had been made, hospital corners and all. There was one desk in the corner, one fake wooden bookshelf and one small window that had a dark shade pulled so she couldn't see outside.

The whole place smelled like cigarettes and unwashed gym socks. She was also pretty sure she picked up the distinctive smell of marijuana wafting through the room.

The man who stood in front of her was somewhere around thirty years of age. Dark-haired and brown-eyed, he had a thin build. He wore black pants and a black shirt with the sleeves rolled up to his shoulders. His arms were muscular, like he lifted things other than weights in a gym on a regular basis. However, his most striking attribute was the five piercings that adorned his face.

One metal rod found its home in his left eyebrow. A dark black hook protruded from his mouth, and a ring of gold dangled from his right nostril. His right eyebrow had two piercings, one that looked like a skull-and-crossbones ring and another that looked like a gold wedding ring that had been altered to hang from his eyebrow.

The woman who had been holding the compress on her eyes was small, dark and delicate-looking. So skinny, Addison was sure she'd blow over in a good gust of wind. Her hair was a golden blonde.

Also in the room were, to her distress, Tara and Holland, who stood in front of five other men who were far enough away that she couldn't quite see them clearly.

She blinked twice more before leveling her gaze on Holland.

"What did you do to me?"

"I knocked you out, and that shouldn't have happened."

"What did it *do* exactly?"

"Knocked you out for three hours. It was just supposed to be a touch of unconsciousness—ten minutes or so—but you never woke up." Holland looked sheepish. He ran his hand through his one strip of hair. Had he said hours? Where the hell was Spencer? Seeds of doubt planted themselves in her brain, and she chewed on her lower lip. Had she been wrong about him? Was it possible he'd abandoned her to these people?

Holland spoke again. "Please don't take it out on everyone else that I screwed up. Please don't have Wade Corporation hurt everyone here."

"She's not going to be hurting anyone, Holland. We're going to kill her first." Every time Tara opened her mouth, she said or did something that made Addison hate her even more.

"We're not going to kill anyone." The pierced man whirled on Tara for a moment before he looked back at Addison. "I'm Jack and this is Marisa. You know Holland and the loudmouthed Tara over there. Behind them are Tom, Ben, Greg, Andy and Russell. We've all been worried about you, and now that we've found out that you're Addison Wade, I guess it would be fair to say that we're terrified of you."

Addison heard voices in the room next door. Female, from the way they sounded, and she wondered if they were the ones who had actually come to Safe Dawn to have sex with Conditioned men. She'd like to see those women. What was it about them that evidently made them think it was okay to pay money to come to an institution? People here could kill you with a thought, and they wanted to engage in sexual activities with them? Was she a prude and she didn't even know it?

"There's no need to be afraid of me in that respect. I'm not going to tattle. At least there's no need for *you* to be afraid of me." She glared at Tara, letting her eyes let the other woman know how afraid of her she'd like Tara to be. "I still want to kick your ass."

Tara's eyes flared red, and the curtain that covered the window caught on fire.

Addison gasped and shot to her feet. The others in the room looked bored.

"Turn it off, Tara, and you're explaining to Rhodes why I need new curtains."

The woman made a noise that was close to a harrumph, but the flames extinguished. "She threatened me."

"I tried to tell you several times that I was here with Spencer, and instead of listening, you sent him." She pointed at Holland. "And he evidently screwed up my eyesight."

Her eyesight was improving every minute, but she wasn't going to discuss that with them.

"Good going, Tara. Really brilliant this time."

Tara looked down at the floor. "I'll take the responsibility with Rhodes right after I tell him how I pay off the guards for you to get the backdoor open and what you're doing with all those women to begin with."

The man she thought had been identified as Russell stepped forward. "If you do that, I'll tell him what I caught you doing. You know, that *thing* you did that I found out about."

Russell had flaming red hair and brown eyes that didn't match. Redheads were almost always blue or green-eyed. Outside on the street, she would think he dyed his hair, but in here... well hell, if Spencer's swirl and Tara's flame eyes were any indication, then nothing was as it was supposed to be.

He reached out and touched her arm. His eyes were lust filled, and she didn't like it. Pulling back a little, she fell onto the bed again.

"Relax, pretty baby, I'm not going to hurt you. You'll like what we do together."

"Russ, stop." Jack stepped forward and pulled the other man back. "You know we don't want you to do that. Sexual manipulation with your powers is akin to rape, and it's not a line I want you to cross, not even to save our collective asses."

"You can sexually manipulate people with your brain?" Addison felt sick to her stomach.

Russell's cheeks got red. "I can make people feel

however I want them to feel, usually. Only you didn't respond to it right off the bat, and that's a little bit odd."

Jack put his hand on her arm. "He's not a bad guy. To my knowledge, he's never done that before."

"Just so I'm clear, you were going to manipulate me sexually so I wouldn't be mad about this whole thing and tell anyone?"

"That was the general idea."

"Pretty dumb."

Addison heard a door slam and female screams. A roar, not animal but fully human and totally male, filled the room. Tara gasped as the door to the bedroom slammed open.

With only one second to register it was Spencer making the almost maniacal yell, she felt herself wrenched out of Jack's grip and pushed behind Spencer. Nearly falling over backward, she was saved from her descent by Roman's quick reflexes as he followed his brother into the room.

"Did you touch her, you sick bastard?" Spencer yelled as he ripped the gold wedding band out of Jack's eyebrow.

Jack hollered and pushed his hand up to stop the blood that poured down his face. "I didn't touch her, Spencer."

"He didn't touch me." Her voice was little more than a squeak in the fray of screaming. Russell moved forward as if to grab Spencer, but Roman was faster. Letting go of Addison—she somehow managed not to fall—he tackled Russell to the floor.

"Okay, I'll stay out of it, Roman. I'll stay out of it." Russell's voice was muffled by Roman's body.

Spencer kicked Jack in the stomach before using his upper body to knock the other man to the floor. "I swear, if you touched one hair on her head, I will destroy you."

"Spencer, he helped me. He was actually the one trying to help me."

He paused for a second as if registering the sound of Addison's voice for the first time. Not lifting his upper body from Jack, he strained his head around to look at Addison. "Why did you need help?"

"Because I was unconscious and I guess I didn't wake up when I should have."

Spencer nodded his head and narrowed his eyes. "You." He pointed at Holland. "That means you did something to her." Jumping off Jack, he lunged for Holland.

Roman grabbed Spencer. "Hold off, Brother. Let's see what's going on here."

Marisa ran to Jack, who was holding one hand over his eye to cover his eyebrow, which was still bleeding. He rocked back and forth, the other hand clutching his gut where Spencer had kicked him.

"Are you calm?" Roman spoke again. "Okay. Maybe we should assess what went on here before you beat up everyone in the room." Roman's voice was low, but they were standing close enough to Addison that she could hear his suggestion to Spencer.

Tom, Ben, Greg, and Andy moved like they wanted to exit the room. Spencer raised a hand. "I've seen all of you. If I find out any of you were involved in this, I'll beat you to a pulp."

Needing no other instruction, the four men scampered away to the sound of delighted female gasps in the room next door. Evidently the women in there were impressed with the new offerings. Addison just wanted the whole nightmare to end.

Moving forward, she touched Spencer lightly on the shoulder. "I followed her"—she pointed to Tara—"in here. I thought you had sent her. She wouldn't listen to me. Holland came, I passed out, and I woke up here. Jack and Marisa were trying to take care of me. Once they found out who I was, they all got a little bit nervous. Then you came." She stared at Russell across the room. She'd deliberately left out his attempt to manipulate her, both because she didn't want Spencer to kill him, and because if she'd learned nothing else under her grandfather's tutelage, she'd learned that it was often good to have powerful people owe you a favor. With that kind of ability, Russell was powerful. The other man nodded silently as if he understood.

Spencer swore. "Tara, if I hit women, I would beat the hell out of you right now."

Tara's already big eyes were huge as she ignored Spencer and stared at Roman. Noticing that, Addison looked back and forth between Roman and Spencer. Tara swallowed before she spoke. "How did he get here?" Considering the fact that Roman was a Fury, she was surprised more people in the room weren't freaking out in silence the way Tara was.

Spencer turned to Addison. "I have so much to tell you." He sighed and shook his head. Pressed up against his arm, she could feel his body shaking. No one else seemed to have noticed Spencer's physical reaction. "I've been looking for you for hours. I don't even want to tell you what I thought had happened. Then I heard about this party. I couldn't find its location, and I've been imagining the worst possible scenarios."

She stared deeply into his swirling eyes. Reaching out, she rubbed her hand against his cheek, wishing they were alone so she could say things she knew he wouldn't want spoken with other ears around.

"These assholes are so disgusting with these parties."

"Hey, dipshit." Jack had sat up and was now holding a towel against his eyebrow. "Not all of us are so lucky as to get to leave this place and meet women who don't live here, as you so evidently have."

Spencer swore again. She'd never heard that particular curse, and she didn't think anyone's body could actually do what he'd said. She stifled a grin.

"All right, Jack, I owe you an apology. I jumped to conclusions, and I overreacted."

Silence filled the air around her.

Tara finally spoke. "Did he apologize?"

"Hey, Tara, if you don't want to be dead, go get me Minnie, Gina and Laurel. We need to meet tonight, after dinner, so I can tell you all what I've uncovered. But just the people in this room and them. No one else."

Roman cleared his throat. "It's hours till dinner. Where are you going now?"

"Out."

Without another word, he grabbed Addison's hand and pulled her from the bedroom. At that moment, she would have followed him anywhere.

FIFTEEN

When they'd walked a sufficient distance from Jack's quarters, which had evidently, at some point, become a place of ill repute, Spencer let himself start to really breathe again. She was okay. Holland had screwed with her mind—kind of unusual for the big guy to mess up like that—but she would be fine. He hoped. His breathing kicked up again. Maybe he should find a medic he trusted and get her checked out?

As if he'd spoken aloud, she answered him. "I'm fine." At his questioning look, she grinned. "You're practically wearing your thoughts on your face. It was a nightmare that didn't happen. I can assure you I wasn't going to participate in the damn sex games."

"You're right you weren't. The only Conditioned guy you're going to bed with here is me."

All the reasons not to become invested in her had flown out the window when he'd finally arrived at the door and she'd been gone. The well thought-out logic had ceased and all he'd been left with was sheer and utter panic that he'd lost her. There was sense, and then there was living the life you needed to live. He'd decided in half of a second that when behaving sensibly no longer made you happy, it was time to stop behaving that way. He needed Addison like he needed oxygen and food.

"But I thought you said—"

He interrupted her, pulling her into the building where he'd lived for the last ten years. He dragged her through the entranceway and up the three flights of stairs to his room.

Addison fell silent, which he appreciated, and he was once again struck by how grateful he was that she was fine and that she was with him. After he pulled her into the room, he slammed the door behind them and pushed her against the doorframe.

He pressed his body against her and leaned his forehead on hers. For a few moments, he just wanted to breathe with the scent and sight of her close to his heart. She closed her eyes for a beat before opening them. When she did, there were tears in them.

"What's wrong?" His pulse beat loudly in his ears. He hoped beyond reason she wasn't actually going to cry. He had no idea what to do with women when they did that, and Addison's tears might actually eat him from the inside out. "Where were you?"

"God, Addison, I got held up and then I couldn't find you at all."

Her eyes flared. "What delayed you?"

Normally, he wouldn't like the accusation in her voice, but after everything she'd been through, he deserved a little blame, and she needed to vent.

"When I got into the building, I was hauled off to Rhodes' office. Roman was sitting in there already."

He'd wanted to kill his brother. For someone who was supposed to be quasi-invisible most of the time, Roman had been around in abundance the past few days. "Mr. Can't-

Mind-His-Own-Business had already told Rhodes about Loretta being involved in Jeremy's disappearance and the whole thing. I walked through the door ready to bypass my post job interview altogether, and instead I found myself involved in an inquisition." He took a deep breath. "I'm not proud of myself. I lost my temper and let Rhodes know exactly what I thought of his involving Roman and not telling me about what was going on. He got even angrier. I questioned his motives; he threw me out of the office."

"Sounds like a good time."

He laughed. No one could disarm him like Addison could. He shouldn't even be breathing the same air as her, let alone depending on her for strength and sanity. "Just your usual day at Safe Dawn. I've never actually been this angry with him before. If I had any kind of threatening condition—meaning if I could do what Tara and Jack can do —he would have locked me up in the static room."

"What's the static room?"

"Static electricity in very high doses seems to affect our powers, dampen them. Did you really not know that?"

"Not at all. Should I have?"

"It was Wade Corporation that discovered that tiny little fact based on the tests they periodically run on us."

She reached out and touched the side of his face, gently rubbing his forehead as she stroked his profile. He shivered from the warmth she created wherever she touched him. "I've never known about anything that was done to hurt you guys here. If you want, I'll put my hand on the Bible and swear to that."

"I don't know that I put much faith in that book, but I don't need anything other than you telling me you didn't know. That will always be enough for me." The weirdest thing was that he meant it. He never could have imagined feeling that way about anyone. Maybe it had to do with having been all but turned over by his mother, but he always doubted everyone. Except now, he had no doubt about Addison.

"You have no faith in the Bible, but you're obsessed with the idea that you're going to Hell. Tell me how that contradiction works." Her eyes stared into his with a mischievous glint. She challenged him, but he knew it was mostly teasing.

"It doesn't have to make sense; it's just how I feel."

She would ask him the same questions as many times as he needed to hear it. "Am I going to Hell, too?"

He shook his head. "Absolutely not."

"By your logic, all Conditioned people are doomed to the pit. Shouldn't I be going, also?"

The thought made his heart pound like he'd been running. "Nope. I won't let it happen."

"Oh, you can control these things now? Are you also responsible for the Earth remaining on its axis?"

He needed to get out of this minefield of a conversation. He was rapidly learning that he couldn't win an argument with Addison, unless he had absolute conviction in his words or facts to back them up. In that way, she was just like her grandfather. She could probably start a small company and, through sheer force of will, build it up to be as impressive as her grandfather's.

Truth was, in some ways Addison was a scary woman

"Anyway, I found one of the guards who owed me a favor. He opened the door for me but you weren't there. I had five kinds of heart attack, and then I turned around and you can guess who was there again."

"We need to put a bell on Roman, or get you more attuned to hearing him sneak up on you."

"I guess it's fair to say he got all the subtlety in the family and I got none."

"You do kind of wear all your thoughts on your face like a picture show."

He sighed. "I'll work on that."

"Don't you dare."

Grinning, he pulled her against him until her head rested on his shoulder. "He said he wanted to reassure me that he hadn't told Rhodes about what you could do. He's not going to say anything. I'm sure he has his reasons, but right now they match my own, so I'm fine with that. He was able to cover up the broken window incident, and he says if we can teach you to control yourself, then he sees no reason to tell anyone."

"Blackmail."

Was his brother really so low that he would resort to that? Spencer had no idea. "If he does that, I'm sure you have Wade ways to make it go away." He inhaled to get a whiff of the aroma that was so intensely Addison. "Once he realized you were missing and I was searching for you, he decided to stay and help."

Addison pulled back to look into his face, and he was struck by the effortless beauty her features contained. Her eyes, which he'd thought of as cold when he'd first met her, were actually sanctuaries of heat, emotion, and fire. Her hair was like a gift of gold sent down from the sun to light the frigid Earth and make it joyful again. He reached out to stroke her cheekbones, rubbing them with his thumbs.

"Addison, I... I don't have the words."

"You don't need them." Her mouth touched his.

For a second, he was stunned. His mind clouded over. What did a man do when he got everything he'd ever wanted, but knew he could never keep?

Life became nothing more than the sensation of her soft lips pressed against his. Her breath smelled sweet and warm. If he wanted to, he could pretend he was fighting for sanity, but he'd already made up his mind when he'd thought he'd lost her.

He decided in one moment that her lips were made just for him. He could get addicted to their caress on his. She was so much smaller than he was—tiny, really. Second by second, he needed her more. He felt desperate to get them both naked so he could feel the heat of her bare skin against him.

He wrenched his mouth from hers and heard her gasp, which gratified him in a purely masculine way. Her lips were already slightly swollen from his kisses. He leaned down as he kissed her neck. She shivered when he found her sensitive spot and he bit down lightly, loving the little squeal she gave at his attentions.

With his tongue, he made love to her skin. Part of him felt like he was asking for permission to continue. If he could just show her how good it could be, maybe he'd be worthy of touching her, maybe she wouldn't feel like she was involving herself with a doomed man who could never be seen with her in public.

She laughed, a low, sultry sound. "You're going to leave a mark."

"I know." That was just what he wanted. If he couldn't *have* her—not in any lasting sense of the word—then he could at least temporarily show the world that she belonged to him. His brand for a few days on her neck would be all he would get. It would have to be enough.

Not that anything could be enough, ever. How was it possible that the more he touched her, the more he wanted? Addison was going to unman him just by the sheer ferocity of his need for her. It was dangerous to need what he couldn't have.

He traced a line from her chin down the center of her still-clothed body to her most sensitive core. Unable to resist, he cupped her mound through the fabric of her ridiculous gray slacks, aching for no barriers. He groaned his frustration. It was too much. He wanted her too intensely.

She closed her eyes and arched her neck until her head hit the wall, giving him a completely uninhibited view of her throat, and the mark he had created moments earlier. If he could, he would capture her in the moment with a camera so he could see her like that for all time, totally unreserved, exposed and gorgeous.

He tugged at the blouse that was tucked into her pants, realizing with a laugh that he'd never get it over her head. The buttons were going to have to be undone. "I'll help you." She started on the top set while his shaking hands went to the bottom. It was fast work, but it still felt like an eternity. She pulled the shirt off her shoulders and exposed the tan cotton bra beneath. Over the years, Spencer had seen all sorts of sexy lingerie, but he would swear until he took his last breath that there was nothing hotter than Addison's sensible beige bra.

"Now you." She tugged on his shirt. Reaching down, he pulled it quickly over his head. Only her bra separated the top halves of their bodies now, and it was still too much clothing. Not bothering to unhook it, he reached inside and took one of her glorious breasts into his hand.

It fit perfectly, and he squeezed it, memorizing the feel of her. "You know, Addison, I've been checking out your figure almost constantly for two days now, and I had no idea you were so well-endowed."

Her laughter was pure heaven, something between a

giggle and a snort but still totally feminine. "It's a breast-reducing bra; it makes me look smaller."

"Why in God's name would you want to do that?" He could barely think given the circumstances, but he wasn't sure that even stone cold sober he could have made sense of what she'd said.

"It doesn't work to be jiggling around in the boardroom. No one takes you seriously."

"Damn." He wanted her in his mouth, immediately. "Could you?"

"I'll get it."

In a maneuver he knew only women could do, she reached behind her back and undid her bra. Sliding it off with her left hand, she threw it on the floor.

His breathing was rough as he regarded her naked breasts. Trying to swallow, he wasn't surprised by the lump in his throat. "We need to move to the bed or I'm going to take you against the door."

"I've never been taken against a door." She chewed on her lower lip. "Maybe our first time we should try for the bed."

He picked her up in his arms and carried her across the room to what the institution called a comfortable bed. He laid her down, giving in immediately to the almost over-whelming need to suck on her breasts. Her nipples were pink and erect as they peeked up at him.

Sucking hard, he heard her gasp. "Too hard? Too much?"

"Not nearly."

He said a silent prayer of relief. Nice women didn't usually go to bed with him. Spencer had no idea whether what he did was what Addison would like. She pulled on his nape, urging him back to the gloriousness of her right breast. He laughed, a low sound, and happily obliged her.

She arched underneath him as he suckled and nipped her areola. "I can see why you have a fan club."

He stopped. "What?"

"Tara said there are hordes of women wanting a romp with Spencer Lewis and you never have trouble finding girls."

"Tara is full of shit." And he wasn't going to discuss other women. "You're the only woman I've brought here. No one comes to my room."

"Why me?"

"Don't you know, Addison?"

Instead of answering him, she reached up and met him mouth to mouth, hard, biting his bottom lip before she let go. God, this woman was hot. His groin was miserably uncomfortable as it strained against his pants.

As if reading his mind, Addison cupped him on the outside of the fabric. He hissed and grabbed her hand. "Do that again and I'm gone before we even get my pants off."

"Really? Is that usual for you? I don't have all that much experience, to tell the truth. This has already gone on longer than most of my sexual experiences."

"Addison Wade, there is nothing 'usual' when it comes to you, and I don't want to think of you ever having other sexual partners."

She blushed, and he wanted to crow. "Do you have a... a condom?"

He nodded, relieved that she'd thought of it.

"Yes, in the nightstand."

He rolled off her, and she gasped and grabbed her head. Immediately, he was concerned. "What's wrong?"

"It's like my condition surged. I was fine—feeling great, actually—and then you rolled off me and everything hurt."

She had no more said those words than the same thing happened to him. Doubling over, he grasped his head. What the hell was wrong? Sitting up, he reached out and touched Addison, immediately relieved when the pain stopped. Realization dawned on him slowly as his head cleared. "It's a psychic thing. We're connecting—like we did in dark space—and it's not finished, so it hurts."

Addison narrowed her eyes. "Spence, are you saying we have some sort of psychic blue balls thing going on here that can only be fixed by consummation?"

He nodded. "I don't know anyone I can ask about this, but I would say that, yes, that's correct."

"Well, then, get the damn condom. I'm desperate for you, evidently on many levels."

Grinning, he kept his hand on her arm as he reached into the drawer in the nightstand. "Got it."

He found her mouth again as he pulled on her pants with his free hand, removing them with three swift tugs. Her underpants matched her bra, and he groaned at his silly excitement over the whole thing. Maybe in a different world he could have introduced her to black lace and leather. What the hell—he could always imagine her in them.

She tugged at the button on his jeans, then pulled them down until they were around his knees. Freed from his painful confinement, he moaned his pleasure into her mouth and was rewarded with a fierce thrust of her tongue. Her hands roamed his body, pausing to brush gently over his chest hair.

Getting her panties down and away awarded him a chance to look at her shapely legs, slender and muscular.

He wondered if she worked out; she had the legs of a runner. He nipped the inside of her thigh.

Thought started to fail him. Only single words filled his brain. *Hot. More. Yes. God. Please.* She seemed just as enthralled, arching her back until only his body on top of her kept her from falling off the bed.

She tugged at his boxer shorts, freeing him completely, and took him in her hands. He thought he might die from the pleasure of it. If they'd had many times together ahead of them, he would have let her keep stroking him. Her face showed she was enjoying it. He could think of only two things sweeter than letting her bring him to release with her hands, and that was letting her do it with her hot mouth or coming inside her tight, warm core.

"Stop." He shoved her hand away. She pouted, and he grinned. Sex had always been intense for him, never funny. Addison had a way of making it both. "I won't make it, Addy. Our first time I need to be inside you—deep inside you."

He loomed over her, taking in the exquisite sight of her nakedness, and realized why people created artwork. They were inspired by the perfection that he'd only ever witnessed in her.

She grabbed the condom package from his hand and tore it open. His hands shook so much he was glad she'd had the foresight to think about it. Pushing him back a little, she rolled the condom onto him. No longer just a means to an end, it was the single most erotic image he'd ever seen. Promising himself they'd make love at least once more so he could take the time to taste her sweet juices without the risk of embarrassing himself by coming early, he leaned over her.

Gently, he entered her. She was tighter than he could

ever have dreamed. She sucked in her breath, and he paused to let her adjust to the size of him. "You okay?"

"Don't stop." Her voice was a whisper.

"Just breathe for a second. We're in no hurry here." He hoped.

She nodded, her eyes half closed. "I'm okay."

Moving slowly, he fitted himself inside her, and for a second, he couldn't move. It was heaven. Like her lips and her breasts, the inside of Addison fit him like a glove. It was akin to... coming home. Perhaps he'd waited his whole life for that moment. He could *feel* her, and not just physically. How could he not have noticed what was happening with his Condition? She was there, psychically in his mind. They were connected. It wasn't a pure mind-merge—he didn't even know if such a thing was possible—but he knew she was inside his mind as surely as he knew his internal dialogue existed. No wonder it had made their heads throb when he'd stopped.

"Can you feel me?"

"In my body and my mind. Are you doing that?" Her voice, when she spoke, had taken on an even huskier sound.

"I think you are."

Then he moved, and all thought ceased. Lost to the sensation of Addison's essence joining his body, in his soul, in his mind, he could think of nothing else but bringing them both the release they craved. Her body worked in rhythm with his, her hips arching to his every thrust. She groaned, and it turned into a moan.

He covered her mouth with his, letting his desire lose itself inside her.

The pressure built. It had never been so intense. Never. He hadn't known it could be. Colors crossed in front of his eyes, and he reached down to touch Addison's mouth with his hand. She bit his finger. He called out her name.

She was his.

Addison threw her head back, eyes closed, and he felt her lose herself to the moment.

One lone tear fell from his eye. How on Earth would he ever let her go? His own release overwhelmed him, and he hit the bed with a thud, managing to hold himself from collapsing entirely on top of her.

How on Earth?

SIXTEEN

The bed was too small.

It was the first coherent thought Addison could fathom. It was too small and there was no way, despite the sated, pleasant look on his face, that Spencer was anything but completely uncomfortable. Twin beds were not made for two grown adults to actually make love or sleep on. The making love part they'd managed, but the sleep—not that they had time for that—was going to prove to be more difficult.

The room smelled like cleaning products, and the amount of sunlight that slipped underneath the shaded window illuminated tiny dust particles floating in the air around them.

The fact that she could even think about sleeping filled her with utter remorse. She was supposed to be completely focused on Jeremy, and she'd just shared the most pleasurable experience of her life with a man who was so delectable, she wanted to eat him like a chocolate bar. She closed her eyes in shame. What kind of aunt was she?

Spencer ran his hand through her hair and hoisted her

up. She opened her eyes questioningly until she realized he was placing her on top of him so that her back lay on his stomach. After they'd resettled, with both his arms around her, he kissed the top of her head.

"Penny for your sad thoughts."

"How do you know they're sad?"

"I'm not the only one who wears what they're thinking all over their face."

She could have told him how wrong he was. She could hide things away so deeply no one would know what she was thinking, but he'd correctly judged her mood, so she wasn't going to argue the point.

Addison took a deep breath, enjoying his heady masculine scent so close to her body. "I'm wondering what kind of horrible person I am that I just shared the premiere sexual encounter of my life, while my nephew is missing and maybe suffering somewhere."

Her eyes filled with tears at the thought. Little blond Jeremy with his adult eyes that told the world he'd seen death at too young an age. He hadn't been there when Jeanne, his mother, had died. They'd gone to tell him, and at just a year old, he'd already seemed to know. Addison had played it off in her head at the time as just part of the strangeness of the experience, but now, in retrospect, she should obviously have focused more on some of Jeremy's early eccentricities.

"We're going to find his location tonight." Spencer said it with such confidence and assurance that she believed him.

"How do you know?"

"I've assembled the right team. After dinner, I'll let them know what's going on and they'll help us get him back."

"Even Tara?" Addison would rather walk on nails than ask that woman for help.

"She'll be useful in the actual recovery. Besides, she's feeling guilty; it's a good time to get her to do what I want."

"That's awfully pragmatic of you, Spencer." He was usually so black and white, so cut and dry. This seemed more like something she would do.

"Must be all the time I'm spending in the company of a certain blonde-haired Wade." As he spoke of her hair, he ran his fingers through it, causing shivers to travel her spine.

He cleared his throat. "Can I ask you about your family?"

She felt her emotional guards click into place. It was always a tricky subject with anyone, and even though Spencer said he wasn't holding her accountable for being a Wade, she still wasn't convinced that was one hundred percent true.

"Sure." She knew her tone had become as cold as ice, but she couldn't help it.

He rubbed her shoulders firmly with his big hands. "Relax—this isn't about your grandfather. I want you to tell me about your parents and your sister."

Swallowing, she tried to ignore the resurgence of her tears. When was the last time she'd talked to anyone about her parents? "Um, they're dead."

"I know that." He sighed. "How did they die?"

"Jeanne was killed in a skiing accident. She took a bad fall." She looked down at her hands. "Into a tree." Addison could still see her sister's neck as she lay by that tree. For a moment, she'd looked like she was sleeping, but no one's neck twisted that way and left them alive to tell the tale. Immediately, she'd known her baby sister was dead.

Her hands had shaken as she'd dialed on her cell phone

for help. It had been so cold that day, below zero on top of the slope, but Addison had felt instantly hot. She'd had to pull off most of her outdoor clothing by the time ski patrol had arrived. The sound of the sirens still followed her into her dreams.

"Were you with her when she fell?" He'd started drawing lines on her stomach with his fingertips, his arms wrapped around her, and his voice was low and soothing.

"No. She was so much faster than me." She grinned as the memory hit her. "She used to say I poked down the hill instead of skiing, but I never liked speed as much as she did."

"I've seen the way you handle that car of yours; she must have been insane."

She laughed. How could she be talking about this and feeling okay at the same time? "Driving is different. It's like boating. I can go fast as long as it's not my own body I'm using for propulsion."

"And you really have no idea who Jeremy's father is?"

She shook her head. "For someone as open as Jeanne, she was completely guarded on that subject, absolutely refused to tell us who he was. I was hurt for a while about it. We were so close, and then she went away to work in England, came back pregnant, had the baby, and never discussed it, not even with me."

"But then Jeremy came, and you really didn't care anymore."

"Exactly."

He squeezed her shoulders again. "And your parents?"

"When I was ten, they were both killed in a plane crash over the Atlantic. They never found the wreckage. Jeanne sat by the window for a week, convinced they were going to show up, but I knew they were gone."

"You don't live with illusions. Even when you're acting like you're not Conditioned, you know you're pretending. You're not the kind of woman who deludes herself."

"How do you know me so well?" She'd never even thought of herself the way he'd just described, but he was completely correct—she couldn't live in the world of make-believe. It didn't suit her.

Gently, he bit her shoulder, and she squealed. "I just do, gorgeous lady."

"Why the questions about my family?"

"It's been sort of eating at me that we don't know who his father is and that Jeanne is dead. Then I started wondering about your parents after you told me about your father teaching you to do your ridiculous shielding."

Addison rolled her eyes. "Okay, so I suppose you could teach me to do a better one?"

"In a heartbeat. But I'm not sure what to do with your Conditioned power. You were in my head while I was inside you."

"And that's not standard Conditioned stuff?"

"Not for me, and not that I've ever heard of."

"Great, just another way I'm strange and different."

He rolled her over until she was beneath him again. His body was heavy, and she loved the feel of him there. They only had a short amount of time together. She'd take any physical contact she could get.

"Why does it have to be about *you* at all? Maybe it's about *us*."

"That's a nice thought." She reached up to grasp his cheek, feeling the scratchy sensation of his five o' clock shadow. His facial hair came in slightly darker than the hair on top of his head, more of a brownish-blond as opposed to the nearly golden locks that hung down in front of his eyes, and which she'd grown so fond of. "But let's face it, it's probably about me if it's never happened to you before."

"Well, you're not going to experiment with any other Conditioned guys to see if it happens again; therefore, this might be a question we never know the answer to."

She laughed. "Your eyes are doing that swirly thing again."

"I think it's just in your imagination."

"You said something about my parents and my lack of shields and whatnot." Lying beneath him, she stretched so she could feel his body even tighter against hers.

"Right." He nodded. "It takes some practice, but you'll get the hang of it. You already have the general idea. When I was a child, I could accidentally slip into dark space. Something would tingle in my head and I'd just go there without another thought. Frankly, I'm lucky I didn't disappear into the vast endlessness a lot sooner. I had to learn to protect myself, to shield my powers from working on their own without direction from me."

"We're not even sure what my powers are. I can bring you a bridge of light to guide you out of the darkness, and I can also blow up a glass window."

"Don't forget merging minds with me during hot sex."

She could only imagine that she blushed, because her cheeks felt incredibly hot. "Of course, let's not forget that."

"In any case, it shouldn't matter; we all shield almost entirely the same. It's a technique." He paused, and as he thought of something, she saw the swirls that apparently only she could see heighten in intensity in his eyes. "It's like learning yoga."

"I'm really very bad at yoga."

He laughed. "Doesn't matter; you'll be good at this. Let's sit up."

Slightly bereft at the loss of intimacy, she did what he asked. He moved until they faced each other, their knees touching on the bed, their naked bodies not bothering either of them.

He raised an eyebrow and grinned. "This feels a little foolish, but it will work, I promise. For most people it's a one-time fix."

"Something is bothering me, Spence."

"What?"

"My father taught me to do that poem, which means he had some form of protection from whatever it was he could do—even though my grandfather is in utter denial about it—so who do you think taught him?"

Spencer seemed to consider the question for a moment before he shrugged. "Maybe he just learned it out of survival. If someone taught him how to do it, we're not likely ever to know who it was. His condition would have shown up before most people knew what it was, before having these afflictions was of international importance. But maybe he knew right away, even as a child, that your grandfather wouldn't handle his differences well. In any case, I'm sure he just wanted to protect you."

She felt her eyes start to fill with tears. She dabbed at them with the edge of the bed sheet, willing herself not to cry. "All right, let's do this, whatever *this* is."

"It's all about imagery. Let's face it, our brains are simply different from those of most people, or we couldn't do what we do, right?"

"Makes sense." She shivered for a moment as she imagined her grandfather finding out she was Conditioned, having her killed, then having her brain dissected.

"Focus, please."

"You do sound like a yoga teacher."

He grinned. "For whatever reason—and we really don't know why, as Wade Corporation hasn't told us the answer yet, we respond really well to imagery. Also sounds, which, although I hadn't thought of it before, is probably why your little rhyme thing worked. It's a repetition of a sound."

"You know I never, ever read the reports that come in from Safe Dawn. I don't look at the rundowns; I don't even know what we're currently working on."

"How can you expect to run your grandfather's major corporation if you don't pay attention to its biggest moneymaker?"

"Whoever told you that is lying."

He canted his head. "What?"

"Only a very small fraction of our holdings in the institutions bring us any money at all. Most of the time, the testing we do here and at the other places is actually a money drainer. The board calls the testing Grandfather's 'pet project.' Very few of the things discovered at this place have had any real-world application on the outside."

She could tell she'd stunned him. He furrowed his eyebrows. Resisting the urge to reach out and comfort him, she let him sit undisturbed for a moment. She had no idea what the people who ran the institutions told them about the testing Wade did, and how it was used for financial gain.

"Then you're telling me that Oliver Wade does this to us out of some sort of morbid curiosity rather than for financial gain?"

She sighed. "He would say that he does it to save society from all of you. If he can find a cure, he can put you back into the real world. If he can't, then he can keep anyone from getting hurt."

"Did someone he love get killed by a Conditioned person?"

"Not that I know of. As far as I know, he loved my grandmother, but she died of cancer, not anything to do with any of this. I really don't have answers about him."

"Then let's get back to you. You need shields. Close your eyes."

She did, with a slight worry that she might actually doze off and fall asleep. It had been a long day, and she was feeling relaxed and sated. Hell, Spencer would be lucky if she didn't start snoring right where she sat.

"I want you to tell me the happiest you've ever been."

"You mean besides right now?" She smiled; she really was feeling sinfully fantastic sitting with Spencer on his bed.

"You're hardly happy right now, but thank you for the compliment just the same. Jeremy is still missing. I have a feeling I won't get to see you truly happy until it's resolved."

A large portion of her liveliness fell away. He was right. She might have been feeling temporarily content, however, the looming truth of what was happening hadn't changed. Biting her lower lip, she tried to concentrate. Happiest she'd ever been?

The memory hit her hard.

Sitting in her father's arms—they'd felt huge and strong to her eight-year-old self—on his sailboat, he'd taught her how to guide a boat as the sun had set behind them. He'd been tall, with dark hair and eyes that laughed more than they angered. Her mother had dressed Jeanne and Addison in matching yacht club clothes for the day, so they'd been clad in blue-and-white skirts that matched their tops. Addison had worn a headband to keep her hair out of her face, but Jeanne hadn't minded the windblown sensation.

Their mother had sat in the rear of the boat, watching

them and holding a video camera to record the day. *What happened to that tape?*

"Do you have the memory?"

She nodded. "I do."

"Wrap yourself in it. Let it fill you up inside. Let your brain absorb it until it solidifies around your insides like a giant, unbreakable wall that no one would dare try to penetrate."

"Why do you make it sound easy?"

He laughed, and the sound warmed her. "Because it is. Your brain is designed to do it. Just wrap yourself in it, live in that moment, go back there in your mind for just a few seconds, and it will happen. Think of it as stretching your brain muscle like you might do with your other muscles in exercise class, or a sensory memory thing in acting."

She tried to take herself back to that evening.

The boat was noisy. The sails flapped, the chains clanked, and the waves splashed against the boat. In the distance, seagulls sang to the universe. Her father hummed in her ear and occasionally remarked on how beautiful their mother looked with the horizon behind her. Jeanne had brought rocks on board with them, and she threw them over the side. *Clunk.* It was the sound the rocks made as they hit the water, followed by the tiniest of splashes.

Her eyes flew open. She could see it all. Spence had been right. It was auditory for her, but there was the memory, as alive as the moment she had lived it. It moved inside her brain until she could feel the memory lodging itself in her head.

"Is it working?"

Spencer's voice startled her, and she jumped. "I think so."

He smiled. Unable to resist the urge, she leaned forward

and kissed him. As he ran his hands lovingly up and down her leg, he held her tight. When she pulled back, he winked.

"Now, if you suddenly find yourself thinking about that time, it probably means you're in danger of having an episode. You can calm yourself down or stop whatever you're doing."

"I do feel sort of... secure."

"Then it worked."

She blew out a breath she hadn't known she was holding. "Now what?"

He leaned over and kissed her on the tip of her nose. "Now, Addison Wade, we go and find out where they took your nephew."

"Just like that?"

"I don't know if it's going to be easy, but we will succeed. I can guarantee it."

"You sound so sure of yourself." How could he be so confident when she was so terrified?

"There are some things in this strange life I live that I can do. Finding missing children is one of them. This case is slightly more complicated than the previous ones, but I can do it."

She swallowed and asked the question that haunted her.

"And after you find Jeremy?"

Something swirled in the strange blue-and-green color of his eyes. "Then you go home, Addison."

"And you?"

"Somehow, I go on."

Only she wasn't sure she ever really could.

SEVENTEEN

Spencer stood at the front of the room, eyeing each of the people he'd called to the meeting with a newfound wariness. Discovering that Rhodes hadn't been completely on the line with him had taken away the security he'd felt about the institutions. How many of the people in them had secrets he knew nothing about?

To be fair, they all seemed to be judging him slightly differently since he'd practically knocked Jack out—not an easy thing to do considering that the man's Condition allowed him to kill with just a thought. Not to mention Spencer had taken Addison as his lover. That had to have everyone freaked out since they didn't know her.

The only good part was that Roman, who hugged the shadows in the corner, seemed equally uncomfortable. Spencer knew he should have been above pettiness, but where Roman was concerned, he might never actually get to that level of maturity.

He cleared his throat. "I don't know what was said after I left here."

Jack laughed, a harsh sound. "Not much. The Fury over

there let us call the people you wanted brought in, but not much else."

"I have a name, dipshit." Roman barely lifted his head as he delivered the set-down.

Spencer wasn't sure he'd ever heard Roman curse before. He tried not to grin.

Roman could get rattled enough to swear. Who knew?

"To make a long story much shorter, I was called out to assist Addison in the search for her nephew, who was kidnapped from their apartment in the middle of the night. I thought it was going to be an easy find—frankly, I thought he would turn up dead—but it's become much more compli-cated than I ever could have imagined. Made even more complex by you kidnapping Addison and nearly getting the whole lot of you killed.

He'd added the last jab on purpose. His panic at her going missing was still a tight knot in his shoulders. It would be a long time before he could forget it.

"It must be serious if you brought *him* in." Holland motioned toward Roman.

"Roman brought himself in." Looking at his brother, Spencer realized for the first time what it must be costing him to put up with such a high level of hostility from the group. He wouldn't want to be on the receiving end of it. "I'm actually immensely grateful for his help." Even if he would have preferred to be able to speak to Rhodes on his own. Roman had concealed Addison's condition so far.

He needed to give credit where credit was due.

Roman nodded, and Spencer suspected that would be the entire acknowledgement he would get. Even as a child, his brother had never been particularly effusive.

"We were initially shocked when I did a reading in dark

space and came up with nothing. It was like Jeremy never existed."

"Are you sure you didn't imagine having a nephew?" Tara directed that nasty remark to Addison, and Spencer wished he didn't have an unbreakable rule about hitting women. Someday, someone was going to smash the woman in the nose.

"I'm sure." Addison gave Tara her most haughty expression, the one that included her ice-cold glare and pursed lips. Tara actually shrank back a bit. He wondered if his woman practiced that, or if it just came naturally to her.

Minnie finally spoke. "Maybe if I went in with Marisa and did a deeper look around..."

A dark space reader like he was, Minnie wasn't as practiced or as good at going deep into the space. Having gone into the darkness with her more than once, he appreciated the offer, but they both knew she could only go as far with a conduit as he could go without one. Marisa flipped her chestnut-brown hair over her right shoulder and nodded.

"I went into the total darkness by myself."

Minnie and Marisa gasped. Marisa's powers were similar to Priscilla's. Usually she worked as Minnie's light path. Spencer had tried to work with her after Priscilla's death, but he'd nearly overwhelmed the woman. He was going to ask her to put herself at high risk today—he hoped she'd say yes.

"How did you get back?" He heard the awe in Minnie's voice. He'd already decided how he would handle that question.

"It's a very long story." He gave Addison a look meant to instruct her to keep quiet. She seemed to understand. She stood, arms crossed over her chest, in a posture that said to the world, "Leave me alone." He could see the insecurity others would miss.

He forced his thoughts back from his admiration for all things Addison to the task at hand.

"Obviously, I did get back. What's important is what I found while I was inside. I located Jeremy."

Tara smacked her hand on the table. "Great. Woo-frickin-hoo. Why didn't you find him and move on? Why drag Princess Addison to our little neck of the woods?"

The girl had never had a sense of when to keep her mouth shut. "Tara, if you let that chip on your shoulder get any bigger, you're going to collapse under the weight of it."

That earned him chuckles from around the room. Even Addison smiled, which impressed him, because he suspected she wanted to kick the woman's behind from Safe Dawn to China.

Minnie and Marisa, as the only other dark space trekkers, were the only ones to see the importance of what he'd said.

Marisa spoke first. "Why was he buried so deep? Doesn't he live in that apartment?"

"What's going on?" Minnie chimed in immediately after Marisa.

He raised an eyebrow. "What if I told you that Jeremy's babysitter's energy was gone from her apartment, too? As well as any sign that Jeremy had ever been there?"

"This is all such existential nonsense to me." Russell shook his head. "My power is so easy compared to this." He looked at Holland, who nodded his agreement.

Spencer didn't care what anyone else thought. He had a role for each of them to play.

But he needed to get the two Ms on board so he could go to work on Laurel. She could heal anyone with a touch—

physical healing—and it hurt her to be too close to others for extended periods of time. If someone even had a hangnail, it could give Laurel a headache. The small, black-haired woman spent most of her time in solitary confinement just to give herself some needed peace. He often thought Laurel's eyes held the sorrows of the world.

His plan was to use Marisa to light-guide them to Jeremy until she physically couldn't do it anymore, have Minnie distract Priscilla so he could get a location, then have Laurel heal Marisa when it was over. The others would come with him. Addison would retrieve Jeremy. It was simple, but in this case, simple was best. There were already too many levels of intrigue.

Marisa sighed, finally answering his question. "I would say it would be impossible unless someone out there could do that, could make people vanish from dark space. I've never heard of such a thing."

"Neither had I until I heard of Loretta. Turns out she's actually not dead... *and* it turns out there are the same doubts about Priscilla and Daniel Monroe."

Tara gasped and covered her mouth with her hands. Tears came to her eyes and disappeared within seconds. Ah... so the rumors had been true. Daniel and Tara had been an item.

She shook her head vehemently. "He wouldn't do that."

Gina scoffed. "He would, and you know it. I knew him better than you without ever sleeping with him. Don't make him out to be a good guy; he's not—alive or dead."

Spencer turned his attention to Gina. She was lounging with her feet up on the couch, her head leaning against Jack's shoulder. She lifted her head and raised an eyebrow. Gina, Jack, Holland and Tara were the final part of his plan. The people with the lethal abilities... well, Holland's weren't quite deadly, but they were scary. He would need all of them with him to get Jeremy back.

He might not have personally had any fatal skills, but he knew how to delegate, how to make people owe him favors, and what buttons to push to get people to do what he wanted. Over the previous two days, he'd realized, as Oliver Wade had filled his thoughts a great deal, that those qualities could be more important than any others.

If Holland could make the whole crew go to sleep, it would provide a way to get out of the situation without anyone getting hurt. Jack could kill with a thought. Russell could make anyone do what he wanted with just a little push of his mind. Tina could set fire to the room around her and not burn herself, and Gina... well, what Gina could do was probably the most frightening, and not something they discussed all that often. Gina could temporarily bring back the dead.

He needed all of them.

Gina stood and walked over to Addison. His love rubbed a hand over her eyes and looked at the other woman. He hadn't told Addison what Gina or Jack could do. It was disturbing enough that he knew.

Gina seemed to have come to some sort of decision. "I didn't want to help you, Addison Wade. When I came in here, I thought, whatever Spence asks me to do, I'm going to say no just to spite the Wades—"

Addison interrupted. "Look, I can't justify what my grandfather has done..."

Gina held up her hand. "But you have a lot more spunk than I thought you would have. I can see it in your eyes. Now I'm hearing that a kid is missing and Daniel is involved. Well, I'll take any opportunity to screw that son of a bitch." Gina turned to look at Spencer. "Count me in. Whatever you want me to do, I'll do."

He cut to the chase. "I want Marisa to host Minnie and me at the same time. Minnie can distract Priscilla, who's blocking me from tracking Jeremy. I'll sneak in, get his location. Laurel can, hopefully, heal the damage to Marisa and the rest of us can go get Jeremy."

Jack stood up from the couch and walked over to where Spencer stood. "You're talking about leaving here—about Gina, Tina, Holland and me leaving Safe Dawn and going out there?" He pointed to the window as if it represented the whole outside world.

A vision of the car Addison had let Spencer drive filled his mind. There had been so many experiences in the last few days. He'd carry them for the rest of his life, and they would help to sustain him.

Holland interrupted his thoughts. "How are you going to get us out of here?"

"I'm going to call in every favor any guard here has ever owed me." He turned to Addison. "Speaking of which, before this is over, I'm going to need to sneak you back out and have you get us some kind of van for transport."

She agreed. He knew it wouldn't be a problem for her. She'd just take the sports car down to the nearest car rental spot and—

The door flew open. One of his least favorite people breezed into the room like a ghost on LSD. Jittery and pale, Simpson Moonarie looked right and left before he leaned up against the wall for support. Laurel followed him in. She was often with him, silently helping him.

Jack put his hand on Simpson's arm. "What are you doing here, man?"

No one ever really knew how to handle the strange

fellow. Barely five feet tall, he was broad-shouldered and he always looked like he'd just gotten over the flu, even when he was in the best of health.

He bent over at the waist like he might vomit, and Spencer sincerely hoped he wouldn't. Simpson pointed at Addison. "He's calling to you, begging you to come to him." His eyes huge, he moved toward her like he wanted to grab her. "He's just a little boy. Why won't you answer him?"

Spencer vaulted forward to intercept him.

"Who's calling to me?" Addison stepped forward, her eyes huge.

"He can hear things the rest of us can't, Addy. Don't worry about it." They needed to get their plan into action; he really didn't have time for this. If Jeremy was psychically calling to Addison, the knowledge would only upset her.

"Jack." He nodded toward the door. Jack was pissed at him, but he still did what he was asked and dragged Simpson out of the door.

"What was that?" Addison grabbed his shirt. "Was he referring to Jeremy? Is he calling to me?"

"Don't worry about it." He brushed her blonde hair off her forehead.

Her gaze fumed. The woman's eyes were a handbook of her emotions. "Don't worry about it? That man just said Jeremy is calling to me."

He nodded. He didn't want to make her mad, but he wanted to keep her focused. "So let's go get him." Everyone spoke, almost at once.

Minnie went first, proclaiming she could do it, while Jack wasn't certain he wanted to have to kill anyone again. He hadn't since he'd gotten control of himself as a child. But it was Tara's statement that stopped everyone in their tracks.

"What's the difference? We're all going to Hell anyway."

Addison jerked at that statement. Whirling around, she stared at Tara. "Someday, one of you is going to have to tell me what religious education they give you people in here."

No, they weren't going there. "Let's not start that again." He glanced at Minnie. "You ready?"

"As ready as I'll ever be."

He looked at Jack. "Are you in or out?"

Jack shrugged. "I'm in."

"Then let's do this thing."

Without a second thought, he gave in to his natural instinct and traveled to dark space in the room. Addison's bright yellow light was the first he saw. Quickly, he counted heads to make sure everyone's light was accounted for before turning to Minnie's dark purple energy. Marisa was right behind her, a burnt orange like the color of a pumpkin.

He called Jeremy's energy from where it was buried inside him and pushed it forward.

He attached his senses to Jeremy's light as he shoved them both onward. "Go find yourself."

Jeremy's energy tinkled but didn't move. Skittish, he reminded himself. This little bit of Jeremy's essence had been all but wiped out; it wasn't going to want to expose itself to the world again.

"Go on. Go find yourself. Let's go find Jeremy."

The child's energy bobbed for a second. Marisa and Minnie moved their energies closer to him. He'd almost forgotten he wasn't alone in dark space this time. Priscilla had been used to his oddball habit of speaking out loud to the energies. Maybe Minnie and Marisa would think he was nuts.

Marisa finally spoke. "It's moving. Hold on."

Grabbing with all his psychic ability, he held on to Jeremy's essence and felt Marisa and Minnie do the same. They flew fast, nearly knocking him on his behind. He'd forgotten how quickly children's energy could move. Utter darkness surrounded him, with only Jeremy's light to hold on to as a guide.

With a screech, they came to a stop. He knew they hadn't reached Jeremy, or he'd see him standing in front of him. No, this was the wall he'd known would be there. Priscilla was good at making them and even better at holding them. Ultimately, with the right conduit and enough time, he could beat it down, but once Priscilla became aware of the attempt she would fortify it, make it even stronger.

"Marisa, are you still holding?" If his conduit was about to fall apart he needed to know about it.

"Barely." Her voice sounded husky, and he knew she was close to breaking.

"Minnie, start beating on Priscilla."

"Right." Minnie took a deep breath as she started to push her energy against Priscilla's psychic wall. The energy field blocking them from Jeremy shivered and flared with white light. He smiled. Priscilla was pissed. All he needed was for Marisa to make a dent or one small fissure so he could slip his way through.

To her credit, Marisa pounded hard on Priscilla. Priscilla was stronger than Marisa in dark space. Spencer was fairly confident that Marisa knew that, but she didn't give up. *Come on,* he silently willed her. He couldn't help her, couldn't fortify her strength or make himself visible to Priscilla.

Smash!

The world shimmered and happiness filled his insides

as he pulled Minnie and Jeremy with him through the miniscule hole Marisa had made. But just as he'd pushed through, his vision became hazy. He stopped moving. The darkness around him blurred, and Jeremy's shimmer phased in and out around him.

He knew this feeling too well. It had only happened once before, but it had been when Priscilla had "died" and dropped out of dark space, leaving only a narrow path of light for him to follow back. He whirled around but didn't find what he was looking for.

Marisa and Minnie were both gone. Damn. He closed his eyes and tried to reorient himself. He'd never chased energy without a conduit. What the hell was he going to do, and how physically and psychically hurt must Minnie be to have completely disappeared? He'd hugely overestimated her abilities, and once again he was struck by just how strong Priscilla must have been.

"Gotcha."

Priscilla's voice filled his mind, and he jerked. Where was she?

"Oh, you can't see me, but I have you now, Spence."

He grasped Jeremy's energy and sucked it back inside him. No way was he going to let Priscilla see it. Loretta might come and destroy it again, and then his efforts would be for naught.

When he was satisfied Jeremy was safe, he decided to answer her. "I see you're not dead." Looking around, he tried to see what she was seeing, why she'd said "gotcha."

"Not even a little bit."

He scoffed. She'd always said ridiculous things. "It's not possible to be a little bit dead."

"All things are possible, Spencer, and the fact that you

don't know that shows just how limited you are. Rhodes has kept you weak."

Her sarcasm irked him. He looked around again. "What do you want, Priscilla?"

"You. So it looks like I've been hugely successful."

"You don't have me, Priscilla."

"Oh, but I do. Take another look."

Narrowing his eyes, he bit down on his tongue to keep from screaming. The walls that had blocked them from Jeremy surrounded him now. Priscilla had put out a psychic net, and he'd walked right into it. Just as she'd said, she had him, and he didn't know if he'd ever get back. His thoughts flew to Addison. She would still be standing in the room, looking at his useless body.

His heart ached at the thought of Addison wondering what had happened. Would he ever see her again, and how could he have failed her so completely? He closed his eyes.

Damn, he was screwed.

EIGHTEEN

Addison watched in horror as Minnie and Marisa fell to the floor. Laurel rushed to the two women, placing her hands on their foreheads. She swore quietly.

Jack hurried to join Laurel.

Addison's gaze flew to Spencer. He hadn't moved, not even slightly. She could hear her heart pounding in her ears. If Marisa and Minnie were back, then Spencer was in there all by himself. Was he okay?

Trying not to show her internal strife, she walked over to him, putting a hand on his arm as if she could bring him back to her by touch alone, which she knew was impossible. She felt helpless and her hands shook with nerves. What was she supposed to do?

Minnie's eyes flew open, and she groaned. Laurel hushed her, but Minnie pushed her arm away. "We lost him. Spencer is still in there." She moaned and closed her eyes. "Priscilla is so damn strong, she all but threw us out of dark space and back into our bodies." As if saying those few words were all she could manage, Minnie made one more pained sound and lost consciousness.

"Spencer won't come back now without a guide." Tara shook her head and glared at Addison as if the whole thing were her fault. "He might as well be dead."

Addison forced herself to stay calm and think. She had guided Spencer back from dark space when they'd been at her apartment, but that had been all instinct. Her body had simply reached out and grabbed him.

She wanted to scream with frustration, never having hated silence more than she did at that moment. She whirled around and grabbed Tara's arm. The other woman looked stunned.

"You're touching me? Are you out of your mind? I could burn you to death."

Addison nodded. "You could, except you won't, because Rhodes' power's dampening this whole place, right?

Jack stepped toward them. "That's right. He keeps us all under a certain amount of control. Prevents uncontrolled power surges and gives us a certain amount of personal strength to decide when and where we do things."

Her gaze met Roman's across the room. He raised an eyebrow, and she didn't have to be a mind reader to know what he wanted to ask. Was she going to expose herself in front of these people for Spencer?

She glanced at Tara again. Not sure why, but Addison believed that Tara was the one to speak to about this problem. She'd caught the curtains on fire with just a thought and put them out just as easily. Obviously, the mean, brown-haired fire controller was not being completely put down. "Can you beat it? Can you get around Rhodes' control?"

"Any time I want to." Tara's eyes narrowed and Addison knew it was now or never. She was going to have to come clean; she'd made the other woman too suspicious. It didn't really matter—for Addison there had never been a choice. She would do anything for Spencer. Even risk her own safety.

Her own life.

"Could you teach me?"

Tara backed away, pointing a finger in Addison's direction as Gina leaped off the couch. Tara laughed once then started to holler. "I knew it. I *knew* you were more than you seemed. You're one of us, you bitch, and your money has kept you hidden from persecution your whole life. Your grandfather abuses us and hides you."

Addison opened her mouth to speak, surprised to find that Gina had crossed to her and placed a comforting hand on her arm, but Roman beat her to it.

"Her grandfather doesn't know anything about it, or he'd have had her in here with the rest of you—either that or he'd have had her killed to spare himself the embarrassment. She just asked you for help to bring Spencer back. Do you want to be a self-righteous prick or do you want to help her out?"

Tara's voice sounded like a scream. "Why am I always wrong? Because I tell the truth? Because I don't want to kiss her ass just because she's Addison Wade? Why does she get to live in New York City while I have to reside in this hellhole?"

"Because your mother gave you up like you were so much garbage. Addison's father helped her to hide."

Addison sucked in her breath at Roman's declaration. She'd have to remember never to piss him off. How did he even know about what her father had done?

Tara looked down at the floor, and Addison wondered if she was about to cry. She didn't want to see Tara lose it; if the woman was nothing else, she was strong in her anger.

She moved forward and grabbed Tara by the shoulders.

"Look, if you want to hate me, hate me. If you want to force Roman's hand when this is over and insist that he bring me into Safe Dawn, do it. It's your choice. However, right now, Spencer needs me. I can bring him back. He's the only one who can find my nephew, and even more than that, I love him. I need him. I'm asking you for help. *Please*."

Tara raised her eyes and stared. Usually Addison had a pretty good idea what people were going to say, but not this time. If the other woman told her to go to hell, she'd have to hope someone else in the room was as strong as Tara and could teach her what to do. Somehow, she doubted it. If anyone else could do it, they probably would have volunteered by now. "It's not easy. Are you strong?"

She shrugged. "Tara, I have no idea. I'm completely untrained."

Roman moved forward. "She's incredibly strong."

"And you're a conduit like Minnie and Priscilla?"

"I think she's a hybrid of powers. She seems to carry a whole slew of abilities, and as far as I can tell, being around Spence makes her stronger."

Roman really knew a lot about her. "How do you know that?"

"I'm not going to tell you, so you should probably not worry about it."

Just like that, he was driving her crazy again. But Spencer needed her, which meant there was no time for Roman's odd behavior.

Tara stepped forward. Addison was a few inches taller, but they still stood almost nose-to-nose. Swallowing, she promised herself she wouldn't let the fire-starter intimidate her.

"You have to want it—badly. Do you?"

"More than I've ever wanted anything." When she said that out loud, she knew it was true. She wanted Spencer back, and she wanted him to find Jeremy, both of which made her want to use her abilities more than ever before.

"Rhodes puts all his energy into keeping this place under control. There are bits and pieces that crack, places where we can slip in and use our powers. You just have to feel it." Tara closed her eyes. "It's like waves of power. Feel the ebb and flow come over you. Marisa, Minnie, and Spencer all had to concentrate on it to enter dark space—even Laurel to heal—but we're all used to it. It's like breathing for us. You're going to need to concentrate."

Addison closed her eyes and matched Tara's stance. With her legs slightly separated and her hips lined up over her feet, she tried to concentrate on the energy moving through the room.

"Can you feel it? It's like a wave moving over you."

Addison searched for the sensation Tara had described. Nothing happened, and she wanted to scream with frustration. Why couldn't this just work? Why couldn't anything be easy?

Roman approached her. "I can feel the tension radiating off you. Take a deep breath. Think of Spencer and Jeremy and their need of you."

If it wouldn't have defeated her purposes, she would have reached out and smacked Roman. Wow, he was aggravating.

Why couldn't he leave her alone?

Didn't he understand this was hard? Couldn't he...

Boom!

Like a freight train moving through her mind, she could feel the energy modulations in the room, but it didn't feel anything like ebb and flow to her. Maybe she'd just spent too much time on the ocean, but this felt more like turbulence on an airplane.

A thought occurred to her. "You did that on purpose?" She hoped Roman knew she was talking to him.

He snickered. "You exploded on Spencer when he stressed you out. I thought maybe the same would work to get you into dark space."

As she paid attention to the steady rhythm of shakes and stops the power dampening took, Addison waited another beat until she knew the psychic hold on her abilities had lessened so she could use her powers.

"Can you feel it?"

Tara's voice called out to her, but she couldn't answer, too intent on throwing herself into dark space.

"Wait, don't," called Marisa, who must have woken up, but she was too far gone to stop.

She realized she was standing in what they called dark space. The first time she'd come, she'd been so consumed with sending light to Spencer, she hadn't noticed where she'd been. Now, however, she could see how this strange reality had earned its name. Everything was simply duller and, for lack of a better description, darker than it had been on the physical plane. Taking a deep breath, she looked for Spencer but couldn't find him.

Damn. He'd had to follow Jeremy's energy to its source. He could be anywhere in the world. What the hell was she supposed to do? She squatted down, leaning her elbows on her knees, head in her hands. It was all too much. How had she thought she was capable of handling any of this? All the years she'd worked at Wade, she'd convinced herself she was strong and capable. Nothing could ever rattle her. Boy, had she been wrong.

Her nephew was gone, the man she was in love with

was all but dead in his body, and she was... No. She forced herself to stand. *No.* She was not going to start whining or feeling bad for herself. Every problem had a solution.

How would Spencer find her if the situation were reversed? She swung around, looking left and then right. The difference, she supposed, was that Spencer could see energy signatures—in colors—and then he could track them. If everyone had one, that meant he did too.

So why can't I see it? Perhaps it wasn't within her power to see such things. Addison sighed. Nothing was ever easy. Why should she expect this to be?

She never gave up—never had and never would. If Spencer could see them, there was every reason to believe she should have been able to catch sight of them as well. After all, she was in dark space. What was the point of being able to enter dark space if you couldn't see energy spectrums?

Maybe she just needed to move a little bit deeper into the shadows. At the very least, she knew she'd be able to light her way back out, which she knew firsthand Spencer could not do.

A hand grabbed her arm. She jolted but didn't leave dark space. Who was distracting her now?

"Addison, can you hear me?"

Minnie. She didn't know the voice well, but she was sure it was her.

"You can't do this alone; you need my help."

A light flashed, and she realized she was seeing Minnie's energy structure in dark space. Bright orange, it kept illuminating brightly and then fizzling out.

"I'm weak at the moment. I'm not going to be able to hold on to this for very long. I'll get you to Spencer—that's all I can promise."

Without warning, Addison felt herself propelled forward through the darkness, dragged behind Minnie's orange form. She hissed in a breath as the landscape around her lost shape and color and became nothing more than shadowed blackness—all-consuming and powerful.

Not even when she'd brought Spencer back from the shadows the first time had she known that blackness had a feeling, a sensation akin to a taste that enveloped her entire body. She hated it. Her insides screamed against the assault on her senses. This wasn't natural. No one should have to do this, ever.

As she came to an abrupt stop, she stared at a giant wall engulfed in a purple light. Her heartbeat picked up but she didn't need the internal signal to tell her how she felt. She already knew. She was scared stiff.

"What is that?" Her voice came out as a strained whisper.

"That's Priscilla. We battered and battered at it." Minnie's voice stopped and started. The woman was clearly having a hard time speaking. "Finally, Spencer got through, but she trapped him inside and threw Marisa and me back into our bodies. I never imagined anyone could be that strong."

"Spencer is in there?" She pointed at the wall; she just wanted to be sure she understood correctly.

"That's right. I'm starting to think we didn't break through the wall at all. If anything, Priscilla let us think we did so she could trap Spencer."

"Why would she want to do that?"

Minnie laughed, followed immediately by a strained cough. "She was always so in love with him. I think she felt if she just hung on long enough, they'd end up together. Anyone could have told her that was ridiculous. Spencer didn't earn his reputation for loving them and leaving them for nothing."

The words ate at Addison, and she forced herself to put away the nagging doubt they created.

She shivered as she dug deep and felt the constant power she carried building inside her. "I can't feel the dampening field at all now. It's like everything I can do is just surging inside me."

"Even though our bodies are still standing in Jack's room, our psychic senses have moved so far beyond Rhodes' reach that we're entirely on our own out here."

That didn't even make any sense. "Then Rhodes isn't really dampening your power at all, not if you can get out any time you want to."

"Kind of ironic, isn't it? He knows it, too. The dark-space walkers have never been under his control, not once we learn to enter the plane."

"Then why do you stay at Safe Dawn, if he doesn't control you?"

"The Fury scares the hell out of us."

Well, she couldn't blame them for that. Roman was starting to scare the hell out of her, as well.

"I can't stay." Minnie's voice had reached a new level of strain.

"Thank you for everything you've done." If Minnie hadn't shown up, she'd never have made it to this wall.

"I don't know if you'll succeed, but someday I hope I meet someone who would do this for me, who would risk so much to bring me back."

Addison opened her mouth to respond, but Minnie's light fizzled away. Not entirely certain how these things worked, she hoped Minnie had found a way to easily return to her body. Hell, who was she kidding? She was making this up as she went along—she'd be lucky if she ever found her way back into her own skin.

Concentrating, she sent her energy forward into the wall. Spencer was in there, damn it, and that meant she needed to be in there, too. As the minutes passed, she'd gotten better and more adept at controlling her own signature. Unlike Minnie, her energy seemed to leave a visible path behind her. Wherever she moved, it followed. It was like her own version of a yellow brick road. Spencer had been able to take it home the last time she'd used it. This time, she'd have to take the path back with him.

That was if she successfully retrieved Spencer and lived to tell the tale.

Forcing all her energy in front of her, she banged as hard as she could against the wall. Surprisingly, it gave way a smidgen. She heard a gasp that was decidedly female. Glee filled her heart.

"That's right, bitch, you didn't expect that."

Her next hit of energy encountered a stronger resistance, but this time she managed to push through.

At first, it felt like she'd barely punctured Priscilla's wall. A small hole; nothing substantial that could cause any damage. But then, like a dam finally bursting from too much pressure, Priscilla's wall fell. Elation filled Addison's veins.

For a moment, all she saw was darkness. She looked around until she located Spencer. His energy signature was entirely blue, but not blue like the ocean—no, his was navy, like faded denim. It fit him.

"Spencer."

His energy pulsated. "Addison, what the hell are you doing here? It's too dangerous."

"That's right, little rich girl." The voice that assaulted her had to be Priscilla's.

"You may have gotten through my defenses, but now I'm going to fry you to ashes."

Addison laughed. "Well, you can try."

She hadn't been feeling particularly happy since Jeremy had been taken, in fact it had been just the opposite. Every day had been terrifying. But it turned out she was really strong and capable in dark space. She'd taken down Priscilla's wall. Whatever the other woman dished out, she could handle it.

Giving her energy a pulsating burst, she felt the rightness of what she was going to do. "Let's do this."

NINETEEN

The situation rapidly spiraled out of control. Spencer pounded on the wall he couldn't get through, even though, evidently, Addison could. Just one day earlier, she'd exploded a glass window because she'd been so overwhelmed. Now she thought she could take on Priscilla?

No way. He wouldn't allow her to hurt herself. He pushed his energy forward, which he could do because Addison illuminated dark space for him. He wished he had solid arms and legs so he could grab her and shake some sense into her.

"What are you doing here? Get out before she hurts you. Forget about me. Roman will help you find another way to get to Jeremy."

"This isn't about Jeremy—well not entirely, anyway—this is about you and me and this lunatic who thinks she can take you from me. I'm a Wade; we don't lose what we own."

He couldn't help the smile that filled his heart. He could imagine her raised eyebrow and pursed, proud expression. As it was, her yellow energy pulsed, and he wanted to kiss her.

Priscilla interrupted. "Such sweet concern, Spencer. If the little troublemaker wants to fight, let her. After all, if she doesn't beat me, I'm going to tell the people I work for that she can move through dark space. Then maybe they'll take her just like they took *poor little Jeremy*."

Spencer didn't even have time to turn back to Addison before his beloved's energy flared and streamed out of her essence into Priscilla. The Wade heir was pissed. He couldn't blame her.

Priscilla sucked in her breath before she flared her own purple surge back at Addison. Their energies smacked together in the center of the makeshift prison Priscilla had created. With her concentration focused elsewhere, the walls around them crumbled.

His heart pounded hard. There wasn't a thing he could do to assist Addison. A hissing noise, akin to the sound a fluorescent light makes when it's getting ready to burn out, filled the space around them.

He moved closer to Addison; he had to shout to be heard. "C'mon, Addy, let's go. I won't let her have you. We'll find another way."

There was no way he could stomach the idea of losing her. The thoughts made his insides go cold. He suddenly realized that for Addison he'd run forever, just to keep her secure. Priscilla was frighteningly powerful. Every protective instinct in his body screamed for him to get Addison out.

"Quiet." Addison's tone left no room for rebuttal.

His temples throbbed with anger. She needed to listen to him. "We are not in the boardroom right now. You have to listen to me."

"I don't know if I should be offended by your lack of

confidence in me or not, but you're destroying my concentration right now."

Priscilla laughed. "By all means, Spence, keep talking."

"I swear, when I get out of here, Priscilla, I'm going to kill you, slowly." He meant it. Priscilla wouldn't just die; he would torture her, painfully.

His former friend's energy pushed forward, consuming Addison in its purple light. Addison screamed. Her yellow light glowed orange as if she were being burned alive.

"No!" He could do nothing to help her.

After only seconds, Addison's wail changed from pain to fury. Spencer instinctively backed up a step as her yellow brightness poured from her body, shoving Priscilla back one inch at a time.

When she spoke, Priscilla's tone had changed from taunting to terrified. "How is this happening?"

Spencer laughed. He should have known better than to doubt Addison. She was full of surprises. The woman was destroying a dark-space practitioner who had been working the space since she was a child. "It's happening, Priscilla."

"I've got to trap her or she'll give us away." Addison sounded exhausted. She'd all but extinguished Priscilla's light. That had to be as hard as hell. "If she can make walls, I can make walls. Roman says I'm some sort of hybrid, that I'm capable of using many powers."

"How does Roman know that?"

"He wouldn't tell me."

Priscilla resorted to begging. "I can teach you how to use your powers. Roman doesn't know what light-bringers can do. That's what we're called. There's so much beyond dark space for us. We connect to people. I bet you've always been very intuitive, and some of us can even use energy in the 'physical' world."

"If you hadn't trapped Spencer and helped to kidnap my nephew, I might have considered your offer. As it is, I'd rather never know." Addison took a labored breath. "Spencer taught me how to do this."

He watched in awe as four large steel walls formed a small box around Priscilla.

"Oh God, no. Please don't leave me in here. Please, please, please, no."

That was the last thing Spencer heard as Addison trapped Priscilla inside an unbreakable box.

He rushed forward. "Are you okay?"

"No." She took a shaky breath. "I'm fading fast, and I don't know what's going to happen. Did you find Jeremy?"

He shook his head. "Not yet."

"Do it. I'll hold on until you're done."

"Addison, you can rest and then we'll try again—"

She interrupted. "No, now. It has to be right away. I may never make it in here again." She groaned. "Not if I have a choice, anyway."

"It can be beautiful to be in here..."

"Just do it. We'll talk afterward."

She was right. He pulled Jeremy out of his energy store as he propelled himself forward, following where the little boy's essence took him. He held tight to Addison; he wasn't going to lose her again. Fortunately, they didn't have far to go.

Moments later, they stopped. Spencer looked around. There was no energy present in the room except the part of Jeremy he'd brought with him. That didn't surprise him; Loretta would be wiping them clean wherever they went.

Tension traveled up his spine. He didn't like the situation. Even with Priscilla out of the picture, it was possible he could push out of dark space and get caught by whoever was with Jeremy. Loretta could obviously manipulate dark space. But he didn't have a choice. If Jeremy's energy thought the real deal was in that room, then he was.

Spencer took the chance. "Hold on, Addison. I have to force my consciousness out into the real world. It's tricky. I don't have a body to move into. I can only hold it for a few seconds, so we need to hope that I can figure out a location really fast."

He forced himself into the light, guiding himself using Addison's energy signature. Alone, he'd most likely have gone the wrong way and ended up farther in the shadows. Addison was a miracle in so many ways.

Blinding light assaulted his eyes. He squinted. Not too many dark-space walkers could actually move from dark space to the physical plane without a body to enter.

He looked around his surroundings. His gaze immediately found Jeremy. The little boy was sleeping on the bed, his blond hair messy and unclean, and he was snoring gently. Spencer couldn't see his face, and there wasn't time for him to do a more thorough examination.

Daniel stared out the window, his eyes glazed over. Spencer wanted to kill the illusionist. He just might do that. Loretta sat on the floor next to Jeremy's bed, looking at a magazine that had a picture of a horse on the cover. He spared her barely a glance before he noticed Priscilla. Her body, now void of its mind and energy, stood silently to the left of Loretta. It might be a long time before anyone realized she was trapped in dark space.

None of that mattered; not until he could find their location.

Loretta looked up, and Spencer shivered. The woman could transverse dark space; it was possible she would feel his presence in the room.

As fast as possible, he sent his senses outward. It wasn't just that he didn't want to get caught; he would be forced back into the darkness at any second. He needed to learn an address before that happened. He pulled back until he saw they were in a warehouse. But what kind? He whirled around, looking left and right to get an idea.

His vision blurred. Damn it, he was running out of time. He couldn't see a thing. Right before he was thrust back into the energy field of dark space, he saw boxes of gin. That wasn't going to be helpful. There could be millions of liquor warehouses.

With no time to worry, he pressed his energy against Addison's. She had faded significantly since he'd traveled into the physical plane. "All right, let's go back."

"Did you find him?" Her voice was no more than a whisper.

"Yes. I don't know if I can pinpoint the location. He's being held, asleep, in some sort of liquor warehouse. I'm sorry that's so vague."

Her energy pulsed. "It's not vague to me. Actually, it makes perfect sense. How do we get back?"

"Like the yellow brick road, we're going to follow your light back home."

"I think I'm going to pass out when we get there."

"I'd be surprised if you didn't."

He hoped all she did was lose consciousness. Addison had definitely overdone it. She could be ready to go into a major power burn and be out of it for days. Spencer doubted they had that kind of time. Once Loretta clued in to the fact that Priscilla was brain dead in dark space, it wouldn't be long before they realized they'd been compromised. Then they might lose Jeremy forever.

He and Addison were slow moving, but after a few

minutes they landed back where they'd begun, each of them falling into their own body. Spencer was used to the feeling of coming back into the solidity of his limbs but Addison wasn't. He had two seconds to reach for her before her knees buckled. He caught her, and she looked up at him before shutting her eyes.

Without a word, and fully aware of the many eyes in the room watching him, he carried her to the couch and laid her down gently. He looked up as he saw the person he'd hoped was still there.

"Laurel, could you?"

Although she looked slightly worse than she had when he'd left, she moved over to Addison.

Minnie struggled to her feet from where she'd been sitting on the floor. "Spencer, Addison is so strong."

His heart lurched. "I know."

"Can you feel her energy in dark space? It's just like being with Priscilla."

"She's better than Priscilla. I doubted her—thought there was no way she could take on someone who'd had so much practice—but Addison all but horse-whipped her in there before she encased Priscilla in a psychic box. It will be a long time until Priscilla gets out, if ever."

He tried to feel sorry for Priscilla, to find some way to have compassion for the woman who had been his partner and friend for two decades. There was none. The sheer betrayal of faking her own death, and then participating in the kidnapping of a child, had killed whatever warm feelings he'd once had for her.

She was worse than a stranger to him now: she was an enemy.

"Did you find the location?" Roman's voice in his ear startled him.

He smiled. "Addison says we should get you a bell."

"That would defeat the purpose."

Spencer thought he heard amusement in Roman's voice, but he wasn't sure. With his brother, it was so hard to tell.

"I didn't recognize it, but when I described it to Addison, she did." He shrugged. "I guess we'll have to wait until she wakes up."

Roman strode away from him, his footsteps loud this time. He stopped right in front of Addison and Laurel. Spencer raised an eyebrow and followed him. What was his brother up to now?

Roman ran a hand over the stubble on his cheeks. Spencer had always thought they had the same color hair, but lately he'd been noticing that Roman's hair had darkened. All in all, he seemed to be aging more quickly than Spencer was. Of course, it could just have been that he was eleven months older. Maybe that was what Spencer would look like in a year.

Clearing his throat and glaring at Spencer like he knew his thoughts, Roman finally spoke to Laurel. "Is she burned?"

"No, she's just sleeping deeply," Laurel answered.

"Wake her up."

Oh hell, no. "Don't do that, Laurel."

"Spencer," she hissed in a whisper. "He's a Fury."

"I'm aware of what he is—believe me, I'm more aware of it than you are—but he doesn't get to say what happens to Addison." She needed to sleep.

Mimicking the look Spencer had given him earlier—and Spencer was quite sure it was deliberate—Roman raised an eyebrow. "Really? You think I can't make this go exactly as I want it to?"

And there was the brother he'd grown accustomed to

over the last twenty-six years. Gone was the man who'd been helpful and informative, and in his place was the nasty, threatening Fury. He wanted to punch him, and it was hard to restrain himself.

"Are you threatening me, Roman? Seems a little beneath you." *Take the bait.* Truth was, he was as tired as hell and didn't know if he was up for a battle of wills with his brother.

"I'm not threatening. I'm letting you know how it is."

Good. "Seems to me like you're threatening, like you're saying if you don't have it your way, I won't like the result."

"Listen, kid, I can haul your girlfriend out of here and have anyone I want awaken her and get the info I want. I'm doing you the courtesy of asking nicely and letting you watch me question her."

Better. It wasn't often Roman lost his temper. He just needed to distract him enough to get his attention off Addison. A groan from the couch drew his focus instead. Addison gripped her head as she sat up.

"Can the two of you stop screaming at each other for two seconds? You could wake the frickin' dead."

Spencer went to her side and sat next to her. Her face was strained; her eyes barely squinted open, and looked red and bloodshot. Under any other circumstances, he would have thought she was hung over. As it was, he couldn't help but be amazed she'd recovered so quickly.

"Ms. Wade, I'm afraid there's no more time to waste. Where is Jeremy?"

"A liquor warehouse."

Spencer wanted to throw something. "How can that mean anything to you? Do you know how many liquor warehouses there must be in this country, let alone the world?"

Addison reached out a hand, and he took it. "Roman knows exactly what I'm talking about, Spencer." Her gaze left his and landed on his brother. "Don't you, Roman?"

His brother's face was a mask of hardness. His eyes were steel, all his attention focused on Addison. When he finally spoke, his voice was barely above a whisper. "But she's a member of the Council."

"Who else could have manipulated this?"

Pounding on the wall above the couch with his free hand, Spencer looked between them. "Tell me what's going on."

"Grace Ann Charters, one of the premiere members of the committee—her family is the largest maker of liquor in the United States. They're hugely rich, hugely powerful." Addison closed her eyes and leaned back against the couch again. "My guess is that your brother isn't going to do anything now."

Spencer stood, releasing her hand. "Is that true, Roman? Now that it's one of them, one of the committee, you aren't going to help?"

"I can't participate in anything related to her. She's exempt from the Fury."

Addison stood next to him. "It's a cushy little rule that I believe Grace Ann added herself a few years ago. No one on the outside paid much attention to it, as most of us believe the Fury is just a myth. I can't possibly imagine why she would have made that rule, can you?" Sarcasm dripped from her voice.

"Roman." Spencer didn't like what he was about to say. "Don't help us as a Fury. Help us as my brother."

He'd counted on Roman—on his stealth, on his knowhow—to get them in and out of wherever they had to go. He had contacts the rest of them could never have. But even more than that, he'd finally decided he could count on Roman again. His brother just kept showing up every time he turned around. Why did he do that? For manipulation?

"I'm only Fury now." An emotion Spencer couldn't identify surfaced in Roman's eyes. He wished it was regret, but that might just have been what he wanted to see.

"Then you need to leave. You don't belong in Safe Dawn, and you know it." If he sounded cruel, then so be it. He wanted him out of his sight. He'd just asked his brother to help him, something he'd never done before, and he'd been unequivocally denied.

Nodding, Roman turned toward the door. He stopped and looked at Addison. "Do you still have what I gave you?"

"Those numbers? Yes, but I have no idea what they are. If you aren't going to be more forthcoming, then maybe you should do what Spencer asked and just get out of here." Roman smirked.

It was the final straw. Spencer launched himself at Roman, tackling him to the ground and punching him hard on the nose. Behind him, he heard Addison gasp.

Laurel yelled, "Addison, you have to stop him! Assaulting a Fury is a death sentence!"

Addison grabbed Spencer's arm, her nails digging through the fabric of his sleeve. He only had a moment to realize how hard she must be gripping him before Roman landed a punch on his nose that made him see stars.

"Stop it," Addison pleaded desperately.

He rolled off Roman as his brother gripped his own nose. He pulled his hand away and realized he was bleeding. He laughed silently. He deserved whatever came out of this. Just because he'd wanted to pound on his brother since he was four years old, didn't mean he actually should have.

Roman stood, tugging on his clothes to straighten them.

"I'm not going to report him, Laurel, so you can stop shrieking like that."

Spencer clenched his fists. "Don't do me any favors, Fury."

"You never did know when to shut up, Spencer." Roman spared Addison one more glance. "With the exception of your feelings for my brother, you seem to be a person who shows great sense and fortitude, Ms. Wade. I'm sure you'll figure out what to do with those numbers."

Tension flowed through the room as they all watched Roman exit.

It was no surprise to him when Tara spoke first. "It's never dull with you, is it, Lewis?"

Addison never gave him a chance to reply. "We don't need him, Spencer. Screw him if he won't take the olive branch you extended to him. Any contacts he has, I have, too."

Unable to help himself, he leaned forward and kissed her. Her lips were soft—as he remembered them—but he could also feel the strength and fortitude in her that he'd been blind to before. His time with Addison might have been limited, but every second was a gift. He regarded her for a moment. "Can you go get us a van?"

She smiled. "I can."

"Hey, Lewis." This time Jack wanted his attention. "What are you going to do?"

"I'm going to sneak all of you out of here. Who wants to go for a ride to retrieve a little boy?"

TWENTY

In other circumstances, Addison might have been amused. The group from Safe Dawn gaped at everything they saw through the car window. She realized that at some point in her life she would have thought their childlike wonder at seeing a fast food restaurant fascinating. It might have reminded her not to take anything for granted.

But at that moment she was just pissed and irritated. All she could focus on was that it had taken two hours—one hundred and twenty goddamned minutes—to rent a van. The incompetence of the man behind the counter had been enough to make her head spin. They'd had the van; she had a really good credit card. Why had the process taken so long?

She gripped her hands in her lap in anger as she stared out the window in the front passenger side. Had the time delay cost them the element of surprise? Would Daniel and Loretta know that Priscilla wasn't coming back to her body, or would they think she was still battling it out in dark space with Spencer?

"You're thinking too much about things you can't

control," Spencer said from the driver's seat. He'd driven only once, but now, outside of Addison, he was the expert in the car. "Or I'm driving really badly. Which one is it?"

She didn't want to smile, but he amused her. Damn. Why was it so easy for him to make her happy? "Two hours, Spence. Two frickin' hours."

He nodded. "So it's not the driving, then?"

"No, you're doing well. If you can drive stick, you can drive automatic."

"This certainly doesn't have the kick of your sports car."

She laughed. That was such a male statement. "You've driven exactly twice in your life, and you're already a car snob."

"Hey, you're the one who owns the car."

A groan sounded from the back seat. No surprise, it was Tara. "Go get a room; spare us all this endless flirtation."

Addison whirled around to stare at Tara and was struck again by how much the car stunk like orange air freshener. She wondered if she'd have to pay a fee for blood damage to the car if she bashed Tara's head against the window.

"You know, we could have left you at home."

Tara crossed her arms. "I can be pretty damn effective when I want."

"Raising the dead is not all it's cracked up to be." Gina had been relatively quiet for most of the trip. "I can only do it for short periods of time. And it's not pretty—they look however they looked when they died... or worse if they've started to decompose."

Addison shuddered.

Tara snickered. "So here's a question, rich girl."

God, she could really do without Tara's new nickname for her. She hoped it didn't stick. "Yes?" She ground the word out between clenched teeth.

"How do you know we're going to the right warehouse? I mean, you're probably right about this Grace Ann person being responsible for it, but don't you think the company has multiple shipping warehouses?"

Holland perked up in his seat. "It's a good question."

Addison sighed. She was going with her gut on this one. Still, she might be wrong. "They only have one warehouse in the Northeast, and it's in Pennsylvania. The rest of them are out west or in Texas. I just don't think they'd want to move Jeremy that far. It seems too risky. Grace Ann is a smart, calculating woman. Whatever her reasons for doing this—and honestly I don't care at this point what they are—she'd want to minimize exposure. Kidnap Jeremy and take him away to a safe, secure location nearby that she can control." Looking down at her feet, she tried to will her pulse to slow down. "Of course, I could be wrong and be dragging you all on a wild goose chase."

Russell spoke first. "Then at least we all got out of Safe Dawn for a cool ride in the car."

She looked up just in time to see the big green sign with the white letters letting them know they had reached Allentown, the location of the warehouse. She took a deep breath as she pointed out the sign to Spencer. He swerved to the right to make the exit. Gasping, she gripped the side of the van, hoping he didn't tip them over.

Jack shouted from the backseat. "What on Earth possessed you to let him drive?"

"Hey, I'm still learning here, okay?" Spencer didn't sound at all repentant, and she wondered if he actually liked the adrenaline of the near miss. It wouldn't surprise her to find out he had the fascination of a teenage boy with things that went fast. "It just has a different center of gravity than Addison's car."

"Hey, Addy." Holland had taken to using her nickname like they were friends.

He had knocked her unconscious; maybe he thought that gave him certain rights.

"When we're done with this, can you teach me to drive?"

Addison had a feeling that when they were "done with this," she wouldn't be teaching anyone anything. She'd be lucky if she got out of there with Jeremy intact, without getting herself hauled off to Safe Dawn, or sent to jail for murdering Grace Ann Charters.

"If I live through this and I can get us to a car, Holland, I will teach you to drive."

Tara snorted. "We'd all like to learn. Can you make a signup sheet?"

She had a vision of herself opening up a driver's education school that specialized in the Conditioned.

She directed Spencer to the warehouse. Ironically, she'd been there once before. When she'd been in high school, her class had done a project on the life of a product from creation to consumption. Her grandfather had called Grace Ann, and she'd gone on a tour of the facility to see where liquor was stored before it was sent out to the stores.

Luckily, she had a good sense of direction. She'd looked up the address and found her bearings by searching the internet on her phone and plugging it in. This place, however, seemed like it had been designed to mess with the phone's GPS. It wasn't locating it correctly. This had to have been manipulated by the Council.

After a few starts and stops, they arrived at their destination. As they pulled up, the people in the car got quiet. The warehouse looked all but abandoned. Even though it was Saturday, Addison was surprised there wasn't at least a little activity in the area. Most of the houses they'd passed in the same vicinity were old and run-down.

The sign on top of the wooden, multi-storied warehouse was only partially lit, making visible only the C, ART, and S of the name CHARTERS. She bit her lower lip as she wished she'd spent a little less time bemoaning the rental car and a little more doing some quick research on the financial affairs of the Charters family. Could this be just a simple case of extortion? Did they want the Wades to pay? Were they going out of business? Why had there been no ransom request?

"Ready?" Spencer cut into her musings. She nodded, climbed out of the van, and followed him toward the warehouse.

Reaching the outside door, Spencer tried the handle. "It's locked."

"Did you think it was going to be that easy?" She was keeping the sound of her voice very low.

He shrugged. "No. This is me, after all. Things don't go that easily for me." Raising an eyebrow, he stared at her with an unreadable expression on his face. "You don't happen to have another hair pin, do you?"

Addison banged on the heavy, partially-rusted, industrial-strength door lock. "I don't think this one is going to open with a hairpin and your nifty finger tricks."

"My nifty finger tricks?" He grinned, and she blushed as she realized what she'd just said. "Girl, you're going to give me a hard-on at exactly the wrong time. Keep your dirty thoughts to yourself for the moment, won't you?"

"That's not what I meant and you know it."

"No one teases you very much, do they?"

She shook her head. Before Spencer, no, there hadn't been anyone who had teased her, not even her parents.

"I would say we could remedy that, but after I get Jeremy out of here, it's unlikely we'll ever see each other again." He walked toward the others, presumably to tell them what was going on.

As soon as they recovered Jeremy, she would cease to have a reason to see Spencer. It wasn't like she could go and visit. Her heart pounded and tears sprang to her eyes. She could feel energy surging inside her. Oh hell, she was going to have another attack.

No, she corrected herself, not an "attack." She had to stop thinking about them in that way. They were powers, and at least with this crew of people, she didn't have to hide them. Priscilla had said that people who moved in dark space could do a lot of things even in the "real" world. She narrowed her eyes as she tried to contain the power surge for a few more minutes.

She'd broken a window. Maybe she could break a lock.

Concentrating, she pushed her energy at the lock, keeping her gaze focused entirely on the hardware. As the energy poured from inside her through her skin, she shook— the pain of trying to contain what, by nature, did not want to be contained was agonizing. She felt her knees start to give and willed herself to stay standing. Strong arms grabbed her around the waist, supporting her in an upright position.

Spencer's angry whisper steamed her ear. "What the hell are you doing?"

"Getting us inside."

With a snap, she heard the lock give as it broke into three pieces and collapsed to the ground. She sagged in Spencer's arms, letting him take all her weight while she collected herself.

"Are you nuts? You practically burned out in dark space

today. Now, you want to play around out here? You're going to give yourself a brain hemorrhage."

"That's possible?"

Spencer laughed and kissed her cheek. "Yes, that's possible, my little naïve Wade girl. Half the people the Fury catch are found in hospitals suffering from brain bleeds. They overdo it."

"Why are you laughing at me?" Really, some day she was going to have to figure out exactly what it was that Spencer found funny, because he always seemed to be laughing at the most inopportune times, and usually at her expense.

"You know so much about some things and then zero about a whole slew of other stuff."

"I've deliberately gone out of my way to know nothing about the Condition. I didn't want to get caught." She took a deep breath and released it a moment later. "You can put me down now. I can walk."

He hesitated, his arms still tight around her. After a moment, he let her feet touch the ground, not letting go until she stood for a few seconds without collapsing. Spencer would hate the description if she vocalized it, but more and more she realized just how kind and considerate he was.

He waved his hand, beckoning the others to the door. Quietly, she pushed it open, slowly at first until she was certain it wasn't going to creak. They stepped into a dark room, empty except for two run-down trucks. One had the hood open, like someone had been looking at the engine, and the other was missing its wheels.

Addison shivered. It might just have been her imagination, but the room seemed ten degrees colder than outside. Spencer pointed to a staircase that stood on the opposite side of the room. Pressing a forefinger to his lips in a gesture for them all to be quiet, he moved forward.

Following so closely in his wake that if he stopped short she was going to topple into him, she let him lead them to the stairs.

"Hey!"

A shout sounded behind them, and Addison whirled around. Three guards holding guns ran through the room, one of them screaming on a walkie-talkie that the facility had been infiltrated.

"Addy, go get Jeremy." Spencer grabbed her arm, pushing her toward the stairs. "Jack, go with her. The rest of you with me."

Spencer charged the guards. What the hell was he going to do to them? She opened her mouth to order them back when she felt herself propelled forward.

Jack yanked on her hand just as the first shot was fired at them.

"You heard him. Don't argue. We have to trust him if we're going to get through this. C'mon, your nephew is upstairs. Let's go get him."

She spared one more look at Spencer, who had taken cover behind one of the trucks. *Please*, she silently whispered to whoever it was that was in charge of the universe, *please let me see him again.*

The gunfire was deafening but she didn't have time to care. All she knew was that she'd covered her ears with her hands, and she was desperately trying to take the stairs two at a time as she kept up with Jack's fast gait. Her breaths came in gasps as she struggled between fury and blind panic not to trip on the dark staircase.

"Jack!" She shouted to be heard. "Why aren't they firing on us?" It made no sense. If Jeremy was upstairs, it would make more sense to attack the two people trying to get up there than wasting time firing on unarmed people in the main room.

"Russell must be compelling their attention away from us."

"Why doesn't he just compel them to put down their guns?"

"I'm not sure. My guess would be that he tried that and failed. Russ can't get people to do something if all their will is directed on doing it. Clearly, they want to be firing their weapons. He's most likely getting them to do it away from us as an alternative to stopping."

The stairs turned and they arrived at the top, the main room down below and a closed wooden door in front of them.

Jack shouted. "Can you do that thing you do to open doors?"

Addison dug deep to find her power reserves. She was all but depleted.

"Honestly, no."

He nodded like he wasn't surprised. "Then I guess we're going to do this the old-fashioned way."

"What is that?"

"We're going to break it down. On three, we ram into this puppy together." He banged on it, and she watched it vibrate. "It's ancient and it's taken on water. We should be able to get through. It's going to hurt, but we'll do it."

"How do you know so much about carpentry?"

"Wood shop in school."

"They teach wood shop at Safe Dawn?"

"I didn't get caught until I was seventeen. I had three years of high school." He looked her square in the eyes. "Are you ready?" At her nod, he continued. "On three. One... two... three."

Together they banged their shoulders up against the wooden door. She felt it give, but it didn't open. Shooting pains traveled up her arm and down her back.

She grabbed her shoulder and glared at Jack.

"That didn't work."

"Thank you, Ms. Obvious."

"Sarcasm doesn't become you, Jack."

"One more time. This time it will give."

Could her shoulder take another assault? She thought of Jeremy's cherubic face and blond hair, of the way he looked when he woke up in the morning after sleeping for twelve hours, of how his little voice sounded when he said "ice cream," since the long C sound in it made him lisp. Yes, her shoulder could withstand whatever it needed to withstand.

Together they charged the door again. This time, it gave way under their assault and they both fell through the center of the door, landing in a collision on top of the splintered wood.

"Don't move."

Addison raised her head to look at Loretta, who was standing above her holding a gun.

"You." Maybe it wasn't the most articulate answer, but it was the best she could muster considering she'd just broken down a door and she'd been on her last legs as it was.

"Ms. Wade, I wish you'd just stayed away. I would never have let anything bad happen to Jeremy. Now I'm going to have to kill you."

Loretta sounded annoyed, like someone had just told her she needed to renew the registration on her car or go to the dentist.

"Addison..." Jack's voice startled her. "You know what my particular power is, don't you?"

Clearing her throat, she looked at Jack, who lay as sprawled out in the wreckage of the door as she did. "I do. I was really hoping you wouldn't have to use it."

"Me too. Listen, when I say run, I want you to get up and run. It's not pretty. She's not just going to fall to the ground."

"What are you two jabbering about?" Loretta looked between them.

Addison was glad Loretta didn't know what Jack could do.

Ignoring Loretta's question, she looked at Jack. "She's holding a gun."

"She'll never get a chance to fire it. Now *run*."

Needing no other direction, Addison did as instructed. She wasn't sure why. Maybe it was that he wasn't as accurate with his power as he'd like and he was worried she could die, too. In any case, she wasn't going to turn around to find out. She heard Loretta let out a scream and Jack's yell of agony before she rounded the corner and ran down a long hallway.

Where was Jeremy? Was he in one of these rooms?

An explosion rocked the hallway, and Addison gripped the wall. It felt like an earthquake had shaken the warehouse. What the hell was that? Pushing herself forward, she prayed she wasn't going to fall over.

"Hello, Addison Wade."

A male voice she didn't know filled the hallway. "Who's there?"

Was it just her imagination, or had the hallway gotten longer and was it swaying slightly?

"Have you come to *play* with us?"

"What?"

"I like to *play,* and I've been expecting you."

Whoever it was speaking to her had an almost childlike quality to his voice. It didn't matter. She had to find a way to move forward. Only now the hallway spun in a series of red, blue and green swirls. Oh God, what was happening?

She fell to her knees, hoping the spinning would stop as a high, maniacal laugh filled her ears. "Oh, we're going to *play*, Addison Wade. I own you now."

TWENTY-ONE

"I thought you had this under control." Spencer looked at the raging fire that had caused the explosion and rocked the warehouse only moments earlier. He wanted to throttle Tara.

"Look, I'm not used to being out of Safe Dawn. I underestimated my power. I guess it grew while I wasn't using it." For once in her life, Tara sounded sheepish. "It got the job done, didn't it? How was I supposed to know there was still gasoline left in that car?"

Spencer looked at the car in question... or rather what was left of it. Thank God they'd taken refuge behind the one that had the tires off and not the one that had the hood open, or they'd all have been toast now. The whole building was burning around them except the small portion where they were momentarily protected by the abandoned vehicle.

Tara was right on one account; it had gotten the job done.

Those guards had been fried.

"Put out the flames so we can get out of here."

Tara stammered. "Here's the thing, Spence—"

He interrupted. "Oh, for fuck's sake, Tara, you aren't going to tell me that you can't? We're going to burn to death because you can't put them out?"

"I don't appreciate that kind of language." Tara's eyes blazed.

"Don't threaten me, Tara. I'm pinned down behind a car, hot as hell, as I get ready to die in a really painful way instead of being up there"—he pointed to the staircase —"with her."

"I can't turn off these flames. They've gotten out of my control, and God forbid I keep you from your little eye-swirly friend."

"What does that mean?"

"When the two of you are together, you both get these weird eyes. They swirl."

"I've never noticed Addison's eyes swirling." Even though she kept insisting his did, but he wasn't going to discuss that with Tara.

"Then you're not looking hard enough."

Russell's furious voice sounded from the left of him. "Would the two of you stop bitching and put out these flames, or do you plan on just staying here until we're all scorched?"

"You be quiet." He wondered if his head could literally explode from frustration. "If either you or Holland had managed to use your abilities, I wouldn't have had to ask Tara to torch the place to begin with. You're not in a position to complain."

Gina swore loudly. "Enough." She stood up.

"Gina, are you nuts? Get down here! You're going to be hurt." Getting his best friends killed had not been on his agenda when he'd woken up that morning.

How was it that everything had spiraled so completely out of control?

Pointing her left hand at the two dead guards on the ground, whose skin had been all but flayed from their bodies, she took a deep breath. "Rise."

As he watched transfixed, the two nearly charred figures stood from their places on the floor. Their skin had almost melted from their bodies, their faces a distorted mess of red and orange muscle and skin tissue that sagged down from their eye sockets. They turned to "look" at Gina, giving Spencer a completely unobstructed view of their melting flesh. It took everything he had not to hurl.

Gina's voice was harsh when she spoke. "Keep it together, Lewis."

Next to him, Tara covered her mouth with her hand and gagged. God, he wished he could cover his eyes.

"Go to the fire alarm and pull it," Gina instructed the corpses. She looked down at Spencer. "This place is way old. It has one of those old-fashioned alarms. Once they push it, hopefully it should trigger water to come out of those valves on the ceiling." She paused. "Assuming they still work."

"And if they don't?"

Gina sighed. "I'll just have the two of them do something else to help until their bones burn too far to be malleable and movable. Then we'll have to think of something else."

Moments later, a shrill alarm bell assaulted his ears, followed immediately by sulfur-scented water falling out of the ceiling. Feeling exhausted, he reacted slowly and didn't cover his head before a flood of water, obviously meant to save equipment, nearly drowned him from above.

The water slammed into the room below at a force that

rendered him unconscious. When he came to, he found he was awash in a flood moving the group toward the truck entrance of the warehouse.

If he didn't think of something, they were going to slam into the wall. Just then he heard Jack shouting his name. Wrenching his neck, he saw Jack running down the steps holding a large piece of what looked like it had been some kind of door.

Jack threw himself onto the ledge of the stairway and held out the front half of the door on the water. "Guys, grab this."

Looking behind him, he counted heads and was relieved everyone was with him and conscious. He grabbed the wood hard, splinters jamming into his hands. At least he wasn't going to hit the wall and be smashed like a fly hitting the windshield of a car. Each of his friends in turn grabbed the wood, except Laurel, who missed it and managed to grab Tara instead.

Jack was brave, but clearly struggling to hold on to the door with the onslaught of water.

"How long can you hang on?" Spencer wasn't a judge of these things, but if he had to guess, it would be a few minutes before the water made its way to the door.

Holland gripped the side of the door and used it to slide toward the ledge where Jack stood. After he pulled himself up, he extended his hand to Spencer. He followed the larger man's suit and pulled himself onto the ledge. "All three of us, we'll pull them up."

He used his back and what remained of his strength to tug the board and those who remained hanging onto the ledge. After they succeeded, he fell backward, breathing hard.

Jack laughed. "The next time you suggest a trip out of Safe Dawn, I'm going to think twice."

Spencer grinned. "Ah... you love the adventure and you know it." Rolling over onto his stomach, he regarded Jack. "Good thing you showed up when you did. Where did you get the board?"

Jack closed his eyes. "Long story."

"I want to hear it, but first things first, where's Addison?"

Lids flying open, Jack sat up. "Hell, in all the excitement, I forgot. I can't get to her. She went down the hallway while I was killing Loretta, and I can't pass the illusion Daniel put on the damn place."

Adrenaline surging through his body, Spencer leaped to his feet. He'd been glad not to see her during the flood, thinking she was safe. Hands shaking, he ran to the steps, taking them as fast as his body could handle. Someone called from behind, but he didn't stop to see who it was.

All of his attention was focused on getting to the woman he loved. He'd never even told her. There was no way he was going to lose her to Daniel. If the man liked death so much he wanted to fake it, Spencer would be happy to show him the real thing. And if he'd dared to harm a hair on her head...

He couldn't let himself follow that thought to its natural conclusion. He'd go mad even contemplating it. Turning the corner, he saw Loretta lying on the floor, eyes open and glassy.

He had no time to dwell on the fact that Jack had broken his cardinal rule of never using his powers. A series of ten steel doors stood side by side on the west wall. Behind one of them was the hallway. He closed his eyes to collect himself. No wonder Jack had had a problem.

Daniel's message was clear. Whoever got in there was going to have to first figure out which of the doors was real, and then get it unlocked to get to Addison. He tried to look at it logically. Daniel was a master of illusion, but he couldn't be absolutely perfect at it. There was no such thing as perfection in anything. There had to be a slight difference between the door that was real and the doors that were not. Unless...

Spencer closed his eyes and forced himself into dark space. His mind was tired—it really didn't want to go—but he fought until he made it inside. He took a deep breath and looked around, joy filling his soul. He'd been right. *None* of the doors were real. They looked real, and he'd bet if he tried to touch them, his brain would think he could feel the door with his hands. But you couldn't hide in dark space.

He could walk right through. He left dark space and clutched his forehead as a migraine began to form. There was no time to deal with that now. With long, confident strides he walked straight through the doors that didn't really exist.

The act of moving through the illusion destroyed it, and when he walked into the hall, the doors disappeared behind him. He heard a gasp and focused his attention on the scene in front of him. Addison lay shivering on the floor, gripping her head and begging Daniel to make the room stop spinning. Standing over her, Daniel looked like a king making a peasant beg for forgiveness.

Seeing Daniel tormenting Addison made him see red. Anger took over his mind with one thought repeating over and over in his consciousness: kill Daniel.

Spencer launched himself at Addy's tormentor.

He charged and had one moment of satisfaction as the other man's face creased with terror before his fist collided with Daniel's chin. As the two hit the floor, with Spencer on top, he pounded Daniel with every bit of energy he had. No part of Daniel's body was left untouched. There was no doubt what he wanted—every part of his soul called out for Daniel's total destruction. The man had dared to harm—no, torment—the only woman who had ever meant anything to Spencer. Not to mention taken part in the kidnapping of a helpless child.

Strong hands pulled him away. He fought like an animal to be free; he needed to inflict more pain on Daniel.

"Dude, he's dead." Jack's voice barely penetrated the angry haze that had formed in his brain. "He's dead."

He tried to comprehend Jack's words. Daniel was dead. Spencer had killed him. He shrugged off his friend's hold as he looked at the bloody mess on the floor. This was real. He had killed the heap that lay beneath him. Taking deep breaths, he tried to make the craziness exit his body. He looked down at Addison. She looked up at him from the floor where she was huddled against Laurel, who had probably tried to heal her after the ordeal.

Searching her face, he tried to see whether there was any condemnation in her eyes.

He couldn't find any, but he had to say something.

"Addison, I..."

She stood. "Don't say anything, Spence. He had me trapped for so long I wasn't sure I was ever coming back. It was hell. I wanted him dead." She swallowed. "Maybe I'm bloodthirsty or sick or something, but I'm so glad he's dead." She rubbed her head against his shoulder, then she closed her eyes. "Are you okay?"

His throat felt tight. "I'm okay." He kissed the top of her head and whispered so only she could hear, "I love you."

He hoped that said everything he wanted to convey; he

hoped she understood what that meant. To him, it said, "I killed for you. I would die for you. There is nothing in this world I wouldn't give you if it was in my power to give. I've never said this to anyone else, and I never will again." It wasn't that he didn't want the others to hear; it was just that the first time a person said "I love you," it should be private. Only he had no idea whether it would be the last time as well.

She kept her head pressed against his arm as she turned her face slightly toward him. "I love you, too."

He closed his eyes. So much had happened in such a short time, and they weren't done. Forcing his heavy lids open, he reminded himself that his job wasn't finished yet. He'd rescued the damsel—after she'd rescued him twice— and now they needed to find the child.

"Jeremy."

It was all he needed to say. Addison nodded and let go of his arm. He regarded the rest of the group. Most of them had made a deliberate choice to look away and give them space. Jack, who was usually the most polite out of all of them, had not. He was looking at Spencer with an unreadable expression on his face.

"What?"

Finally, Jack smiled. "You're a lucky man. Most of us in Safe Dawn will never get that, ever."

"I know."

Addison moved ahead of him, opening and closing the doors of empty rooms.

She'd gone through three unsuccessfully. Opening the fourth door, she ran in, and he heard her laugh out loud. He followed her, closing the door behind him to give them privacy.

Addison embraced Jeremy as if she feared he might

vanish into thin air if she let go. His blond head lay on her shoulder, his eyes open but clouded, like he'd been drugged. Spencer believed he had been. Not that he was a doctor, but how else would they have kept a four-year-old so quiet?

"Auntie, Loretta said we were going on a trip." He closed his eyes and snuggled closer to Addison. "I don't like it here. I don't want to come here anymore."

Tears rolled down Addison's cheeks. "Okay, little guy, we won't come here ever again."

The door slammed open and men dressed in black rushed into the room. Coldness filled Spencer's veins. He knew those uniforms—Roman usually wore one. They were Fury guards. Addressed as simply a number, not a name, to preserve their anonymity even from each other, they were fierce and unbeatable.

"You're not going to be taking that child anywhere."

Grace Ann Charters sauntered into the room like she was shopping for shoes. Spencer didn't have to guess where his friends were; the Fury with power-dampening abilities was probably already hauling them into the back of a van.

"You kidnapped him." Addison looked like a lioness prepared to fight anyone who came near her cub.

"Is it really kidnapping? After all, he's my grandson, and nothing bad happened to him."

Addison laughed, a long, hard sound. "I don't know what planet you're from, but I'm afraid it's the one called Delusion. He's not related to you at all, lady, and I'm taking him out of here."

"Didn't your slut sister Jeanne tell you anything before she gave him to you? She seduced my sweet son, Craig, before he was so abruptly taken from us, and the result is in your arms. Now give him to me."

"You don't have a son named Craig. I know all your

children." Addison backed away from Grace Ann and the Fury. There was nowhere to go except out the two-story window, and he wondered if she was going to jump. If he could, he would find a way to help her.

"From my first marriage—the one I never discuss—I had Craig when I was eighteen. He was just twenty when he died. Way too young for your sister to have seduced. Not to mention that she polluted my blood line with that *thing*." The last word was directed at Jeremy. Spencer wanted to smack her—hard.

He scanned the crowd of Fury looking for Roman. He was nowhere to be found. He was both relieved and annoyed. The former because it meant his brother wasn't participating, and the latter because he might have—even remotely—helped them a little bit. As it was, he and Addison were majorly outnumbered and clearly screwed.

"That's why you sent Loretta to us—so you could monitor your 'grandson.' Is that it?"

Grace Ann lifted a perfectly sculpted brown eyebrow. How did women of her ilk do that? "Well, yes, but also because it afforded me a chance to spy on your grandfather. Now give me the Conditioned, Addison. We have plans for him."

"What plans?" Addison continued to back away. "You don't believe the Conditioned should even be left alive."

Spencer stepped forward. She was getting crazed. He couldn't have her doing anything stupid or desperate. Three men in black moved forward.

"I'm not going to do anything. I'm moving to Ms. Wade, okay?"

"That's right." Grace Ann wasn't done talking yet. "I don't think they should be left alive, and that's why I need Jeremy. You see, his disgustingness is quite interesting. He can eliminate—not just dampen but eliminate—powers in all Conditioned people everywhere. Once he gets a little trained, I'm going to wipe the Conditioned from the face of the Earth."

"Oh hell, Grace Ann, do you realize you sound like a megalomaniac?"

"Shut your mouth, Addison Wade, or I'll have someone shut it for you."

Urgency compelled him to speak. "Wade Corporation has shown over and over again that to remove a person's Condition leaves them dead, or at the very least in a permanent vegetative state."

"And your point?"

She really was a sick bitch. "You're going to kill all of us, every one of us?"

"The world will be better off without you."

Addison hollered, "No wonder my sister never told us who his father was. She must have known you were crazy."

"She did have some choice words to say to me—as did your father all those years ago when I presented a similar, albeit less simple, plan of elimination to him. That's why they both had to die."

Spencer watched Addison turn three shades paler. He moved forward again, terrified she was going to faint.

"You killed my family?"

Grace Ann nodded. "Yes, dear, and if you don't put down the child, I'm going to have these men kill you." She glanced sideways at Spencer. "After I have them kill *him,* since you two seem to like each other so much. Touching show in the hallway. I never took you for having a Condition fetish, Addison."

A banging noise sounded in the hall, followed by the

sound of footsteps. "You're not going to kill anyone, Grace Ann."

Spencer could have cried with relief. In his life, he'd never thought he'd be so glad to see Oliver Wade. "Gentlemen, step away from Grace Ann. I'm putting her on committee arrest, which thereby removes your loyalty to her."

Grace Ann blinked rapidly and her mouth formed a perfect O of shock. "You can't do that, Oliver. This boy— he's my grandson, too, and he's one of them. He's Conditioned."

From behind Oliver, Roman moved into the center of the room. He didn't spare a glance in Spencer's direction.

Oliver continued to speak. "I know that, Grace Ann, and that's why number 3 here"—he nodded toward Roman —"is going to take the child now and deliver him to William Rhodes at Safe Dawn for securing."

"No, Grandfather, please," Addison shrieked. "Don't take him. I won't let you take him!"

The Fury moved fast. Two of them grabbed her from behind, pulling her arms back. Roman yanked the child from her arms. Having gotten what they wanted, the two Fury holding her let her go immediately.

"Roman, you can't do that." Addison was begging, but Spencer knew it wouldn't do any good. His brother was a Fury first, second, and third.

Turning his back on the room, Oliver issued one more command. "Take the Lewis fellow, too. He needs to be locked up. He's broken all kinds of rules here today. It might be time to put him down."

"No." Addison's pleas were becoming almost incoherent. Stumbling forward, she grabbed her grandfather's arm. "Take me instead. I'm Conditioned. Not Jeremy. It's me."

"She's lying, Mr. Wade. I've been with her for days." Spencer took a deep, steadying breath. He could do this. Somehow, it wouldn't kill him to say what had to be said. "She's just an attention whore. God forbid this not be about her for two minutes. You guys don't have to take me in—I'll come quietly. Even death would be a relief after listening to your granddaughter yap for so long."

Without sparing her a second glance, he proceeded down the hall. He couldn't let himself look at her or he'd be destroyed. Thank God he'd told her he loved her. *Please*, he prayed for the first time since he was a child to a God he wasn't sure didn't hate him, *please let her remember how I feel*. All he could do was hope his deception had been enough to save her life. Even if his was over.

TWENTY-TWO

Spencer's words struck Addison like a physical blow. She shook her head. She knew what he was doing. In his own way, he thought to protect her. But it was just nonsense. Did he think she could just go on if he was taken away and killed, or "put down" as her grandfather had disgustingly said? There was no way in hell she could let them take Jeremy.

Ears ringing and chest tightening, she ran forward, tears streaming down her face. Spencer walked so quickly toward the waiting Fury van that she barely caught him before he stepped inside.

"Don't do this, Spencer. Tell them the truth. Tell them you were helping me, that this was my fault. Tell them I'm one of you."

Spencer shrugged off her arm as one of the guards opened the back of the armored vehicle and pushed him inside. He looked up at the guard, his expression unreadable, the swirls she'd come to count on missing from his eyes.

"Will you please get this person away from me?"

"Ma'am," one of The Fury addressed her. "We need you to unhand Mr. Lewis immediately." Strong hands grabbed her shoulders and pulled her backward. She fought as hard as she could as she caught Tara's eyes. Tara sat in the truck, her hands cuffed together. Releasing Addison, the Fury moved in front of the truck so she couldn't get near it.

"Tara," she shouted into the truck. "Tell them what I can do; tell them the truth. Make them take me, too."

Tara cleared her throat. "I don't know what she's talking about. She's as normal as they come, except whinier than most."

Why the hell were they all doing this? Would no one help her, no one tell the truth? "Tara." Her voice was strained with frustration as she begged one more time.

Sitting forward in her seat, Tara looked her straight in the eyes. "I hope you'll remember all of us, Ms. Wade, when someday you take over your grandfather's place on the committee."

Addison shuddered. They were all doing this because they thought she could help them on the committee? No, she'd rather die than sit on any board that was headed up by Grace Ann and her grandfather. She whirled around. Maybe it was too late to reason with Spencer, but she wouldn't let them take Jeremy—not when she'd just gotten him back.

Roman approached another truck, her nephew still in his arms. A crack of thunder sounded in the sky, and the clouds opened, pouring rain down on them. She realized numbly it was the perfect ending to a horrible day. No way was she finished. She couldn't be this ineffectual. It just wasn't possible.

She raced to his side and grabbed Roman. He glanced at her, his eyes blank as if he was looking at a person who meant nothing to him; someone he'd never spent any time with at all. "You can't take him, Roman, please."

He spoke to the crowd that was forming behind her. "Committee Member Wade, I do believe your grand-daughter is hysterical."

"Please, Roman, he's just a little boy. We don't actually know that he can do what she says he can do. She could be making it up."

"Jeremy Wade will be tested like any person brought into the institutions. You're welcome to file an appeal with the committee for reconsideration, and I'm sure, especially given your personal relationship with the members of the board, that they will take your concerns into consideration."

Abruptly, he climbed into the truck, Jeremy asleep on his shoulder. Her grandfather grabbed her arm as the roaring of the engines filled the air around them. The sound made her cold inside. Everything she'd had for such a short time, the things that had become the most important elements of her life, were being ripped away, and she would never get them back. They were going to be destroyed. She swallowed the lump in her throat and made her hysterical tears stop by sheer force of will alone. The rain would do her sobbing for her.

When her grandfather spoke, she could hear the deri-sion in his voice. "I'm going to assume all this is out of some misplaced concern for your late sister's child and because you are exhausted."

"He's your great-grandson." Didn't that count at all?

"We are not above the law we help to enforce. If Jeremy is Conditioned, he belongs where others can be kept safe from him, and certainly he's too dangerous to be around you."

She bit her tongue to stop the words she wanted to fling at him. Quickly, she made a crucial decision. Her grandfather and the Fury might have won the day, but it wasn't over —not by a long shot. One way or another, she would get them all back. She *would* triumph over this.

She raised an eyebrow as she placed her practiced superior expression on her face. She regarded her grandfather with the same remoteness that he used on her. "What about Grace Ann? She's all but confessed to murdering Jeanne and Mom and Dad. You can't let that go unpunished. It would be so humiliating for you."

"You let me handle Grace Ann."

She nodded like he'd told her he was going to handle a business account instead of commit murder. That was fine by her. If ever anyone deserved what they clearly had coming, it was Grace Ann Charters. In some ways, it was a relief not to have to handle it herself.

The ride home in her grandfather's car was silent. She noted he had a new driver and wondered briefly if he'd had Gregory killed or if he'd just fired him. How would her grandfather weed out who had betrayed them and who hadn't? In the quiet darkness, she shrugged. It didn't matter. As soon as she figured out what to do, she would leave and never come back.

Finally back in their apartment, she paced around her room, trying to come up with some sort of cohesive plan that she could actually implement. If nothing else, she was a type A, task-oriented person. Surely, she should be able to work through this and come to some sort of conclusion. When her head finally pounded beyond the point that she could stand it, she lay down in the bed with a cold compress over her eyes and let sleep take her.

When she woke with a start, it was still dark outside. She ripped the cool cloth from her eyes. She stood up and rushed to the chair next to her desk.

Methodically, she reached for the sweater she'd abandoned there earlier. Feeling in the pocket, she found what she'd sought: the piece of paper containing Roman's scribbled numbers. Was it too late? Spencer had been taken away. Was it past time to use them? She sighed. It wasn't like she knew what they meant.

She stared at the paper but nothing changed. It was still 18, 22, 64 and 50. Not long enough to be a phone number. No matter how many times she rearranged them, she couldn't seem to form any codes or words based on the numbers. Besides, why would Roman have encoded a message in numbers when he could have just written down what he wanted to tell her using letters?

She set the paper down next to her computer as she went to the kitchen to pour herself some water. She leaned against the counter and tried to recall everything Roman had ever told them. He was such an oddball. She'd discounted most of what he'd said as sibling rivalry with Spencer and his being a valued member of the Fury. But what if it was more than that? What if he'd actually been trying to communicate some information that was relevant?

They'd been standing in Jeremy's room. She'd just brought Spencer back from dark space and he'd come in full of information they'd needed but not known. Realization hit her hard. He'd mentioned a name to Spencer, had wanted to know if he knew who it was. Spencer hadn't. In typical Spencer fashion, he'd been uninterested because it came from his brother. Roman had said it out loud. If he hadn't wanted her to hear it, he wouldn't have done that. If nothing else, he was careful about what he said and did.

Even when he'd taken Jeremy away—something that would always make her blood burn—he'd been gentle with him. The name. She needed her mind to remember. What was it? Like a light dawning, it hit her. Guy McKidd.

Who the hell was Guy McKidd?

Addison rushed to her computer. Spencer might not know him, but this was the time of technology. You could find anything and anyone on the internet. Opening up the search engine, she typed in the name and instantly she saw five hundred pages pop up.

The first few seemed inconclusive. Several people on multiple social networking sites had the name, but a quick review proved they were unlikely candidates. Nothing about them screamed *a-ha*. The next few sites were business sites. Several Guy McKidds worked in business, one was a physician in Cincinnati and two were serving in the armed forces overseas.

None of this was setting off any bells in the "A-ha, I've solved it!" department. She moved to the next page of results, becoming convinced she'd made a mistake and was wasting her time. Her hand paused on the mouse and she read the blurb about the page the browser had suggested. "Conditioned man still missing—police warn public he is extraordinarily dangerous."

Gasping, she clicked the mouse and let the website load. It was a site devoted to the goings on at Earthquake, the institute for Conditioned people on the west coast of the United States. Looking quickly, she knew almost immediately that it was a conspiracy-driven website, and the counter at the bottom of the page showed her it didn't get very much traffic. It didn't matter; in her current circumstances, even weird internet conspiracy theorists knew more than she did. She scanned down the page until she got to the section that dealt with Guy McKidd. Evidently, ten years earlier, a man by his name had escaped from Earthquake and vanished. The police had no leads and no idea where to find him. There was, of course, no mention of the Fury, as the average person believed them not to exist, but Addison knew now beyond a shadow of a doubt that the Fury would have looked for him.

Lower on the page was a follow-up article in which, in two sentences, the police declared that the suspect was dead. The website author had written in a strange font over the article the words "Why so brief on the story of his death?" Addison sat back in her chair, chewing on her lower lip. Actually, that was a pretty good question. Where were all the gory details of his death? Surely, there had to be more to the story than that.

Noticing that Guy McKidd was underlined on the page, she sat forward again and clicked on the link. The website changed to a picture of a man who looked to be in his late twenties, with long hair that went past his shoulders. He stared at the camera, giving whoever had taken the picture the finger. Addison couldn't help smiling as she wondered if they'd run that picture in the newspaper.

She racked her brain and still couldn't remember the story ever making national news. There had to be more to it. She groaned and leaned on the desk, holding her head in her hands. Maybe she was deluding herself. Maybe Roman had just been thinking of two different things, and the numbers had nothing to do with Guy McKidd's disappearance. Snippets of that conversation came back to her. Right after he'd given her the numbers, he'd remarked that he knew she'd sent her crazy aunt to the Caribbean. Well, maybe she was embellishing with the crazy remark. Roman would never have said that out loud—at least not to her.

Addison made herself focus on that point. It was odd that Roman had brought it up at all. Why had he mentioned it?

"Wow. That's it. That's it!" She jumped from her seat. Could it be that easy? She looked down at the numbers again. It had to be. She couldn't have come to this conclusion if it weren't true.

She ran back to the computer. Her aunt was in the Caribbean, and she would bet any money that if she plugged those numbers in as longitude and latitude coordinates, it would take her to a place in the Caribbean. That was where Guy McKidd was hiding, and Roman had been trying to tell them that was where they could go to get away.

18, 22, 64 and 50. 18°22 N 64°50 W placed them smack in the middle of the ocean, just north of St. Croix in the American Virgin Islands. It was international waters with no major landmasses to speak of. She rubbed her nose. The Caribbean was littered with small, nothing islands— some owned privately, some not. She didn't bet—what was the point of giving someone the money you'd earned for nothing? Except in this case, she'd wager any money that Guy McKidd was on one of those islands and the Fury couldn't touch him because they only had American jurisdiction.

Every country had its own version of the committee— well, the ones that didn't execute the Conditioned immediately. If that island belonged to no one—if it was privately owned and the people on it were "dead" and not paying taxes—the possibilities were endless. Why didn't every Conditioned person escape there? *Duh.* She felt like smacking her forehead. Because no one told them, no one explained it, and the people who knew—like William Rhodes—were in the business of making sure it didn't come out. What would Rhodes be without Safe Dawn? Just another Conditioned man not welcome in America. As it was, with the status quo, he was important, relevant...

She blinked and got back on track. This still didn't solve the problems in front of her. Spencer and Jeremy were locked up in Safe Dawn. Spencer was probably due to be executed. Even *if* she could somehow get a boat and *if* she was right about all of this and Guy McKidd really was on that island and they could go there and hide away to live their lives, it still meant she had to get them out of Safe Dawn. Somehow, she suspected she was no longer going to be welcome inside. Not to mention, she couldn't leave the others—they all belonged to her now. The crew that had helped her deserved their freedom, too.

Like a child with a toy, she spun around in her chair until she got dizzy and jerked it still. Every problem had a solution, and so did this. How could she sneak them out? It would take bribing the guards. No. She shook her head. It wouldn't.

She knew what she needed to do; she just had to get inside the walls. Grinning from ear to ear, she rose from her seat. There was a way into Safe Dawn. She knew that from firsthand experience.

Once again, she turned to the internet. Typing the words "sex with Conditioned men" into her search engine made her cringe. When this was over, some authority would likely seize her computer and find that in her cache—even if she tried to disguise it, which she didn't intend to do. They'd write her off as a sexually depraved loony based on that search alone.

Message boards where women discussed and described

their sex with Conditioned men popped up on the screen. She clicked on the first one, distressed to see that Spencer warranted his own section. For a moment she debated looking at it before deciding it was a really bad idea. He said he didn't participate in the sex parties, and she believed him. Instead she clicked on the phrase "Sex Party."

After moments of searching what she was certain were illegal websites, she found a phone number to call if she wanted a good time with Conditioned men. She looked at the clock; it was four in the morning. *Oh well.* Whoever was running this thing couldn't be keeping regular business hours.

After two rings, a man answered. "Hello?"

"Yes, hello, I got your number from a website called deviancealliance.com." She took a deep breath. "I want to have sex with Conditioned men."

She closed her eyes as she said it out loud. Even the day before, she couldn't have imagined having this conversation. Now it wouldn't even be amongst the strangest things she had done.

"Then you called the right place. You're lucky, we're about to take the number down. It's been up for too long. Periodically we have to change websites."

"Yes, well, then it's my lucky night." She cleared her throat. "I want to have sex with Conditioned men."

"Right, you said that. It doesn't come cheap. To get into an institution, you'll need to fork over one thousand dollars."

Okay, not a problem. "Wow." Better not to seem too interested. "Okay. If that's what it costs, that's what it costs. When can I get into Safe Dawn?"

"Wait a minute, girlie. Who said anything about Safe Dawn? I heard that place has gone into lockdown. Not sure what's going on over there. I can get you into Earthquake or Silver Dust."

"No, it has to be Safe Dawn." She left the unspoken "damn it" out of her speech. "Look, mister... what is your name?"

"You can call me Prometheus."

"Is that some kind of Frankenstein reference?"

"What?"

"Never mind." She sighed. "It has to be Safe Dawn. It's the only one I'm interested in."

"I told you, no can do."

She looked at her clock. Five minutes had passed since she'd gotten on the phone. Enough was enough already. "I'll give you twenty thousand dollars for Safe Dawn tomorrow."

Prometheus sucked in an audible breath. "I'll make it happen, but you have to hand-deliver the money right away."

"I'm in the New York City area."

"That'll work." He gave her an address in the Village and told her to ask for someone named Zeus. She rolled her eyes. She was going to a drag club at four in the morning to deliver twenty grand to a man named Zeus. Life had never been so completely out of her control.

She hung up the phone and looked at her computer one more time. There were two things left to do. The first was to break into Wade Corporation's mainframe. When she was done, it would take them six months to locate their boats and weeks to determine that she'd stolen one. Her grandfather had thought it a waste of time for her to learn how the system operated, but it was going to turn out to be time well spent. After that, she needed to make a phone call to her friend who helped run one of the morning news segments.

Tomorrow night, she would either have broken them all

out and be on her way to her new life, or she'd be locked up with them.

Either way, she was through.

She was Addison Wade, and she was done hiding. Screw the world if they didn't like it.

TWENTY-THREE

Oliver waited to see Grace Ann's eyes flicker open. Her head hung down in front of her body, her neck no longer able to support the weight of her head as she was tied sitting up in a chair. For a moment, a blank, confused expression crossed her features before memory and realization reconvened in her eyes.

"Oliver." Her voice was no more than a croak. Torture and abuse at the hands of the Fury could do that to a person. He wouldn't know from personal experience, just from watching the events he'd ordered to take place on twelve different occasions. Not too many, considering he'd been on the committee for thirty years.

He yawned. "Yes, Grace Ann?"

"Surely as two reasonable, rich, powerful people, we can work something out between the two of us?"

"No, Grace Ann. You see, *I'm* a reasonable, rich, powerful person." He stood up from the wooden chair that made his back ache. At his age, that was happening more and more often. Maybe it was time to find a chiropractor. "All you are now is a talking corpse." He looked at the Fury—number seven, the one he always called on for this kind of activity because of the joy the man seemed to take in using the instruments. "Finish her."

He walked down the hall and then through the steel doors that led outside.

Someday, he supposed, he'd have to tell Addison about these secret rooms. She would need to run what went on down here. He rolled his eyes. The way the girl had acted at the warehouse, it might be another decade before he hardened her up enough to take over Wade. She clearly needed more time in the trenches. Perhaps it was time to send her back into the stock houses to do cattle inventory again.

Not that it had helped the last time he'd ordered her there. Rather than letting it beat her down, she'd reorganized the cattle houses, making them run at top efficiency. The memory made him grin. He might give her a hard time, but she was a credit to him in many ways.

He heard the click behind him that meant the steel doors had resealed. He was surprised to see the Fury with designation three standing in front of him, holding some sort of translucent ball in his hands.

He pointed to the object he didn't recognize. "What is that?"

"Wade Corporation made it. It's a static electricity ball. It gives out just enough of a push to make a Conditioned person better able to control their unusual abilities."

"I never gave the order to have that made." It was a stupid waste of money. He didn't want them getting control of themselves. That would mean people would start to demand they have rights, and no one knew better than he did that the Conditioned should never be allowed back into society.

"Addison suggested it be made five years ago when she

first started at Wade. I doubt she even remembers she did it. Probably she just signed a piece of paper authorizing the money and didn't look at it again."

"That's Ms. Wade to you, number three."

Number three nodded. "As you say, Committee Member Wade. You're right, it's Ms. Wade. Needless to say, when I read about it in the Conditioned reports, I never forgot that she did that."

"It was wasteful spending, and when she gets back to work, I'm going to speak to her about it."

"Shall I just get rid of it from the building?"

Oliver narrowed his eyes. "What is your Condition, number three? Remind me. I always think of you as the smart one, and I can't seem to fathom why you were locked in Safe Dawn to begin with."

The Fury smiled. "Among other things, I'm a power dampener. That's my main ability."

Oliver's head felt fuzzy. The usual buzz that allowed him to reason out any problem was eluding him. Maybe he needed to see a doctor, or maybe he was just getting old. In any case, he was going home. "What was it that you asked me?"

"Sir, I inquired as to whether or not you wanted me to get rid of this?" He held up the strange-looking ball. "To remove it from the building?"

Waving his hand in a dismissive gesture, he nodded. "Do whatever you want to do with it, Fury."

"Yes, sir." Number three smiled at him, but there was no joy in it.

"Oh, number three, before you go, tell me something. Why is it that you suddenly look so familiar to me? I know I've known you, seen you trained since you were nine but why now is there also this 'otherness' about you that I find familiar?"

The blond man cleared his throat. "Maybe it's because you just signed my younger brother's death warrant. I'm told we have a very similar look."

"Lewis is your brother?"

"Spencer is, yes." Still holding the ball, the Fury walked toward the exit. "We're both Lewises. Don't worry, though. I'm Fury through and through. I swore an oath to be, and I always keep my promises. I won't interfere in Spencer's punishment. If he's in Safe Dawn tomorrow morning, he'll be executed with no help from me."

Oliver nodded. They were good sentiments—just the kind that years of training and drilling and brain manipulation in the Fury academy programmed into the young men and women selected for it.

"Very good, then."

"Good night, sir."

He didn't answer. What business was it of his whether or not he had a good night?

Walking toward the exit, he hummed the opening song of *The Sound of Music*.

Funny, he hadn't thought about that musical for years. Why was it in his head?

———

"YOU KNOW, if you had come to me, perhaps I could have helped you."

Spencer looked up from his study of the floor tiles in his prison to see William Rhodes standing in the room. He hadn't heard him come in. That was how out of it he currently was.

"Come to you? Like you came to me and told me your concerns when Priscilla," he couldn't help his dark laugh, "died? I walked around here like the living dead for months, feeling responsible for that, and you didn't utter a word." He paused as a thought occurred to him. "Or was it that you weren't sure you could trust me? You didn't know if I was involved in it, too?"

Rhodes shook his head. "Emphatically no. I knew you weren't in on her deviousness. I just wasn't sure you would believe me without proof. You believed her, and one of your biggest faults—and strengths—is that you hold tight to those you consider friends."

Spencer sighed. He was sitting on the bed. It was, after all, the only place to sit in the room, which contained only a bed and a toilet, not even a window. He laid his head against the wall. "So you decided to go to Roman?"

"Is that what bothers you the most about this? That I went to your brother?"

"No." Spencer sighed. "What bothers me the most about this is that Jack and Tara are going to die along with me, and Gina is going to spend the rest of her natural life locked up in the static room."

He knew unequivocally that had they been able to prove that Minnie and Marisa had been involved, they would be joining Gina in the static lockup. Laurel, Russell, and Holland were in trouble for leaving the institute. They'd probably have clean-up duties for years but weren't in any physical danger.

"Then maybe you shouldn't have dragged them out on a suicide mission with you."

"There was no way to get Jeremy without them."

Grace Ann was a sick, deranged woman and rescuing

Jeremy would have turned out to be a blessing for all of them. The woman was going to use Jeremy to kill them all.

Rhodes pounded the wall with his fist, his eyes flashing and his skin flushed. "You could have come to me."

Wow. Spencer raised an eyebrow. Rhodes was really angry. He actually couldn't remember ever seeing the head of Safe Dawn so mad before.

"I couldn't."

Even now, he wouldn't tell William why that was. Addison had to be kept safe at all costs. If his life was over, she still had hers in front of her, and maybe someday she'd be able to fix things on the committee. Not to mention that his love for her was such a large, palpable thing that even hours away from where she was, he could feel her filling the places inside him that should have long ago died from emotional neglect.

Rhodes crossed the room and sat down on the bed next to him. "You know I had you as one of the candidates to take over for me when I stepped down."

Spencer cracked up. "That's ridiculous."

"It wasn't. Everyone here respects you. They listen to you. You solved all those cases on the outside, giving you a certain amount of respected notoriety, not to mention that I think you would have liked the job." Rhodes rested his head in his hands, leaning on his knees. "Now, instead, I get to walk you down the hall to where they'll end your life tomorrow."

"How will they do it?"

"They'll inject you with something."

Spencer nodded. He supposed he should have been more worked up about his death. The week before, he would have railed against the unfairness of it all. Since he'd met Addison, things had changed. Even though it had been brief, he'd really lived for the first time in his life; he'd finally known what it was to feel like a man and to know the love of one of God's angels on Earth. That was how he'd think of Addison for the next few hours of life: as a gift sent down from Heaven for him alone.

He wouldn't have believed it possible, that someone like that existed for him. Because of her, he had to question all the other things he'd believed. If Addison was Conditioned, then there was no way that all Conditioned people were doomed for Hell. The divine wouldn't be that cruel. She was obviously a creature of goodness and light. Maybe that meant he was, too.

Shrugging, he realized that one way or the other, he'd know soon. He'd either go up or down when the time came. There were still some questions he needed answered before that happened.

"Let me ask you a question, if I could."

William looked up at him, straight in the eyes. "Ask."

"Have you ever heard of a scenario where a Conditioned man and woman met and they sort of changed each other, even physically? Strange manifestations, like swirling eyes and stuff like that. I'd heard a rumor that such a thing could happen."

Rhodes smiled. "I haven't heard about it happening for years, but yes, thirty years ago, when we first opened these places, we saw it start to happen with some of the teenagers. They would connect—grow stronger—and their eyes would change. It was like an external signal of the internal strength."

"What happened to all of them?" It might have been nice to think about a "what if" scenario while he waited for his time to be up. Actually, he was amazed he'd never heard these stories before. To his knowledge, he'd never seen anyone with swirling eyes walking around Safe Dawn.

"They got to be too strong as a unit. Also, the committee does not want you guys breeding, and something about the connection leads to an almost unstoppable desire to procreate." Spencer gulped silently. That hadn't happened with them yet. A baby? What would that have been like?

"So then what did you do about it?"

"We separated them. One stayed here, the other would get sent somewhere else." The sadness of the world seemed to cross Rhodes' face. "Once parted, they died off quickly. Heartsickness, even though that was impossible, was the cause of death. I would swear it. Sure, it was always something like pneumonia or the flu, but in actuality it was always—as cheesy as it sounds—a broken heart."

Spencer's palms sweated. He wanted to get up and pace even as he made himself stay still. No, that was not acceptable. Addison couldn't mourn for him until she died. That wasn't how he wanted to pass on thinking of her. She wouldn't, couldn't, let that happen. There was Jeremy to consider. He knew the woman; she would never rest until she'd gotten the committee to free that little boy. Yes, he tried to believe, that would sustain her for a time. His breath came quickly. Then what? What would happen to her after she either succeeded or failed to help Jeremy?

Rhodes stood and moved to the door. "I guess I'll see you tomorrow, kid."

"William—is there any chance you could do me one more favor?"

Laughter hit Rhodes' eyes and made them glow. "What can I do for you now, Mister Lewis?"

"I want to see Jeremy Wade." He stood. It was pivotal.

"I just rescued the kid. I'd like to see him for ten minutes. I can't go anywhere. What's the harm?"

"You don't have to sell me. I'll grant you a last request."

Spencer exhaled loudly. "A million thanks. Rhodes, one more thing."

William cocked his head to the side. "What's that, Spence?"

"Can't you do anything for Jack and Tara? She only did that to save our lives, and Jack killed a Conditioned fugitive who didn't have rights to life anyway."

Rhodes' face fell, showing every year of life on his usually jovial features. "The committee thinks they are too dangerous to live. There's nothing else I can do." He turned back to the door before stopping one more time. "You never told me how awful it was hanging out with Addison Wade. Was she a nightmare?"

Spencer hid his grin. "It was something out of a dream, that's for sure."

Rhodes sighed, a glint coming to his eyes that Spencer had never noticed before. Anxiety peaked at the top of his spine. Rhodes had always held a reputation for being ruthless and brutal. The stories were that when the institutions were first opening, he'd killed anyone who hadn't complied with his orders.

"You were right not to come to me." Rhodes turned on his heel to face the door. "I would have told you Addison Wade—or any of the Wades—aren't worth the trouble. I wish I didn't have the kid here. He's going to be nothing but trouble just by existing."

"So you admit it, then—you wouldn't have helped me?"

"Honestly, no, I would have forbidden you to pursue it any further and you'd have disobeyed. As much as I love you kid, I would have had the whole lot of you put down earlier than today."

Spencer wasn't sure what, if anything there was to say about that. He would have been scared, except he was already doomed for death. What more could the man do to him?

HOURS LATER, when the guards finally came to get him to take him to Jeremy, he was still amused over that comment. Rhodes had nodded, missing the subtlety. If everything went well, Spencer would be able to give Jeremy some quick advice and assure his aunt did nothing to harm herself after he was gone.

The room where they put the new juveniles was bright and cheery. It had to be. The kids endured hours of physical and mental testing every day for a year before they were released into the enclosed juvenile hall where they would remain until they were eighteen. During that time, they'd learn to read and do basic math as well as some other "necessary" schooling. They'd also be taught a useful trade. Spencer had thrived at the textile work and failed in the license plate making. It hadn't mattered. As a dark space mover, he hadn't had to participate in the adult slave labor that went on inside the walls. He'd made money for Safe Dawn using his abnormal skills.

Stepping into the room, with its yellow walls and star painted ceilings, was like walking into his past. Twenty-six years earlier, he and Roman had been dragged in kicking and screaming. Well, he'd been crying. Roman had been kicking and screaming. He'd climbed into Roman's bed that night and held on to his five-year-old big brother like he had all the answers in the world, like he could make all the monsters go away.

What would Roman think about his death? Spencer shrugged. What did it matter?

Jeremy sat removed from the three other children in the room. One little boy, dark haired, and two redheaded girls—sisters, he would guess—sat around a table coloring together. Some of the Conditioned considered "safe" enough had designations of caretaker or teacher to the children. None of them were around at the moment. Maybe that had been on purpose. Rhodes wouldn't want to give him access to any adult contact when all he'd promised him was ten minutes with Jeremy.

Jeremy sat on his bed, staring through the bars at the world outside. Spencer sat down next to the little boy.

"Hey, buddy. I don't know if you remember me. I'm Spencer. I'm a friend of your auntie."

Jeremy turned to look at him, and Spencer got a view of the needle marks on his arms and the bruising on his cheeks. The tests had begun quickly. They must not have wanted to waste any time. His eyes were red, and tear stained streaks ran down his chubby face. Spencer's heart clenched. He wouldn't cry in front of the boy; it wouldn't do any good.

When Jeremy smiled, it almost destroyed him. That mouth was all Addison—or maybe it was a Wade trait, not that he'd ever seen Oliver smile—and he looked so much like his aunt in that moment that it hurt.

"I remember you. You were there when Auntie came, before they took me away from her again." The little boy turned to look out the window. "She'll be coming soon."

"No." Spencer's voice broke, and he cleared his throat. "She won't, buddy."

Jeremy turned, regarding him with a very adult, proud

expression that again must have been a family trait. His blue eyes, shaped differently from his aunt's, had an entirely different shade with their gray speckles. They looked older than his four years.

"She's coming."

Okay, he wasn't going to argue with a four year old. He didn't have much time, and the kid would learn fast enough the realities of his new life. "Well, until that happens, I thought maybe I could give you some advice."

"Sure." Jeremy regarded him with interest shining in his eyes.

"Don't eat the meatloaf. It's gross. William Rhodes has a big heart. Make friends with him and then with whoever takes his place. Try to make friends; they will get you through the days here. The housing lottery, when you get old enough to get in it, is completely rigged. Give up your food rations for a good room—you won't regret it. Learn fast and don't make trouble. The guards are not your friends. They'll turn on you for a pack of cigarettes. And last but not least..."

"Yes?"

"Don't lose yourself in here. You don't get what that means yet, but try to remember I said that. If you do see your aunt, can you give her a message for me?"

"You're going to see her, too."

Spencer laughed. "I'm going to have to argue with you on that point. I'm not going to see her. That much I'm sure of. Anyhow, can you tell her she's not to follow me where I'm going until she's good and gray-haired? Can you tell her that?"

"Auntie has blonde hair, not gray hair."

He ruffled Jeremy's golden locks, which matched his aunt's. "I know that."

The door opened and a guard stood in the entrance. "Time's up, Lewis."

"All right." Wow, it had gone quickly. "Take care, little man."

He didn't look at Jeremy again as he walked out of the room. He couldn't.

Losing his cool wouldn't do him any good anymore. The cards had been dealt and his hand was up. There was no use obsessing over things he'd never have. The memories would have to be enough.

TWENTY-FOUR

Addison waited by the secret door. The trepidation she'd felt the first time she'd entered the building was gone. She was focused. The door opened, and she grinned. It was Russell. Fate was clearly on her side.

"Addison," he hissed. "What are you doing here? I'm supposed to be waiting for a woman who paid twenty K for a sex party. Not that anyone here feels like doing that just now..."

"It's me. I'm the girl who paid the money." She grabbed his arm and walked inside, pulling him close to her so she could whisper and not be overheard. "Are there guards around?"

"At the end of the tunnel, waiting for us."

"Listen to me closely. Do you want to get out of here?"

After a few agonizing moments, he spoke. "More than you can possibly imagine."

"I can't free the hundreds of people who live here, but I can take care of our little group if you help me."

"What do you need me to do?"

"Well, first I need you to get me past the guard who's waiting at the end of the hall."

Russell pulled her into his embrace, wrapping an arm around her like a lover might do; she was taut up against his body as they walked through the darkness. Coming into the light of the courtyard, she blinked several times to clear her vision.

"Keep your head down just in case anyone recognizes you," Russell hissed in her ear.

Addison did as he instructed. He pulled her even closer, blocking her from the guards' view.

"I've got her, guys; did you get your money?"

Two voices assented that they had while they whistled and hooted at Russell, telling him to "have a good time" and "give it to her good." When they'd traveled far enough away, she pulled out of his embrace.

"Why do you do it? Why do you have sex with those women?"

"Not all of us are Spencer. Most of us will never get out of here to meet our own version of Addison Wade. Some of us have to take it where we can get it."

Her head spun, and she didn't want to dwell on what he'd just said. She hated to think of Spencer alone in the world, or any of them for that matter. "Where are Spencer, Jeremy and the others?"

"Jeremy is in the juvenile ward. Everyone else is scattered around except Spencer, Tara and Jack, who are all awaiting their executions."

The news made her blood turn cold. She'd heard her grandfather make the proclamation about putting Spencer down. Evidently, he'd meant it.

When she'd composed herself, she answered him. "Tara

and Jack were sentenced because people died when they used their powers."

It wasn't a question. She knew the committee rules; she just needed to say it out loud to mark the moment as the exact spot she gave up any hope that her grandfather could ever change. He'd turned in his great-grandson. She'd hoped in her deepest heart that he'd done it because others had been there to witness it, that if they'd been alone, he would have let her leave with Jeremy. She knew better now. He'd condemned three people to death for saving the little boy. It wasn't that he was heartless. It was that he was devoted, in an almost religious sense, to the system he'd helped to create. He couldn't possibly see that there was any other way to live or that anything might be inherently wrong with the way things were.

"We need Holland, and we're going to need a distraction."

Russell laughed. "He's always good for those."

Moments later, enclosed in Holland's quarters, which were significantly smaller than Jack and Spencer's had been, she explained her plan. It was simple. They needed to create a major distraction. Something large enough that William Rhodes temporarily lost control of his power dampening. Then Holland would knock out some of the guards, giving them the chance to free everybody and make their escape. If it came to it, Russell could use his abilities to convince the guards they wanted to let them walk out the front gate.

Holland nodded, his face serious. "It's so simple it might work."

"Assuming you want to leave, of course." She'd already considered the idea that maybe everyone wouldn't want to.

There was no way she was going to drag anyone out of Safe Dawn who didn't want to go.

"I want to go, no question about that whatsoever."

That was a relief. Her plan, now that Jack and Tara were out of the picture, was going to rely entirely on Holland and Russell and what little she'd be able to contribute.

Holland regarded Russell. "Go get Minnie, Marisa and Laurel. Tell them to stay by the door. I'll go with Addison to the juvenile hall and the execution wing. After you stick them by the gate, go do your thing on the guards watching Gina."

Russell raised an eyebrow. "Who put you in charge?"

Addison rolled her eyes. "No one. I'm in charge." She smiled, touching Holland's arm. "However, I appreciate the help. Let's do what he suggests."

Russell nodded, but his eyes told her he was pissed about having to listen to Holland. She sighed. If they managed to pull this off, it was going to be hard keeping them all from exploding with temper during their escape.

She needed to get him out.

Following close behind Holland, she kept her head down and avoided eye contact with anyone she saw. "Holland, what are we going to do for the distraction?"

"I don't suppose you have any matches?"

"Ah... no, I'm sorry. I didn't think to bring any."

"I didn't think so." He shrugged. "Then we're going to have to get the only one of us who can set fires."

"But I thought Tara was trapped, awaiting a death sentence?"

"She is." He ran a hand through his hair. "Even though that's true, she's the only one of us who can work around Rhodes' power blockage for long enough to create a large enough distraction to break through the dampening. I mean, you saw what happened when I tried to work on you inside the walls here—I screwed it up because I couldn't get proper control."

"How are we going to get to her?"

They arrived at a set of locked steel doors. Holland took a deep breath, smiled at her, then knocked on the door.

"You didn't answer my question. How are we going to get to her?"

"As soon as they answer, I'm going to start throwing punches. Get ready to hide or fight. Your choice."

The door swung open, and a guard who looked to be in his fifties with gray hair and a visible potbelly stepped through. "Holland, you know you can't be here."

"Yeah, I know. You've always been decent to me. Sorry about this, my man."

Without another word, Holland swung his large fist at the guard's head. Not seeing it coming, the older man did nothing to block Holland's attack and crumpled to the floor like a sack of potatoes.

Holland turned back to her. "It won't all be that easy." He raised an eyebrow.

"Coming?"

She nodded. "Absolutely."

For a section of Safe Dawn that was reserved for people "warranting death," the hallway was remarkably quiet and serene, reminding Addison more of a hospital wing than a jail. Holland directed her to the left. They turned the corner and ran into another group of guards. There were three, all much younger than the first guard had been and each one shouting that they shouldn't be there.

Without another thought, she jumped on top of the smallest of the three. He'd been unprepared for her assault and flailed around as she grabbed his ears and scratched his face with her fingernails. He pushed and pulled at her, trying to get her off him. Holland had the audacity to laugh at her as he easily knocked out one and then the other guard in quick movements. Having finished, he stood back as if he were watching a show as she tried to take her guard down.

"Little help here might be appreciated."

Holland glared at the guard, who hit the floor hard, Addison collapsing on top of him.

She sat up and gave Holland what she hoped was a look of death. "I thought your powers weren't working."

"I said I couldn't control them. This man could be out for hours and hours, or just seconds. I have no idea." He gave her his hand, and she stood up. "Tara should be in one of these rooms."

Holland bent and removed a key chain from the belt of the guard she'd attempted to beat down. He handed the keys to her, and at her questioning look he said, "My hands are shaking. I'm not sure I can hold the keys."

She touched his arm. "What's wrong?"

"I guess I'm more worked up than I realized."

Nodding, she said nothing in reply to his confession. She might not know everything there was to know about men, but she knew enough to know that when a six-foot-five, two-hundred-and-fifty-pound man confessed to being overwhelmed, you didn't make too big a deal out of it; you just did what he asked you to do.

There wasn't going to be any way to find Tara than to simply try all the doors until she found her. Fiddling with the keys, she tried them on one door lock until it opened. Turning the key, she pushed open the door and gasped.

Spencer. She hadn't been prepared to see him yet; she'd been so focused on Tara. The room was lit, but dimly, and he slept on his side, facing the wall. His head rested on top of one of his arms, his breathing was deep and even. For a man who was about to be executed, he seemed remarkably undisturbed.

Walking to his bed, she sat on the edge of it and ran her hands over his face, feeling the two days' worth of stubble. The rough texture on her fingertips sent a thrill into her core. Maybe he should leave it like that. Scruffy worked really well on him. Her pulse picked up. In her heart of hearts, she had been terrified she wouldn't see him again, and just to have this moment was a gift she couldn't waste.

His eyes opened, and after a moment of recognition, he grabbed her arm. Whispering, he still managed to sound like he was shouting. "Addison, what the hell are you doing here?"

Joy pulsed through her veins. "Rescuing you."

Holland poked his head through the door. "Glad you found him. Judging from the screaming and cursing, I think Tara is two doors down and Jack is somewhere in here too. No time for cute reunions if we're going to get to Jeremy before we get caught."

Spencer acted like he hadn't heard Holland. "You're serious. Are you out of your frickin' mind?"

"Come on." She stood. "No time to waste."

Without turning around, she heard Spencer get up from the bed and follow her. Holland was standing in the hall outside a door. Tara was screaming and yelling inside. Unlike Spencer, Tara wasn't going to spend her last hours on Earth sleeping peacefully. Using the same key that had opened Spencer's door—what she now thought of as the master key—Addison opened the door.

Spencer grabbed her arm again. "This is insane. There's no way it's going to work."

"You don't even know the plan, so stop with the negative energy." She turned the doorknob, and it opened.

Emotions traveled over Tara's face. First shock, then pure relief, followed by anger. She pointed at Addison. "I did not tell those lies to the Fury so you could risk your goddamn life. Everyone here needs you to inherit your grandfather's committee seat."

"Your life is worth more to me, Tara, than the committee seat."

She waited for the snappy response or the negative comment. When none came, she decided she'd gotten her point across. Tara's face went blank. Addison wasn't going to push her for a response.

"Come on. We still have Jack and Gina to find, and we need to set something on fire so we can get Jeremy out."

Tara rushed forward. "You're serious? You're breaking us all out of here?"

"Didn't I say I was?"

Spencer sighed. "I think it's crazy, too. That's why I love her."

Addison turned around to smile. "You're adorable, and when we get out of here, I'm going to kiss you. Until then, we need to hurry."

"This way." Holland ran down the hall, and she followed. They opened several more rooms before finding them. Jack raised an eyebrow at their entrance but didn't say another word. Gina was quite vocal, cursing and yelling, but happy to have been released from her static-filled prison.

"Time to go." Addison smiled and sprinted down the hall. This would either work or it wouldn't.

Spencer ran next to her, grabbing her arm, pulling her

out of the way so she didn't trip over one of the guards who lay unconscious on the floor.

"Addison, if we don't get through this," he called to her, "I want you to know how much it means to me that you tried..."

She stopped running and looked at him. "There's no 'if' about this. I cannot live out there without you and Jeremy, so either we make this work or it ends tonight."

Spencer opened his mouth to speak, and she placed her hand over his lips to stop him. "There's nothing else to say on the subject."

"This is it," Holland called. "This is juvenile hall."

"Okay." Addison chewed on her lower lip. "Take Jack and Tara and go wait with the others by the gate. If we don't make it out of here, get out that back door. There's a van waiting. Jack told me in the warehouse that he wasn't institutionalized until he was seventeen. I bet he can drive, or you guys can figure it out. You're smart." She would have suggested that Spencer go with them, but she knew what she would have said if he'd told her to go without him.

Spotting Russell, she smiled. He hadn't let them down.

"Hey, everyone." He nodded at them. "The alert just went out on the radio that you all broke out. They don't know about Addison yet. So since they just think it's Spencer leading the whole thing, the guards have gone on alert looking for you in all your regular haunts. Rhodes is getting ready to make an announcement."

Spencer ran a hand through his hair. Addison could see the worry lines starting to form around his eyes. She'd woken him, and she suddenly wondered when he'd last slept.

"How do you know this, Russell?"

Russell pulled a radio out of his coat pocket. "I stole it months ago. Just had a feeling maybe I might need it."

"Can you get us inside?"

Russell shook his head. "No. All the buildings are locked up now."

"I can get the locks undone."

Spencer started to object. "Addison..."

"I practiced all over my apartment. I'm good at it now. It won't leave me exhausted, and even if it does, you can go in and get Jeremy."

She moved to the lock. Compared to the safe in her apartment, this one was child's play. Closing her eyes, she sent her energy into the lock and smiled when it released. "Let's go."

Spencer put his hand on Russell's arm. "Go with the others."

"I can help."

"I know you can. Get the others out. Do this for me. I need to know they're okay."

Understanding lit Russel's eyes. Probably none of them knew the aching guilt she was sure filled Spencer's soul over the deaths he'd nearly caused. Russell turned on his heel and headed toward the exit.

Watching him leave, Addison sighed. "You know, I thought he could get us in and out by making the guards think they wanted to let us through."

"I guess we'll just have to be more creative than that."

"When Tara lights the flames, we'll need to escape in the chaos." She took a deep breath and let it out. "I assume you know where Jeremy is."

"I do. I visited with him yesterday."

"You did? Why did you do that?"

"I thought I was going to die, and I wanted to make sure he was okay and give him some advice on how to live here."

Tears filled Addison's eyes. "Were you born this way, or did you just learn how to think about everyone but yourself as time went along?"

Spencer took her arm and hustled her through the door. "What are you talking about? It was incredibly selfish. I just had to see a part of you again."

"Liar."

A siren sounded in the hall, loud and distracting. She wanted to cover her ears. Instead, she took his hand and let him lead her down long hallways. Jeremy had always hated the fire alarm in their apartment, so the noise must have been making him crazy.

He opened a door, and they walked in together. "In here."

They stopped short, Spencer sticking his body in front of hers.

"Move, Spencer, or I'll put a bullet in his head. Right now, the boy's unconscious. I could also wake him up."

Addison sucked in her breath as she heard Rhodes' voice.

"I knew you'd come here."

"You were right, Will. Listen, no one has to get hurt. I'll go back to my cell, and Addison will leave. It will be that simple."

Spencer forced her more tightly behind him, placing himself between her and the doorway.

She couldn't see Rhodes' face, but she could hear the disdain in his voice. "That simple, Spencer? Do you think I'm going to let you make a fool of me? It might be too late for me to keep Jack and Tara from leaving, but I'll be damned if you and Ms. Wade, who has caused me endless amounts of trouble, are going to leave here. Now move before I put a bullet in his brain."

Not letting Spencer say anything else, she pushed around him to see the scene, her heart pounding harder than it ever had before. Rhodes stood over Jeremy, gun in his hand, his eyes bloodshot. When she'd first met him, he'd been so cool and collected. Addison had spent enough time with disgruntled employees to know that in front of her was a man who had come unglued.

"I'm going to put an end to this, Ms. Wade... or maybe I should call you Addison; everyone else seems to. Enough is enough."

She'd always heard that time slowed down in serious situations, but not for her. Rhodes raised his gun and fired it. Everything seemed to speed up. The moments between the bullet exiting the gun, the deafening sound of the shot, Spencer's scream, and the realization that she'd been shot were the fastest of her life.

Her hands instinctively covered the blood-soaked hole in her abdomen, and long before she felt the pain that would bring the darkness, which would end her life, she saw the truth that she'd grasped echoed in Spencer's blue eyes.

She was going to die. No last words, she sank to her knees, and only Spencer's roar of agony as he grasped her arms carried her into nothingness.

TWENTY-FIVE

Spencer's ears rang. *No!* His internal voice screamed out a protest. He would not allow this to happen. It couldn't be allowed to happen. Laying Addison down on the floor, he pressed his hand against her abdomen. Her blood, bright red and sticky, flowed out around him.

"No!" he screamed, but didn't recognize the sound of his own voice. "No, baby, hold on, you can't die, you're not allowed." He looked at her beautiful face. Her eyes closed. He could still see the pain etched around her features. Fury made him fast. Jumping from the ground, he leaped on top of Rhodes. He ripped the gun from his hand and pointed it at the old man's head.

"Why?" He couldn't form more than one word.

"None of this happened until *she* came." Rhodes' eyes were bulging out of his head. Spencer had always heard rumors that the man could be like this. They said Rhodes was capable of killing anyone who got in his way, which was why the committee liked him, but up until that instant, Spencer had never seen it.

"God, I loved you like the father I never knew."

He hadn't let himself make plans with Addison, imagine a future they could have together, and he had no idea whether she'd thought of him or not. But there were things they could have done together if they could have escaped, places they could have visited, babies they could have made, ones with her shade of blue eyes and his ability to tease her. She'd actually made him believe it might all have been possible, and she lay dying on the floor.

There was nothing in the world he wanted more than to have taken that bullet for her. He couldn't do that, and he wanted to wail that fate was unkind, except he already knew that. He'd known it since he was four years old. Rhodes had always made it bearable.

His face was wet. Maybe he was crying; he had no idea.

Addison was gone and nothing could undo it. All that was left of her was one small, innocent boy.

Rhodes stared at him, his red-glazed eyes intense and determined. "Spencer, the Wades are evil. They should all be put down. Let me up so I can finish off the boy."

Spencer placed the gun to Rhodes' temple and fired.

God, he could hardly breathe. Leaping off the body whose life he'd just ended, the body that had once contained the essence and life of a man he'd loved since he was a child, he rushed back to his beloved.

Addison looked paler than she had moments earlier. The blood continued to seep out of her. He wasn't a doctor, but he knew he was losing her and he had no time to waste. He picked her up in his arms just as Jeremy made a groaning noise. God, he couldn't get them both out. Hell, who was he kidding? He couldn't get any of them out of there. He wouldn't make it two feet out of this building carrying Addison before they caught him.

Jeremy's eyes fluttered open. He looked around, confusion falling onto his features. "Spencer?"

"Hey, buddy, listen, your auntie is sick. We need to get her some help." Laurel could help her if only he could get to the woman in time. She'd be waiting by the gate with the others.

"You'll save her, Uncle Spencer. You know what to do."

He'd never told the child to call him that, and what's more, where on Earth would he have gotten the notion that he could save her?

"Don't you remember what the lady told Auntie in dark space? There's so much more that you can do."

He did remember that conversation. Priscilla had been begging for her life, telling Addison she could teach her things about her power she didn't yet know. Addison had boxed her anyway. But he and Addison had different abilities... not to mention, how the hell did the kid know what they had said in dark space?

"Jeremy. How do you know this?"

The boy blinked twice, his eyes innocent and confused. "How do I know what, Uncle Spencer?"

Addison was dying in his arms, yet somehow, he had to find patience for this little person who couldn't possibly begin to understand what was happening around him. "How do you know what the lady told Auntie in dark space?"

"What do you mean? The voices told it to me, like they always do."

Crap. There was so much more to Jeremy that they didn't yet understand, and he had no time to work it out now. "Okay, kiddo, what am I supposed to do? Can you ask the voices?" He needed to count to ten to keep from screaming.

"What you've always known you could do."

What did that even mean? What he'd always known he could do...

He could move through dark space, so much faster there than he could in reality. He could move at the speed of light, so fast others got dizzy. There was no way that could help him. His body stayed put where he left it. Addison would still be there, and even though he could momentarily look at the new location, he couldn't communicate in it and was immediately thrown back into his body.

Without Rhodes alive to dampen his power, he could feel it surging inside him. It was different, stronger and more efficient.

Jeremy stood and grasped his leg, holding on to him. "Do it, Uncle Spencer. Move us through dark space."

He'd always felt that with just a little more power he could move, physically move himself and others through the shadows to where they needed to go. Yes, he could, or he'd die trying.

"Okay, Jeremy, hold on to me. It's going to be very dark and scary, but as long as you hold on to me, we'll get where we need to go."

"I won't let go."

He closed his eyes, and when he opened them, the landscape of dark space was laid out before him. It had to be different this time. The shadows couldn't be allowed to consume him. Even in the shadow space, he had to keep things solid. He had to maneuver his whole body in the space. Actually, not just his body—he needed to move Addison and Jeremy as well. There was nothing like jumping off the deep end without learning how to swim.

Looking down at Addison's nearly lifeless form in his arms gave him strength.

"I'm going to do this for us, baby. I'm going to get us to Laurel."

It felt different, harder, but he was still able to move, and that was key. If he could get where he needed to go in the darkness, then no one in the "real" world would know what was going on. He could take Addison to where she needed to be, unhindered by the guards and anyone else who felt like getting in his way.

"Faster, Uncle Spencer—you can go faster."

Jeremy had been right so far. Thank goodness for his "voices." Clearly there was more to Jeremy's powers than the ability to take away the powers of everyone else, if he could do that at all. Who was to say that Grace Ann knew what the hell she was talking about?

He moved faster, his muscles adapting to the new environment. If anything, he felt lighter, as if gravity moved differently inside dark space. Laurel—he needed to move to Laurel. He knew her essence; he'd seen it many times.

Following it now proved to be no problem.

Within moments, he saw it glowing, pulsing a bright yellow-and-purple light that told him he had reached her. This would be tricky. He had to move them all back into the light. Looking down at Addison, he almost stopped breathing. Her yellow, sunlight essence was almost gone. Only a sliver of her intensity was left.

The thought alone pushed him out of the darkness.

Blinding light filled his eyes and he nearly dropped Addison, tripping over Jeremy, who was still hanging on to his leg.

"Spencer? Holy shit, what's going on?" Tara's unique phraseology filled the air.

"Can't see. Moved us all through dark space. Help her, need Laurel." He could barely form sentences due to the pain in his head. Okay, so he wasn't meant to move through space like that unscathed. It didn't matter, as long as Addy was going to be okay.

"Laurel."

"I'm with her, Spencer. I can feel your pain. Close your eyes. Don't try to see yet."

He'd never been so happy to hear her voice.

"The bullet is lodged in her abdomen. I can see it so clearly. Why are my powers so intense right now?"

Spencer groaned. He wasn't ready to tell anyone about what had happened with Rhodes. He might never be.

"Uncle Spencer, are we there?" Jeremy's high-pitched, little boy voice called his attention.

Opening his eyes a crack, he looked at him. Things were somewhat clearer.

"We're there, Jeremy, we're there."

He sat up. The world spun, but he didn't care. Addison wasn't awake to care for Jeremy; she would want him to do it.

"Laurel?" He was sorry if he was being annoying, but he needed constant updates. The woman literally had his reason for living in her hands. She damn well needed to tell him what was going on.

"She's going to be okay, Spence, but I'm concentrating, so hush."

His eyes were tolerating the light better, so he dared to move, picking Jeremy up in his arms.

"We went on an adventure, didn't we, bud?"

"We did." Jeremy had dimples. They were so cute. He reached out and poked one with his forefinger and was delighted when the little boy giggled.

"I hate to bring up a bad subject here, but we need to

move. Aren't I supposed to be setting something on fire?"
Tara was clearly getting impatient as she tapped her feet.

"Only problem is, only Addison knows where the car is
and where we're going."

"The van is in the bushes," Addison croaked.

Spencer set Jeremy down and rushed to her side. "You
okay, sweetheart?"

"I should be dead, but I'm still here, so yes, I'm okay."
She sat up. "Are you okay, Laurel?"

"I'm a little worn out. Don't let her walk yet, Spencer."

Picking Addison up in his arms felt right. It was just
what he wanted to do, even though Laurel had ordered him
to do it. Jeremy squealed and ran to them.

"Hey." Addison's voice shook. "Were you scared,
kiddo?"

"No. Uncle Spencer moved through dark space. It was
cool."

"Oh." Addison looked at him, questions in her eyes.
"What happened to Rhodes?"

Hearing his name caused a pang in his gut. "We'll talk
about it later. Tara, the fire, please."

"You've got it."

Tara looked behind her and he watched as the walls
went up in flames, first one and then all of them. The
orange bursts of light would have been beautiful if they
weren't so incredibly dangerous.

She hissed. "I didn't mean for it to be that strong."

"We're all going to be stronger now. Rhodes is dead."
Behind him, he heard the guards shouting to get everyone
out. "Let's move."

The group seemed to move in unison, running toward
the van.

As they piled into the vehicle, Spencer took one last

look behind him at the place that had been both his home and his prison for twenty-six years.

"Take me with you."

Spencer jumped, jarred out of his reverie. It was Simpson. He rolled his eyes. Wow, he hated the little man.

"How did you find us? No, don't answer that—you had a vision, right?"

"I did." His shifty blue eyes seemed to float inside their sockets. "I can help with the boy; he's going to need me. Take me with you."

"This is Addison's show." He looked down at the woman he held in his arms and knew the answer before she nodded. There was no way she would leave anyone behind who wanted to come. Hell, if the woman had her way, she'd probably bring the whole institution with her.

"Come on, Simpson. Let's go."

They got into the car, the sound of fire engines growing closer by the second. Jack was at the wheel, a grin on his face. He couldn't blame the guy; he'd like to drive too. Although at that moment, all he really wanted to do was hold Addison on his lap and keep Jeremy next to him.

"Where are we going?" Jack asked as he jerked the van onto the road. "Sorry, I'm a bit rusty at this. It's been... well... over a decade, but I'll get it together."

Addison turned to look at Spencer as she answered Jack. He had a feeling this was not by accident. She wanted to watch his reaction when she said it. Her eyes alight, she stared at him. "We're going to the ocean. Drive east. We need to get to the Jersey Shore."

Silently he tried to digest what she'd said: the ocean. He'd told her it was his dream to see it, and now he was going to. Not wanting anyone to see how emotional he was, he leaned down and kissed the top of her head, holding her as close to him as he could. If it were his choice, he'd never let go.

———

SPENCER WAS IMPRESSED. The ocean was extraordinary, vaster than he could have imagined, and the love of his life was beyond competent at all things she attempted, it seemed.

He was impressed and also slightly seasick. After they'd boarded her boat, Addison had turned out to be quite the sailor. She'd taken them out to sea with very little trouble and spent the next hour explaining to the group exactly how they were going to operate the two hundred and forty-six foot, fiberglass, twin diesel engine vessel they would reside on until they arrived at this island of Guy McKidd's.

When she explained all his brother had done, it had made his head spin. Closing his eyes, he let the breeze off the ocean hit him in the face. He was supposed to be dead, and instead he was nauseated on a boat in the ocean. "Penny for your thoughts?"

He jumped. "I was thinking about the fact that I'm supposed to be dead and instead I'm here."

"We're both supposed to be dead."

The statement hung between them. The image of her nearly lifeless body would haunt him forever. Pulling her into his arms, he held her tight. "You do realize you're my entire world?"

"That goes both ways."

As he stared at her, he could see the swirls everyone else had noticed. How had he missed them? Her blue eyes were alive and dancing with light, swirling like a child's pinwheel in front of him.

"But..." Her smile said she was feeling mischievous. "You're not getting out of telling me what happened. I also have something to share with you."

"Which you won't tell me if I don't tell you what happened?"

"I didn't say that."

He sighed. "But you implied it. All right." He kissed her cheeks, first one then the other. "I killed Rhodes. It was different from killing Daniel, harder, but I would do it again in a heartbeat. He intended to kill Jeremy as well. In that moment, I realized I didn't know him. I spent twenty-six years with him, practically worshiping the ground he walked on, yet the man I killed was a complete stranger."

She stroked his face, the sensation sending shivers down his spine. "It's going to be hard to live with."

He nodded, not surprised that she understood. "It is."

"And then?" she prodded.

"Then Jeremy started sounding like a prophet and told me that I could walk us all through dark space, said the voices said I could." He shrugged. "I believed him, and it turns out he was right."

Addison lowered her voice. "Do other people hear voices, or do I need to find us a therapist when we get where we're going?"

"I think it's safe to say it's part of his power somehow."

She bit her lower lip before she pressed her head against his chest. "I hope I didn't massively screw up and this is all going to turn out to be a big disaster."

Russell spoke from behind them. "Well, if you did, at least it's a nice ride on a boat."

Spencer jumped, and Addison yelped before they both burst out laughing.

Neither of them had heard Russell approach.

Addison grinned, showing her straight, white teeth. "You're easy to please, Russell. First you liked the car, now the boat. I wish I could find you an airplane and a train."

Russell's face turned serious. "Do you think that's a possibility?"

"I would say no, but I never thought this was a possibility, so I'll say maybe. How about that?"

"Addison, everyone wants to come out to talk to you, to say thank you."

In his embrace, she stiffened. "Russell, please don't. Please tell everyone I don't need their thanks. I'm grateful to them. Jeremy is sleeping downstairs because of all of you. You're all my friends now. I don't know what I'll do if you all start thanking me."

Russell paused for a moment. "I'll tell them that, but you may have to take it from Tara. She's worked up like I've never seen her before."

Spencer ran his hands through her silky blonde hair. Was there any chance they'd ever be alone? "Hey, Addy, who's driving the boat?"

"Holland. I showed him how to use the GPS. It's kind of point and click after that."

They'd worked up a schedule so everyone took their turn and everyone piloted. He'd promised to teach Marisa and Minnie how he traveled through dark space in his body. It was a large boat, but everyone was going to have to share rooms. Addison wanted to be with Jeremy, which he completely understood, but that meant that he wouldn't be ravishing his love in the quiet of their dark cabin.

Addison looked at Russell. "Give me a minute?"

He nodded and headed back down below. She handed Spencer a box.

"What is it?"

"I kind of noticed that my powers felt more under control, subdued even."

"Is it Jeremy?"

"He's asleep." She pointed to the box. "There's a note."

Spencer opened the box, pulling out a circular, transparent object. It looked like the crystal balls he'd seen on television. When he touched it, his skin felt warm. He pulled out the note enclosed in the box.

Wade Corporation authorized this object five years ago. It was one of the first things Addison Wade ever did there, and even if she doesn't remember doing it, I'll never forget that she did. I am a Fury through and through. I've taken oaths and made promises you'll never understand. I am a man who keeps the oaths I make.

But before I swore allegiance to the Fury, I made a promise to someone else. I promised Mother I would keep you safe. Before today, I have been unable to keep that promise. Now I have fulfilled it.

The object you are in possession of is a static ball. It will help you—and whoever is with you—control your abilities. Say hello to Guy McKidd. Ten years ago, I did him a service and told him someday he would pay me back by taking you in. I think you will be a good team.

Don't return to the United States. If you do, I will hunt you down and re-institutionalize you or one of us will die.

William Rhodes is not your friend. He promised me five years ago that he would tell you of Guy McKidd. His agenda and yours do not match.

Good luck. You've found a worthy woman. Such a thing is rare.

Your brother, R

#3

He looked up from the note. "Did you read it?"

"I did. When I found the box, I didn't know what it was, so I read the letter."

He pulled her close. "I guess we're done, then."

"With him, maybe. Life is long. You never know what's going to happen."

He was good at burying his emotions, but it was going to be hard. He didn't trust Roman, hadn't since he'd returned to Safe Dawn as a Fury. However, something about the note was so final. For a moment, he saw his brother as he had been. The little boy pulling him through the crowd to protect him, bringing him food and holding him while he'd cried in the juvenile ward. Had Roman ever been a child? Spencer had thought he himself had never been. Maybe, in reality, it was Roman who had never been allowed to be small.

He crumpled the note in his hand and tossed it overboard just in case they got caught. No one would ever know Roman had helped them. That much he could do for his brother.

Addison pulled him close in her arms. "How do you think he knew we were on this boat? I buried the boat records so far in Wade's database it'll be six months before anyone realizes it's missing."

"He's Roman. I think he's been planning this for a long time."

Behind him, he heard someone running up the stairs. Jack stood in front of them, out of breath. "Addison, I was watching the satellite news to see the pictures of Safe Dawn —it's totally gone. Un-frickin'-believable. By the way, you're on the news."

Spencer jerked. How had they found out? When he looked at Addy, she didn't look surprised. "What did you do?"

"I gave an interview. Come on, let's watch it."

They walked below deck hand in hand. The others were gathered around the television. Addison's assured, classic features looked like they had been made for television.

She looked directly into the camera. He recognized the background as the living room in her apartment.

"My name is Addison Wade. I am speaking out today to let you know that I am and always have been Conditioned. Although measures were taken, unbeknownst to my grandfather, to hide me from discovery, I find I can no longer hide the truth of who I am.

"The rules against Conditioned people are barbaric. The Conditioned can learn, with age, to control their abilities, and before that both medical and scientific measures can be taken to protect the general public and the Conditioned person themselves.

"It has never been acceptable that we lock them up or that we force parents to either break the law or separate themselves from their children. It's time to change the laws. I am capable, smart, and continue to be as I always was, not in spite of but maybe *because* of my Condition.

"I urge you to take measures to change our barbaric, inhumane laws. Thank you."

The camera pulled off her, and the commentators went crazy discussing what she'd just said in relation to the burning down of Safe Dawn.

He kissed the top of her head. "You do know that now your destiny is the same as ours, regardless of what happens."

He couldn't help wishing it were different. Addison had to be safe. Everything else was secondary. "It always was, Spence."

TWENTY-SIX

Addison's first impression of Guy McKidd's island was that it was pink. The group had been on the boat for several weeks. All of them were tanner and, for the most part, much more relaxed. But as the destination had neared, a tension had re-formed. Roman had said that Guy would take them in. Would he? Did they even want to be there?

She directed the boat into the dock, noting three others. On the edge stood a man. Although it was hard to tell from a distance exactly how tall he was, she would guess over six feet. His face was familiar to her. She'd seen it in the newspaper article. He was darker skinned than he had been then, and ten years older. His hair, which had been long and to the middle of his back, was completely gone. Whether that was by design or Mother Nature's choice, she didn't know. Guy also had a gold earring hanging from his left ear.

All in all, he looked like a pirate in his light woven beach trousers and cotton shirt with the sleeves cut off.

As they maneuvered the boat, two men joined him. One

was tall and redheaded, the other shorter, stocky with black hair.

"Let me get off the boat first." She wouldn't expose everyone else if things didn't go well.

"Not without me." Spencer's declaration made it sound like she'd suggested she wanted to walk by herself into a volcano, not three feet from the boat.

She knew enough to know he wouldn't budge on the matter, so she nodded and took his hand.

Her legs wobbled when she stepped onto dry land.

"Guy McKidd, I'm—"

He interrupted. "Addison Wade, I know. I'd have to have missed the last two weeks of news reports not to know you. Of course, I knew who you were before then, even though I didn't know you were one of us." His accent was southern, which surprised her considering he'd been residing in the western United States.

"And you're Spencer Lewis," he continued, though he still hadn't shaken hands and that the men behind him were silent. "I've been waiting for you for ten years." He smiled then, and it lessened the intensity of his face, made him look younger and less scary.

"I didn't know about you until two weeks ago." Spencer's tone told Addison he was tense, not sure what to make of Guy.

Guy raised an eyebrow. "That surprises me. In any case, you're all more than welcome here. We're a small group by some standards, too large according to others. How many are you?"

"Ten, including us." Addison moved forward. "And a child."

"We have five children here. I wish it were more. All in all, we're fifty, now sixty with you."

He looked to the man to his right. "Go make beds. We'll figure out their particular talents later tonight. They've had a long trip."

"And the boat?" the stockier man inquired.

"We'll have to strip it, disguise it and remove the HIN number."

"I'll get to it after they disembark."

She still had a lot of questions before they took everyone off the boat. "What do you do here?"

"Now that you're all here, we'll do a lot more. I don't have any dark space travelers, and we're desperate for one."

He would get four now, but she wasn't ready to give away that information yet.

"You didn't answer my question."

"Now that we've amassed a certain amount of strength, we're what I guess you would call the Resistance. A war is coming. We won't let our brothers and sisters languish in those places anymore. Good job, by the way, burning down Safe Dawn. A lot of folks here see that as a sign that the time has come to fight back."

Spencer spoke. "What did my brother do for you to make you take us all in?"

"I would have taken you in anyway. Roman just let me know to expect you." He sighed. "I was caught. I'd almost made it over the border into Mexico. I was about to take the final steps. Not that I wouldn't have had to fight my way through Mexico, but at least it wouldn't have been the world-famous Fury. A hand grabbed my shoulder. It was Roman. He told me who he was. I thought I was done. Then he let me go and explained to me the rules of where the Fury could and could not go. That was how I found this place. He also gave me twenty thousand dollars."

Addison looked up at the large houses on the hill. "Looks like you've made more than that to afford all of this."

"Yes, we've made some good calls money-wise, but we could use more. Can you help us with that, Addison?"

She smiled. Between her natural ability to turn one dollar into a hundred every time she tried and the accounts she'd hidden all over the world, she was certain she could do that. "I think I could help with that."

"And if we don't want to fight?" Spencer voiced the question she'd held on her tongue. It wasn't likely that Laurel, for example, was going to want to participate in violence.

"As long as you're loyal, the fighting can be left to other people."

Spencer regarded her seriously, running his hands through her hair in the way that made her shiver and sweat. "I think we've reached our destination." Looking back at the boat, Spencer motioned for everyone to get off.

"You know you've all been declared dead," Guy said in passing. "You're not going to be transferring funds—we're going to need you to use that Wade brain and invest *our* money until we have *your* kind of money.

"I can do that, I promise." She took a deep breath, confused. "That's good, right, that we're dead?" That meant they were free.

"It depends. Spencer, explain it to your woman." With that, Guy turned his back on them and walked toward the boat. He still hadn't shaken their hands.

Turning around like he could read their thoughts, he grinned. "I can't shake hands, sorry. I'd rather not know everything about you. As it is, I know too much."

Addison regarded Spencer, her arms slipping into their

natural position around his waist. "What does it mean that we're dead?"

"It means the Fury will make us that way if they catch us. No one comes back from the dead."

"Spence..."

Concern filled his swirling blue eyes. "Regretting your decision?"

How could he even think that? Some day he would be confident and wouldn't wonder if he was worthy or if she was going to leave. It would just take time. She would wait.

"Don't be ridiculous. What I wanted to say is that now that I'm dead, I'd really rather not be Addison Wade anymore."

"You want to change your name?" He looked so confused she almost laughed.

Men were so clueless.

"I want to change my last name."

He shook his head. "To what?"

"Lewis."

Understanding dawned fast in his eyes. "Oh. It never occurred to me to ask. The Conditioned can't get married."

"So does that mean you want to?"

He grinned. "Hey, Guy," he called, "anyone ever get married here?"

Addison laughed. Whatever happened now, she had Spencer, and they were finally somewhere that no one would keep them apart. Even if there was fighting to do, they would do it together.

Looking at Spencer, she saw her whole future—love, laughter, tears, promises and babies—float back to her in his eyes. She'd found herself, even though she hadn't known she'd been lost.

Why was she surprised? Spencer found lost people. He was good at it.

She kissed his hand.

Life was good like it had never been before.

EPILOGUE

The new rules did not come as a surprise to the general population. The committee was relieved about that. After all, under Oliver Wade's direction, the committee had all but created panic about Addison's declaration and the destruction of Safe Dawn.

This time the notices went out via email and internet chat boards.

To Whom It May Concern:

New Rules to the management and handling of the Condition:

Any person caught with the Condition outside institution walls will be executed on sight.

All female Conditioned will be sterilized at the age of twenty and any Conditioned woman found pregnant before then will be executed.

The life span of the Conditioned will be terminated at the age of forty.

The Fury is real, and They are watching you.

Only people given particular permission, written

consent of the committee, will be allowed to hire the services of the Conditioned for their personal use.

These rules are for your safety.

Do Not Disobey.

And the world watched, again. Only this time, the Resistance on a small island in the Caribbean Sea had other plans. Things would change. Soon.

AFTERWORD

Thanks so much for reading. I hope you guys loved Addison and Spencer as much as I loved writing them. The good news is that book 2 in the Illicit Minds series is already available for purchase. You'll get to see Roman, Addison, Spencer, Guy and others again. They all make appearances (Roman a rather big one) in Illicit Connections. You can grab it here: https://amzn.to/2NDMse1

Also, please come and join me in my reading group on Facebook. https://www.facebook.com/groups/RebeccasRandomness

Turn the page for a complete list of my books and to learn more about me. Hugs!

ABOUT THE AUTHOR

As a teenager, I would hide in my room to read my favorite romance novels when I was supposed to be doing my homework.

I am the mother of three adorable boys and I am fortunate to be married to my best friend. I live in Austin Texas where I am determined to eat all the barbecue in town.

I am in love with science fiction, fantasy, and the paranormal and try to use all of these elements in my writing. I've been told I'm a little bloodthirsty so I hope that when you read my work you'll enjoy the action packed ride that always ends in romance. I love to write series because I love to see characters develop over time and it always makes me happy to see my favorite characters make guest appearances in other books.

In my world anything is possible, anything can happen, and you should suspect that it will.

I'd love to hear from you! Please visit my website at www.rebeccaroyce.com to sign up for my newsletter and learn about my books!

Here's where you can find me online:

Rebecca's Randomness Reading Group https://www.facebook.com/groups/RebeccasRandomness/

https://www.rebeccaroyce.com

https://www.facebook.com/authorrebeccaroyce/

www.twitter.com/rebeccaroyce

Instagram: rebeccaroyce79
MeWe: RebeccaRoyce
Cheers!!
Rebecca

OTHER BOOKS BY REBECCA ROYCE...

Wings of Artemis

Kidnapped By Her Husbands https://amzn.to/2BQdUxy

Rescued by Their Wife https://amzn.to/2Rr9as4

Crashing Into Destiny https://amzn.to/2VkyXRL

Meeting Them https://amzn.to/2BLPaXm

Reclaiming Their Love https://amzn.to/2GKAw8E

Loving Them https://amzn.to/2BKDmEK

Ship Called Malice https://amzn.to/2BNputj

Saving Them https://amzn.to/2SsrBtH

Dark Demise https://amzn.to/2VidXv3

Light Unfolding https://amzn.to/2GO6Yqr

Still Waters https://amzn.to/2CFePT8

Rising Tides https://amzn.to/2MCdTlM

Lost Star (coming soon)

Pointed Arrow (coming soon)

Last Hope (completed series)

Tradition Be Damned

Past Be Damned

Destiny Be Damned

Compassion Be Damned

Future Be Damned

Dragon Wars (completed series)

Forever

Eternal

Always

Evermore

Endless

Wards and Wands (completed series)

Hexed and Vexed

Curse Reversed

Meow, Baby (novella, co-written with Ripley Proserpina)

Tragic Magic

Safe Haven

Everywhere and Nowhere

Dimension X (coming soon)

More coming soon....

Soul Bound

Prisoner of the Dragons

More coming soon....

Shadow Promised

Strange Days

Weird Nights

Bizarre Years

More coming soon...

The Warrior (completed series)

Initiation

Driven

Subversive

Redemption

Justice

Warrior World (spin off of The Warrior, completed series)

Deacon

Micah

Jason

The Westervelt Wolves (completed series)

Her Wolf

Summer's Wolf

Wolf Reborn

Wolf's Valentine

Wolf's Magic

Alpha Wolf

Angel's Wolf

Darkest Wolf

Lone Wolf

Fallen Alpha

Alpha Rising

Alpha's Strength

Haunted Redemption

Phoenix Everlasting

Fragility Unearthed

Persuasion Enraptured

Reverse Harem Story (completed series)

Unconventional

Unexpected

Undeniable

Kiss Her Goodbye (completed series)

Hard Truths

Dark Truths

Deadly Truths

Shifter World

Planet Bear

Planet Wolf (coming soon)

The Swamp

Hidden

Pursued (coming soon)

Stand Alone Titles

Under The Lights

No Quitting Allowed

Mr. Wrong

Bite Marks

Bitten Surrender

The Vampire and The Virgin

Demon Within

Crimson Lust

Call Me Crazy

The Storm (writing with Ripley Proserpina) **completed series.**

Lightning Strikes

Thunder Rolling

The Deluge

www.ingramcontent.com/pod-product-compliance
Lightning Source LLC
Chambersburg PA
CBHW011430240626
47153CB00011B/2927